About the Author

CARLA BURGESS was born in Solihull and now lives in Chester with her husband, three children, dog and bearded dragon. Her love of books was sparked when she borrowed *Ghost Ship to Ganymede* by Robert Swindells from her primary school library and devoured it in one night. It was just after this that she started writing her own stories and inflicting them on family and friends. She began her working life as an editor on a trade magazine where she dreamed of writing about romance instead of tubing, but still felt privileged to be working with words. She has a degree in English literature and psychology, and loves animals, the countryside and the sea. Carla's debut novel, *Marry Me Tomorrow*, released in 2016, became a bestseller. For more information about Carla, you can follow her on Twitter @MsBear123 and on Facebook at www.facebook.com/carlaburgesswriter/

Also by Carla Burgess

Meet Me Under the Mistletoe
Stuck With You
Marry Me Tomorrow

Meet Me at Willow Hall

CARLA BURGESS

ONE PLACE. MANY STORIES

HQ
An imprint of HarperCollins*Publishers* Ltd
1 London Bridge Street
London SE1 9GF

This edition 2018

First published in Great Britain by
HQ, an imprint of HarperCollins*Publishers* Ltd 2018

Carla Burgess asserts the moral right to be
identified as the author of this work.
A catalogue record for this book is
available from the British Library.

ISBN: 978-0-00-831006-6

MIX
Paper from
responsible sources
FSC www.fsc.org **FSC™ C007454**

This book is produced from independently certified FSC™ paper

to ensure responsible forest management.

For more information visit: www.harpercollins.co.uk/green

Typeset by Palimpsest Book Production Ltd, Falkirk, Stirlingshire
Printed and bound in Great Britain by
CPI Group (UK) Ltd, Croydon, CR0 4YY

For Fifi, the super fan

Rachel,

I've been thinking a lot about us recently and I've come to the conclusion it's not working. As you know, I was never looking for long-term commitment, and I really think now is the time to part ways. We had four great months together, but since my accident I just don't feel like carrying this on any longer. You know I don't love you. I will never love you. I need to be alone. I'm sorry to be writing this in a letter instead of telling you face to face, but I thought it would be worse for you to drive all this way to visit me here in hospital, only to have to drive home again knowing you'd had a wasted journey. It's been good of you to visit me, but the truth is that seeing you exhausts me. I've told the nurses I only want to see close family, so please don't come again. I don't want a big discussion about this. Please, just accept that it's over and move on.

Goodbye and good luck.
Anthony

Chapter One

One year later

'*Make Willow Hall the stage for your love story!*' I made my voice dramatic as we bounced along the narrow country lane towards the hall in Elena's little car. Turning slightly in my seat to face her, I cleared my throat and adjusted the glossy brochure in my hands. '*Set in the green, rolling hills of the Shropshire countryside, and with a past steeped in history and romance, Willow Hall is the perfect venue for your wedding...* Oh, please!' I broke off. 'Steeped in romance! Honestly, what a load of rubbish! You can tell Anthony's had nothing to do with this!' I laughed and looked again at the photograph of the Georgian manor house on the front cover. I couldn't deny it was a beautiful house and would make an ideal wedding venue, but the fact that it belonged to my ex-boyfriend's family made me ultra-critical. It was unbelievable that Anthony's family home was going to be hosting weddings when he was so against any sort of commitment himself. 'I bet he's horrified by it all. He hates weddings.'

Elena gave me a sidelong glance, pushing her long dark hair behind her ear. 'Are you sure you want to do this? What if Anthony's there? What will you do?'

'He's not going to be there,' I stuffed the brochure into the glove compartment and slammed it shut, feeling jittery all of a sudden. 'He hates Willow Hall. He never once visited his mum there when we were together. She always came to us. He didn't even want to tell me about it.'

'I know, but things might have changed since the accident.'

I stared silently out of the window for a moment, watching a buzzard hover over a field. 'He won't be there,' I repeated, with more assurance than I felt. This morning I'd been positive this would be the case, but as we drew closer to Willow Hall, doubt curdled my stomach and I was suddenly nervous. I wiped my clammy palms down my bright-red, halter-neck sundress, suddenly wishing I'd worn something a little less conspicuous. Usually I was happy to stand out in a crowd, but I'd rather keep a low profile today.

What if he was there? What would I say?

A surge of nerves set my heart racing and I swallowed hard. Lifting my sunglasses, I examined my winged eyeliner in the tiny sun-visor mirror, relieved to see it hadn't smudged in the heat. A few tendrils of my red hair had escaped from my bun, but it still looked okay. Sitting back, I reopened the glove box and pulled out the brochure for Willow Hall once more. It was a wedding fair, for goodness' sake! Everyone was welcome. We had every right to be there, and with Elena getting married in a few months' time we had the perfect excuse. Nobody needed to know Elena had almost everything organised already and that we were just going to be nosy.

I couldn't believe it when I'd seen the advertisement for Willow Hall in one of Elena's wedding magazines. I thought there must be a mistake, or perhaps another country house of the same name. But after a bit of sleuthing on the Internet, I found it was the same house and still seemingly owned by the Bascombe family. It seemed ironic it was now being used as a wedding venue when Anthony had been so against marriage and commitment of any kind.

Still, like Elena said, maybe things had changed. A year had passed since I'd last seen him. He could have had a whole attitude change since then. He could have met someone who'd changed his mind about commitment. He might even be married himself by now.

I drew in a sharp breath as pain sliced through me. My mind shied away from the thought of him being with someone else. I couldn't deal with it. A year might have passed, but my feelings for Anthony Bascombe were still very much in existence. His letter telling me it was over had come as a massive shock, as had visiting him at the hospital and being turned away by the nurses. His lovely mother, Cath, had kept me updated on his progress for a few weeks afterwards, but then contact had dried up and I'd seen and heard nothing of him since. I'd sent him one letter, wishing him well, but had received nothing in return.

So, I'd let him go. And I'd been hurting ever since.

The lane widened out and we entered a chocolate-box-pretty village, with stone cottages lining each side of the street. Daffodils waved cheerfully from the grass verges and pink and white blossom decorated the trees. The village seemed quiet. A dog tied up outside the post office, and an old man sitting on a bench outside the quaint-looking pub, were the only signs of life. A large church stood at the end of the high street, its spire reaching up towards the clear blue sky and its neatly tended churchyard filled with daisies and cowslips.

'Wow, this is pretty!' Elena leaned forward over her steering wheel to peer through the windscreen.

'Mmm, it is,' I agreed. 'Quiet, though! I hope we've got the right day. I thought there would be more people around than this. Willow Hall should be on the left, just before the church, according to the brochure.'

Elena shrugged. 'We've definitely got the right date. Maybe everyone's up at the hall.' She flicked her indicator as we passed the last of the stone cottages and a gated entrance appeared signposted Willow Hall. A rhododendron framed the green sign, its bright-red flowers bobbing in the breeze. Willow Hall was printed in large gold lettering, with 'Civil Ceremonies, Wedding Receptions and Events' in smaller white print underneath.

'The sign looks very new,' Elena said as she drove in through the tall, wrought-iron gates. A stone lion stood on each gatepost and trees rose up on either side of the driveway, forming a green, leafy archway through which the hot, midday sun glinted, bathing the inside of the car with dappled green light. 'I wonder if they've done any weddings yet.'

'I don't think so. Their website didn't have any wedding photographs on it, so I think they must be just starting out.'

The drive snaked through the trees until the woodland gave way to gently sloping sheep-grazed meadowland. Ahead of us, the wide Georgian façade of Willow Hall appeared, its soft red brick glowing warm pink in the hot midday sun.

'Wow!' Elena said in surprise.

It took me a moment to speak. I gazed open-mouthed at the huge house with its neatly manicured gardens and parkland. 'I didn't expect it to be quite so big!' I said, stupidly.

'Well, you knew it was a mansion.'

'Yes, I know but… it's a huge stately home.' I blinked in disbelief. I didn't know what I'd been expecting really. Certainly nothing as beautiful and grand as this. Built over two storeys, it had eleven bays on each floor and an arched entrance with wide stone steps leading up to it. The photographs were pretty impressive, but Anthony's hatred of the place had made me think it couldn't be quite as grand as they'd made it look. He'd seemed embarrassed by it, in fact, like it was some kind of guilty secret. I'd only found out about it by accident, through something his mum had said when she came up to visit, and that had been towards the end of our relationship. When I'd asked to see it, he'd refused to bring me, saying he hated the place and never went there willingly. He'd led me to believe it was some kind of rundown relic, but this was beautiful.

'I can't believe we know – *knew* – someone who grew up in a big mansion like this. It's unbelievable!' Elena followed the driveway round to the side of the house. Her tyres crunched on the gravel and dust clouded up behind us as we entered a large square car park, already half-full of cars shimmering in the heat.

'I know. I mean, I've seen pictures, obviously, but they didn't prepare me for this.' Gathering up my handbag, I climbed out of Elena's car and gazed up at Willow Hall. The air was full of birdsong and butterflies. It was hard to imagine why Anthony hated this house so much when it was so lovely.

'Imagine getting married somewhere like this,' Elena said wistfully as she locked the car. 'It would be a perfect venue. Just imagine sweeping up the drive towards this big house. Daniel and I could never have afforded anything like this, though.'

We took the path leading around the front of the house, following the signs directing us to the wedding fair at the back. I was very aware of the crunch of my footsteps on the gravel path and the volume of Elena's voice as we passed by the ground-floor windows of the house. I had a sudden urge to tiptoe and, as we walked past the front entrance, I realised I was holding my breath.

What if Anthony *was* here? What if he was just behind that door or window, and just happened to look out as we passed by? My heart thumped at the thought and I gave myself a mental shake. There was no way he would be here. And even if he was, so what? I didn't have to speak to him. From the number of cars in the car park, it looked like there were loads of people here. Avoiding him would be easy.

Elena tucked her arm through mine as we rounded the side of the house, taking a path bordered by pink, flowering rhododendrons. Music and laughter floated on the spring breeze, and we found a large white marquee standing in the middle of a green-striped lawn. People were standing around, sipping champagne and laughing, while besuited waiters circulated with trays of champagne and orange juice.

'Ooh, this is lovely!' Elena said enthusiastically as we walked towards the entrance of the marquee. I gave a tight smile, my heart bungee jumping to my toes and back up again as I spotted Anthony's brother, Julian, talking to a group of people to the side of the marquee. Why was he here? Surely he still lived in Scotland? Readjusting my sunglasses, I turned my face away and hoped he wouldn't notice me.

'Are you okay?' Elena asked as we accepted a glass of orange juice from a passing waiter.

'Yes, of course.' I smiled brightly and did my best to blend in with the groups of people sipping champagne around us. Everyone seemed to be dressed in pastel shades. Even Elena was wearing a pale-blue maxi dress instead of her habitual black jeans. What was I thinking, wearing red? I stood out like a sore thumb!

Taking a deep breath, I squared my shoulders and attempted to pull myself together. It wouldn't be so bad if Julian saw me. He'd always been lovely and I had every right to be here. I wasn't snooping. Not really. No, not at all.

There were lots of dewy young brides-to-be, eyes bright with love and excitement, holding hands with their fiancés or else with their mothers or friends. But there was also a contingent of tweedy local types who'd obviously just come for some free booze and a nosy.

'They'll never make a go of this,' I heard a severe-looking lady say to her friend. Her iron-grey hair was tightly curled and she had a bristling border terrier on the end of a long leash that kept yapping loudly at passersby. Pausing next to her, I pretended to check the heel of my shoe so I could listen to what she was saying.

'Oh, I don't know. It all looks very professional,' her friend replied, obviously impressed by the large marquee and decent number of visitors.

'Hmph! They'll sell it before the year's out,' she said, darkly.

'Those no-good sons of Cath's will be off before she knows it. They never could stick around.'

Sons? As in plural? Did that mean Anthony was here too? Good God, no! I glanced at Elena to see if she'd heard, but she'd walked on ahead and was disappearing inside the marquee. Not wanting to be left alone, I darted after her to catch her up.

Inside, the ceiling of the marquee was swathed in twinkling fairy lights and the round tables were laid out with beautiful wedding products and services. Pretty wedding cakes of all different designs towered on the table next to the entrance, while a photographer displayed artistic black-and-white wedding shots on the stall next door. Everywhere I looked there was wedding stationery, bridal flowers, balloon arches, chocolate fountains, rose-petal confetti and photos of wedding cars and horse-drawn carriages. I wanted to tell Elena what I'd overheard, but she was deep in conversation with one of the stallholders. As I gazed around at the beautiful stalls, I realised this would be Anthony's idea of hell and there was no way he'd be making an appearance here. If he was at Willow Hall, he'd be skulking inside the house, keeping well away from all this wedding nonsense.

Taking a glass of champagne from a passing waiter, I forced myself to relax and enjoy the happy atmosphere. Everyone was so friendly and Elena and I wandered from stall to stall, discussing ideas.

'Ooh! Let's check out that dress stall,' Elena took my arm and towed me towards the back of the marquee. 'They might have a bridesmaid dress for you.'

'I doubt it. It all looks rather bridal,' I said, allowing Elena to lead me towards the racks of dresses.

'Hi!' Elena greeted the sales assistant cheerfully. 'Do you have any vintage-style bridesmaid dresses? Preferably tea-length. It's for Rachel here. She's my bridesmaid and, as you can see, likes a vintage look.' She indicated my fifties-style sundress with a sweep of her hand. The sales assistant smiled at me but shook her head.

'We have a tea-length bridal gown but no bridesmaid dresses here with us today. Would you like to try the bridal gown on to see if you like the style?'

Elena's face lit up. 'Oh, could we? That would be wonderful. Thank you.'

I started to protest, but Elena just grinned and shooed me on to follow the assistant, who was at another rack searching through the plastic-covered dresses. 'It's here,' she said, pulling out an ivory silk dress. My heart skipped a beat as I looked at the lace bodice and full tulle skirt. 'Come this way.'

She led me towards a makeshift dressing room behind the racks of dresses. I felt a bit of a fraud as I stepped into the ivory silk gown and allowed the woman to do me up at the back. It felt wrong to be trying on a wedding dress when I didn't even have a boyfriend, let alone a fiancé. But as the zip went up and the lace bodice moulded to my body, I realised I loved it.

'Ooh, that looks beautiful!' the assistant murmured, standing back to look at me. 'Fits you like it was made for you. Hold on, stay there.' She ducked out of the little room for a moment, reappearing a moment later with a tiny silver tiara. 'Here, pop this on,' she said, placing it on my red hair. 'Your hair looks lovely up like that. Here, let's pull a few tendrils down around your face and you're good to go. In fact, you could get married like that right now and everyone would be blown away. You look amazing!' She put her hands to her face, visibly moved, while I blinked at her in disbelief. If this was a sales pitch, it was wasted on me. I loved the dress but there was no point in buying it when I didn't have a man. 'Now, go and show your friend. Come on!'

'Oh! Can't she come to me?' I said, quailing at the thought of parading the dress in front of everybody in the marquee.

'No, you don't! You don't get away that easily!' She laughed. 'You're the perfect model for this dress and there's a roomful of brides-to-be out there, so come on. You can be my model.'

Whipping back the curtain, she beckoned me out. Elena was

waiting patiently at the front of the stall as I padded barefoot towards her. I was aware of people stopping to look, but I kept my eyes on Elena. Her face lit up when she saw me and she covered her face with her hands before placing them over her heart. 'Oh, isn't it gorgeous? You just have to wear something like that. It's so you.'

'I do love it,' I said, turning slightly so the skirt swished from side to side. The silk whispered around my bare legs and I flexed my toes self-consciously as people gathered around to watch.

'And here we have a tea-length bridal gown in ivory silk,' the sales assistant said to the crowd of onlookers. 'This is from our vintage collection and is also available in white or oyster. If you'd just like to turn around, Rachel, and let everyone see the detailing on the back.'

Obediently I turned while the sales assistant pointed out the pearl detailing on the buttons at the back of the dress. 'I should get you to model some more really, shouldn't I?' she said to me cheerfully. 'Well done! You can take a bow now.'

Turning back round to face Elena, my smile froze on my face as I found myself looking into the bright-blue eyes of the man standing directly behind her.

Running a hand through his dark-blond hair, Anthony Bascombe looked on in startled disbelief.

'Rachel?'

Chapter Two

I couldn't speak. All I could do was stand and stare at him in shocked silence, and all he did was stare back.

My brain seemed to have shut down. I was dimly aware of the sales assistant talking about the dress, but she seemed very far away all of a sudden. Everything seemed to fade out, leaving just me and Anthony staring at each other beneath the twinkling lights of the marquee. I didn't know what to do or say. And, seemingly, neither did he.

'Oh, my God!' Elena said in a shocked voice as she turned to see who I was staring at. 'Anthony!'

He seemed to gather himself then. Shaking his head slightly, he looked at Elena and switched on his smile. 'Elena!' Stepping forward, he kissed her on both cheeks. 'How lovely to see you. And you, Rachel.' His eyes returned to mine. 'You look… you look…' He indicated the bridal gown, his eyes travelling the length of my body down to my bare feet and back up to my eyes. '… Very well.' He nodded slightly and took a deep breath in. 'So, you're getting married! Congratulations!' Nodding again, he flashed the briefest of smiles. 'Well, must dash. It's good to see you.'

And then he was gone, striding purposefully away through the crowded marquee. I stared after his retreating figure in heart-pounding disbelief.

'How do you know him then?' the sales assistant asked as she continued to fuss about with the back of the dress. 'He owns the hall, doesn't he? Very handsome man. Some of the girls were talking about him earlier. And his brother too. Nice-looking family. Great genes, obviously.'

I couldn't form the words to answer her question. Luckily, she was distracted by someone else asking to try on a bridal gown. I looked at Elena. She was staring at me in wide-eyed horror. 'Are you okay?' she murmured, stepping closer and taking my hand. 'You've gone really pale.'

'Errm, I err…' I shook my head, unable to find any words. I was lightheaded and trembling all over.

'Shall we take this dress off now, my lovely?' said the sales assistant, steering me back towards the dressing room and starting to unbutton the back of the dress. 'Oooh, are you cold? You've got goose bumps all over! If you give me a minute, I'll get you the details for the bridesmaid dress in this style. You'll have to order it online, but at least you'll know the size now you've tried this one on. Here, step out and I'll leave you to get dressed.'

'Thank you.'

She left me alone and I stood with my eyes closed, sucking in deep lungfuls of air and trying to calm my racing heart. I felt panicky and there was a deep ache in the pit of my stomach that seemed to be anger, despair and longing all rolled into one. Because no matter how many times I told people I was over him, that I hated him and never wanted to see him again as long as I lived, I knew none of that was true. I was a long way from getting over Anthony Bascombe, and his sudden appearance just now had proved that beyond a doubt.

What did I do now? Just leave? Just walk away like it had never happened? I wasn't sure I could do that. I needed to see him again. I needed to talk to him. I needed to know why he'd finished with me so abruptly.

Dressing quickly, I took a moment to steady my breathing before going back out to Elena. She was chewing her fingernail and looking worried. 'Do you want to go?' she said, her dark eyes wide with concern. 'We can go. I don't mind.'

I shook my head. 'No. I'm fine.'

'Are you sure?' She raised her left eyebrow sceptically. 'The lady's given me the details for the bridesmaid dress so there's nothing we really need to do now. We can go.'

Taking a deep breath in, I shook my head again. 'No, it's okay. I've seen him now. It's done.'

'Well, I doubt we'll see him again, anyway.' Elena tucked her arm through mine. 'He practically ran away.'

I forced a smile and looked over at the flower stall. 'Let's have a look at the flowers. She might have some ideas I can use in the shop.'

'You should start exhibiting at these wedding fairs. I told you that at the last one we went to.'

'Yeah, I know.' We paused next to the flower stall, but I was more interested in scanning the crowd for signs of Anthony than taking much notice of the flower designs.

'You could send Bobbi if you didn't want to do them yourself,' Elena added, mistaking my distraction for disinterest.

I laughed. 'Maybe. Shall we go and sit down outside and have something to eat? I think they're serving food from the back of the house.' I led the way back out of the marquee. Small round tables had been placed on the lawn so guests could eat. I found one that was empty and sat down. Elena glanced around before taking the seat opposite me.

'I can't believe he was here!' she hissed. 'After everything we were saying in the car.'

'I know.' I opened my eyes wide and inhaled deeply. All around us, people chatted and laughed while sipping champagne, completely unaware that my life had just been thrown into turmoil. I was so stunned and confused, my head was spinning. But really, I had no right to be feeling this shocked. There was always a chance he'd be here. This was his family home, after all.

And maybe, just maybe, part of me had hoped he would be.

I'd often wondered how I would react if I saw him again. How many nights had I lain awake, missing him and wondering where he was and who he was with? Even while I was furious with him, I missed him. I cried myself to sleep, night after night, thinking about him and longing for him to come back to me. As weeks turned into months and it became clear he wasn't going to change his mind and come back, I'd tied to convince myself that, even if he did, I wouldn't want him. That my feelings had changed and I wouldn't feel the same way about him. Too much time had passed and he'd hurt me so much I was bound to feel differently. The connection would be severed and there would be no attraction. It would be like looking at a stranger, and his blue eyes would no longer have any hold over me.

But it hadn't been like looking into the eyes of a stranger. I'd felt exactly the same way as I had twelve months ago. It was so strange to feel that same connection. How could I still be in love with him after all this time? What kind of masochist was I?

Of course, he was still as handsome as ever. The high cheekbones and square jaw. The sparkling blue eyes and neatly cropped fair hair. But it wasn't just about his looks. It was more than that. If it had been only that, his brother would have had the same effect on me – they looked so alike. As soon as I saw him, the good memories had come flooding back, overpowering the words in his letter.

They were serving afternoon tea from the terrace at the back of the house. Elena went up to join the queue while I stayed at the table, trying to regain some control over my emotions. I wasn't even hungry. My stomach had lurched so violently when I'd seen Anthony that it felt sore and bruised.

15

'Rachel? Is that really you?' Julian, Anthony's brother, appeared next to our table, looking down at me in disbelief. 'How wonderful to see you again. I just saw Anthony and he said he'd just seen you, and I had to come and find you and say hello. How are you?'

'I'm fine. Thank you, Julian. How are you?' Standing up, I kissed him on both cheeks. His broad, happy grin was so infectious that I found myself smiling back at him. He looked so happy to see me that I felt truly touched. He was such a lovely man.

'Very well, thank you! Wow! This is wonderful! And you're getting married, I believe? Congratulations! Do you have a date set yet?'

Blinking rapidly, I opened my mouth to tell him I wasn't getting married, just trying out the style of dress, but at that moment Elena arrived back at the table, abandoning her place in the queue.

'You haven't set a date yet, have you, Rachel? Hi, I'm Elena by the way.' She reached out to shake Julian's hand. 'I'm getting married at the end of August, though.'

'This coming August?' Julian's eyes lit up.

'Yes.'

'Do you have everything booked already?'

'Yes, pretty much. All sorted really.'

'Oh, lovely. Whereabouts are you getting married? Forgive me if that seems like a nosy question.' He pressed the palm of his hand to his chest, looking embarrassed. 'It's just that this is our first foray into being a wedding venue, and I'm interested in hearing why people choose the places they do.'

'Oh, well, it came down to cost in the end. We've been renovating a house so most of our money has gone on that. It made sense to get married at the local golf club to keep costs down.'

'Oh, okay. Fair enough. What about you, Rachel? What will you be looking for when you choose your wedding venue?'

My mouth dropped open. 'Oh, I don't know yet, really. Willow Hall is so beautiful, though.'

'It certainly is. An ideal venue, I'd say. And Liz and I got married here, so I know it's perfect. How about I give you the guided tour and we'll see if I can tempt you into booking your wedding with us? After all, what better revenge than to get married at your ex-boyfriend's family home?' He winked at me and I laughed.

'True.' I felt my cheeks flush. What had I got myself into now? I wasn't sure I could keep up the pretence of being engaged. I opened my mouth to tell him we really ought to be going home now, but Elena jumped in before I could get my words out.

'We'd love to look round,' she said eagerly, her eyes lighting up.

'Great!' Julian looked delighted. 'Are you ready now?'

'Yes!' Elena said, before I could back out.

'Great! Well, as you can see, we have the pavilion here laid out on the lawn,' he said, gesturing to the marquee. 'We call it the pavilion rather than the marquee because it's a semi-permanent structure, with its own toilets and electricity supply. We can cater for up to one hundred and eighty guests in there, with space for a dance floor and a stage for a band or DJ. You've been in there already, haven't you? What did you think?'

'It was beautiful,' Elena said. 'Especially with all the lights on the ceiling.'

'Yes, that's our starry-night theme. Perfect for creating a romantic ambience. We're really pleased with it.'

'Do you conduct the civil ceremonies in there?'

'No, we're planning on holding them in the orangery or the library. Although only the orangery is ready at the moment. If you'd like to follow me, I'll show you now.' He led us to the end of the house where the orangery jutted out, surrounded by flowering shrubs. Crocuses flowered in the lawn, blue and yellow flowers poking up from the green grass. 'It's quite shady down here,' he said, gesturing to the large oak tree nearby, 'so it doesn't get too hot in the midday sun. Ideal on a boiling hot summer's day. Will you be having a civil ceremony or a church service, Elena?'

'Church.'

'And you, Rachel?'

'Err, haven't decided yet.'

'Oh!' Julian shot me a surprised glance. 'You really are in the early stages of planning, aren't you?'

I laughed nervously. 'What about you, Julian? Did you and Liz get married in here?'

'No, we were married in the parish church, which is just down the road. You'll have seen it when you turned into the drive. It's a lovely church and we've had a word with the vicar, who seems quite open to marrying couples from out of the parish, so that's also an option if you choose to book with us. So, what's your fiancé's name, Rachel?'

I gulped, my mind immediately emptying of all possible names.

'Jayjay,' Elena said helpfully.

'Jayjay?' Julian turned to look at me, eyebrows raised. 'Where did you meet?'

'In my flower shop, The Birdcage,' I said truthfully. I had met Jayjay in the shop, but only because he was Bobbi's boyfriend. Bobbi worked in The Birdcage with me and had been seeing Jayjay for a couple of months now. They made a lovely couple, and Jayjay was cute but certainly not my type.

'Lovely.' Julian opened the door to the orangery and let us inside. It had been laid out as though ready for a wedding, with rows of beribboned chairs and an aisle left for the bride to walk down. 'This can seat sixty guests, so obviously, if you wanted more guests, it would be best to choose to have the wedding in one of our other rooms, such as the library or the Great Hall when it's finished.'

'Great Hall? That sounds very grand.'

Julian grimaced and then laughed self-consciously. 'Well, it's possibly not quite as grand as it sounds. We're still in the process

18

of restoring it. We're nearly there, though, so by the time anyone books a wedding we'll have it all back to its former glory.'

'How many weddings have you booked so far?'

'One today, so far that is. But that's for next year and we were rather hoping we'd get someone booking for this year. Probably a bit of a long shot. Most people book their weddings at least a year in advance. But still, we live in hope. If we could get someone to book with us this summer, that would be a great start.'

'You could advertise,' I suggested. 'There's bound to be someone who's left everything to the last minute.'

'Liz suggested that. I'm not sure it's the best idea, though. It makes us sound a bit desperate to be so public about it.'

'Where is Liz, by the way? Is she here or is she at home with the kids?' Julian and Liz had two children and lived up in Scotland. 'How are they all?'

'Oh, Liz is fine. But this is home now. We all live here.'

'Here? Really?'

'Yes. It all came to a head last year. After Anthony's accident, we realised we couldn't stay living so far away. It put a lot of things into perspective and made us all sit up and open our eyes.'

I nodded. 'How is he?'

'He's doing well. You saw him before, didn't you?'

'Yes. But we didn't really speak.'

'Oh, really?' Julian looked surprised, as though he'd imagined Anthony and I having a good old chat. 'Well, he's fine, anyway. Recovering well. His accident made us see we'd been living our own separate lives, carrying on like it was fine to leave our mother here, managing this massive hall and twenty-two acres on her own. The more we visited, the more we realised Mother wasn't coping quite as well as she claimed, and the old place was rather falling apart. So Liz and I moved back. We're living in the east wing with Mother and Arthur.'

'Arthur the gardener?' I interrupted, remembering a bit of gossip from the Christmas before last where Julian and Liz were speculating about him and Cath being in a relationship. Anthony had been appalled by the idea.

Julian laughed. 'Yes, we all live together now, like one big, happy family. It's only temporary, though. Liz and I are renovating one of the houses on the estate to live in.'

'Does Anthony live with you too?'

'No, he's moved into Arthur's old cottage to be miserable on his own.'

'He lives here, though? On the estate?'

'Oh, yes!' Julian looked surprised at the question. 'Yes, we all live here now. Got to make a go of this place or else we'll have to sell it.'

'I kind of thought that was what Anthony wanted? He hates this place, doesn't he?'

Julian shrugged. 'Hmm, well, we can't sell while Mother's still alive. It would kill her. Right, I'll show you the Great Hall if you want to see it?'

I glanced at Elena, who was looking eager and excited. 'Oh, yes, please.'

He led us into the house through a side door, and we walked through long, wood-panelled corridors with high ceilings and threadbare carpets. It was gloomy, and the air smelt musty and stale, as though this part of the house was rarely used. Julian stopped at the end of the corridor and opened a door on the left.

'Here we are,' he said cheerfully, as we stepped into darkness. He flicked a switch on the wall, but the room remained dark. 'Oops! Just a moment. I'll open one of these curtains and let some light in.' We watched as he wrestled a long, dark drape to one side, releasing clouds of dust as he did so. It sparkled in the air as the light poured in, revealing a large, rectangular room with mystery humps of furniture hidden beneath dustsheets. As my eyes slowly adjusted to the light, I started to make out family portraits hanging on the walls.

'Wow!' Elena said, looking round, impressed. 'This is a great room, isn't it?'

I turned a slow circle, taking in the sadly neglected room. It could be a great room, but right now it just made me feel sad. As a florist, I'd delivered many wedding flowers to venues like Willow Hall, and their rooms were all sparkling silverware and polished floors. It was sad to see this beautiful old house so uncared for and a shame they couldn't have sorted it out before this wedding fair. A beautiful big room like this had the potential to convince people to have their wedding here. Especially a winter wedding. I imagined a roaring fire in the big fireplace at the end of the room, decorated with garlands of holly and mistletoe.

'What will you be offering this room for? Wedding breakfasts?'

'Yes. Well, eventually, anyway. It's not ready, as you can see. This is next on our list.'

'It's a pity you couldn't get it ready for today. A lot of people would have liked to have seen it,' I said, staring up at a huge oil painting of a man riding a horse. It looked like it had been painted centuries ago, but with the bright-blue eyes and chiselled features the man's resemblance to Anthony and Julian was uncanny. I was just about to say something about it when the door swung open and Anthony stalked in.

'Ah, here you are,' he said to his brother. 'What are you doing in here? I thought we weren't showing anybody in here today.'

'I know, but I'm trying to convince Elena that she wants to get married here this summer.'

Anthony pulled a face and glanced disdainfully around the room. 'By showing her this horrible, creepy room?'

'It's beautiful!' Elena said, spinning round as though she were a Disney princess. 'You can really see the possibilities this place has.'

'It would be great for a winter wedding,' I said, pleased when my voice didn't squeak or tremble with nerves. I took a few steps forward, feeling awkward, and clasped my shaking hands behind my back.

'I suppose so,' Anthony said, stiffly. 'We haven't used this room for years and years, have we, Jules?'

'No. I can barely remember using it, to be honest. I expect that's because I'm younger than you by a good few years, though, isn't that right, Anthony?' He grinned cheekily at his brother and Anthony laughed.

'Only by three years. Let's not exaggerate.'

Julian chuckled. 'Apparently we used to have family parties in here at Christmastime. It's a bit big really for general family use, don't you think? I think we'd all lose each other.'

Anthony shivered slightly. 'It gives me the creeps.'

'That's because it's so dark. If you pulled open the curtains and uncovered the furniture it would be lovely. Especially with a big Christmas tree and roaring fire.'

Anthony dipped his head. 'If you like that sort of thing.'

I felt guilty then. I knew very well that Anthony hated Christmas because his father had died at Christmastime when he was fourteen. The last thing he needed was me trying to make his childhood home look like a scene from a Christmas card.

'Well, even a bit of sunlight would make all the difference. Just look at these amazing family portraits. Do you know who they all are? This one looks just like you two.'

Julian laughed. 'Yes, that's our great-grandfather. He made his fortune in the shipping business.'

'Oh, really? So you're not dukes or earls or whatever?'

'No. We don't have titles.'

'Thank God,' Anthony muttered. 'So are you having a winter wedding, Rachel?' he asked.

'I… no, we don't have a date yet.'

Anthony looked surprised. 'And yet you're trying on wedding dresses?'

I blushed. 'We're here for Elena today. I was looking for a bridesmaid dress but they didn't have any in that style.'

Elena shot me a look as if to say I should be making up loads of wedding details, but I ignored her. I didn't want to get involved in some elaborate lie. I was uncomfortable enough about the Jayjay thing as it was.

'But I thought you had everything sorted already, Elena?' Julian said. 'Are you addicted to wedding fairs or something?'

'Pretty much!' Elena laughed. 'We have everything except Rachel's dress, but I think we've got that sorted now, thanks to today. Besides, Rachel's only just got engaged. It's all about my wedding right now. We'll think about Rachel's after my honeymoon.' She laughed to show she was joking.

Anthony smiled. 'How is Daniel? Well, I hope?'

'He's great, thanks!' Elena beamed. 'We've moved into our house together and it's lovely.'

'Oh, it's finished then? That's great!'

'Yes, just a few bits here and there to finish off, but it's wonderful to be in our own house at last.'

'Excellent! Give him my best wishes. I always liked Daniel.'

'He liked you too. He was gutted when you and Rachel broke up.'

I felt my cheeks flare and Anthony looked away, obviously uncomfortable with the subject. Julian laughed and slapped his brother on the arm.

'If you and Daniel had such a bromance going, you should have no trouble persuading him to get married here instead of his local golf club.'

Anthony shrugged. 'Are you actually thinking about it, Elena? Would you move your wedding to here?'

'I'd love to but I'm not sure how practical it would be. It's a bit late to reorganise everything now. All the invitations have gone out and it's a bit cheeky to change the venue on the guests, especially when it's an hour away.'

'It's your wedding,' Anthony said. 'You should be able to get married wherever you like.'

'Well, I doubt we'd be able to afford it anyway. A place like this must cost a fortune!'

'Not if we do you a deal,' Julian said. 'How about you get married here this summer and be our first marriage. If you agree to be photographed and videoed for our website and perhaps featured in a magazine, we could offer the venue for free.'

'For free?' Elena blinked at him in amazement. 'Why would you do that?'

'To get publicity, of course. We're just starting out and we're pretty desperate to get this up and running. Honestly, you'd be helping us enormously. You'd need to pay for catering and your flowers and stuff like that, but we wouldn't charge for the use of the hall.'

My mouth fell open in disbelief. It was an unbelievably generous offer, and I almost wished I really did have a fiancé so I could be their first wedding. It was ironic that my commitment-phobic ex-boyfriend's family home was now the wedding venue of my dreams.

Elena laughed. 'Wow! That's a good offer.'

Julian's eyes lit up. 'What would you lose? Your deposit? I bet it would still work out cheaper in the long run.'

Elena grew serious again, chewing her lip. 'It's still a bit far for all my guests, though.'

'It's only an hour from Chester!' Anthony said over his shoulder. 'Besides, they could stay over. We have plenty of rooms in the hall and we're converting the stable block into accommodation.'

'Would it be ready in time, though?' I looked pointedly around the dusty hall. 'Elena's wedding is only four months away. That's a lot of work.'

'It will be finished by then,' Julian said. 'We're looking at the beginning of July for completion so it would fit nicely with an August wedding. So, as long as you don't want to get married in this room here, Elena, you'll be all set.'

'How many guests can you accommodate? Surely not eighty?'

'Not at the moment, but there are a couple of good guesthouses in the village, so I'm sure between us we could manage.' Julian looked across at Anthony. 'Our holiday cottages can accommodate four families of five and we also have four double bedrooms within the hall itself, on top of the honeymoon suite. I can show you that now if you'd like to follow me.' Julian led us towards a door at the opposite end of the room and into a wide, oak-panelled hallway. A large staircase with an intricately carved banister wound its way upwards. Elena and I followed him up to the first floor, with Anthony walking slowly behind us. It felt like all my senses were attuned to him: the thud of his footsteps on the stairs, the squeak of his hand on the polished wooden banister, the sound of his breathing. It made the hairs on the back of my neck prickle and my pulse race.

The day had taken on a surreal quality. After all this time, how could this be? How could I be walking up the stairs with Anthony? My brain couldn't process it properly and I kept thinking I must be dreaming.

We reached the first floor and Julian led us along a red-carpeted corridor flanked by doors leading to different bedrooms. 'Okay,' he said, when we got to the door at the end. 'This is the honey-moon suite, and it's the room Liz and I stayed in on the night of our wedding. This was one of Liz's first projects so it's looking pretty good in here.' The door swung open with a creak to reveal a beautiful cream-panelled bedroom with a king-sized bed. Gold jacquard curtains hung at the huge window, which had sweeping views of the rolling hills and woodland surrounding the hall. 'As you can see, it's rather nice. There are tea- and coffee-making facilities on the dresser, and a lovely en-suite bathroom.'

'Ooh, it's lovely!' Elena wandered in, looking around her in delight. She seemed entranced by everything she saw and I wondered if there was any possibility that Daniel would agree to move their wedding to Willow Hall. It was clear she loved it and I hoped she wasn't going to be disappointed if he said no. His dad's golf club had never been her first choice of venue.

Crossing to the window, I looked out at the view.

'Yes, Liz designed it all. She wouldn't let me or Anthony near it. I don't think she trusts us with the design side.' Julian laughed as he opened a door next to the bed. 'Take a look at the en suite. It's got a roll-top bath!'

'Very nice!' Elena said, following him into the bathroom, leaving me and Anthony in the main bedroom. I stayed by the window, staring out at the view with my back to Anthony. Even though I couldn't see him, I could feel his eyes on me. I rubbed the back of my neck. The atmosphere grew hotter and heavier with each minute Elena and Julian were out of the room. They seemed to be taking their time. I could hear them discussing the gold taps and the fluffiness of the towels. *Hurry up, for heaven's sake!*

'Do you like the view?' Anthony's voice came from just behind me, making me jump. I hadn't realised he was quite so close. I half-turned before quickly facing the window again, my heart thumping.

'Oh! Yes. Yes, it's really lovely,' I said, far too heartily. 'The whole place is beautiful. You're so lucky to live here!'

He laughed and I felt his warm breath on my neck. My knees trembled and I shut my eyes, trying to block him out. 'There was a time I wouldn't have agreed,' he said. 'But the old place has grown on me over the past year. It's quite nice to be back.'

'It's great that you and Julian are back to make a go of things,' I said, surprised my voice sounded relatively normal when I felt so breathless.

'Yes, well, it was time I grew up and faced up to my responsibilities. I suppose I have the accident to thank for that.'

I nodded. I didn't feel like thanking the accident for anything. As far as I knew, we might still have been together now if it hadn't been for the accident. But perhaps that was another thing he was grateful for. He never had wanted a long-term relationship.

Elena and Julian emerged from the en suite, still discussing the fixtures and fittings. 'Where have you booked to stay on the night of your wedding?' he asked her. 'A local hotel?'

'No, we're just going home after the night-do,' she said, slightly glumly.

'You can't *just* go home after you get married!' Anthony protested. 'What an anticlimax! It's supposed to be the most romantic, most memorable day of your life, Elena!'

I turned to look at him in surprise. Since when did he care where people spent their wedding night? Was it just a sales pitch? A new angle to convince Elena to move her wedding?

Elena shrugged. 'It will still be a memorable day. We'll be really tired anyway, so I don't suppose it will matter. Besides, we're going on honeymoon the following day.'

'Where are you going?' Julian asked.

'Portugal.'

'Lovely. We went to Portugal on holiday the year before last. Where are you staying?'

Elena began talking about her honeymoon plans but I was so focused on Anthony's presence that I was unable to follow what she said. Every cell in my body seemed to be straining towards him, like flowers to the sun. I wasn't sure why I found him so attractive after all this time. I'd spent most of this past year feeling angry with him, so why should seeing him again have such an effect on me? I turned back to the window and stared out at the distant hills and the blue, blue sky. I kept getting wafts of his aftershave, subtly competing with the new-paint smell of the bedroom. I pressed my fingertips to the windowsill, my nails whitening with the pressure.

'Do you have a room where the bride and bridesmaids can get ready beforehand too?' Elena asked.

'Oh, yes, we're preparing that at the moment. It's just down the corridor. Follow me.'

I turned to follow, only to find myself nose to collar with Anthony.

27

'Sorry!' I blurted, backing away instantly.

'My fault. I was just trying to catch a glimpse of something in the garden below. So sorry.' He stood back to let me pass and I scuttled away, cheeks glowing like distress flares. *Oh, God, please let this be over soon*, I prayed. It was too awkward and intense.

The bridal suite, as they called it, was a large cream room, similar to the honeymoon suite, but with a huge dressing table and pewter-framed mirror. I tried my best to focus on what Julian was saying, but my nerves were shredded. The only thing I cared about was the fact that Anthony was leaning casually against the doorframe like some kind of male model.

'Ooh, I like the window seat!' Elena said, pressing her hand into the cushion, which was still covered in plastic.

'Yes, Liz said it's a good photo-opportunity.'

'Oooh!' Elena spun round enthusiastically. 'And we could stay over the night before? Rachel and I?'

I swallowed. Was Elena really considering moving her wedding to Willow Hall?

'Of course!' Julian answered. 'Guests could stay too. And the groom, of course. Although you'd have to be careful to keep out of sight of him before the wedding.'

'Guest accommodation wouldn't be free, though,' Anthony put in with a glance at his brother. 'Although we would offer it at a reduced rate.'

Elena nodded. 'Well, I think you've given me plenty to think about. I'll have to talk to Daniel about it, obviously. I'm not sure... it's the golf club where his dad goes, you see, so he might not want to change.'

'Well, bring him down and we can convince him. Otherwise, it's down to you, Rachel.' Julian turned his blue eyes on me and smiled. 'You've got us excited now and we're counting on one of you to have your wedding with us here this year.'

'No pressure then!' I laughed nervously and turned quickly

away from Anthony's gaze. 'Someone might well book with you today and you won't need us at all.'

'I doubt it. Most of them are locals who've only come to have a good old look around. They don't really approve of our new venture. They think it will cause too much traffic in the village.'

'I bet the owners of the guesthouse will be happy. And the pub.'

Julian wrinkled his nose and looked at Anthony. 'You'd think so, but they're a bit sceptical. I think most of the villagers think we're going to fail and sell up anyway. But we're determined to prove them wrong, aren't we, Anthony?'

'We are.' Anthony inclined his head and looked down at his shiny black shoes.

Julian led us back down the stairs and out of the front door and along a shady gravel path towards the stable block. He kept up a stream of cheerful chatter the whole way, while Elena walked beside him, laughing and looking around her excitedly. It was a relief to be outside. I felt like I could breathe again.

'I'm sorry if I seemed rude when I saw you earlier,' Anthony said in a low voice as he fell into step beside me. 'It was just such a shock to see you.'

'Oh, no, you weren't rude at all!' I glanced up at him in surprise. 'It was certainly a shock. I didn't expect to see you either.' I swallowed nervously and touched the back of my hair to check it wasn't falling down. Should I apologise for turning up unannounced on his territory? At least I'd known there was a slight possibility he might be here. To him it must have seemed like I'd fallen from the sky. Still, he appeared to be over his shock now and looked quite relaxed, whereas I still felt raw and emotional.

'No, well, I suppose you wouldn't have expected me of all people to be at a wedding fair, even if it was on my property!' He gave a rueful laugh. 'I must admit it wasn't my first choice of business. I was thinking more along the lines of conference facilities and countryside pursuits. You know, clay pigeon shooting or paintballing. Maybe even a golf course.' He sighed longingly and I laughed.

'Why didn't you go for those then?'

'Julian and Liz can be pretty persuasive when they get going. They managed to convince me weddings would be lucrative and probably the least labour-intensive of all the options. I'm not sure I believe that. I think it's just a line they fed me to get me to agree to it all, and now I'm up to my armpits in wedding paraphernalia!'

'Oh, dear! Is it that bad?'

He laughed. 'It hasn't been so far. It's been quite satisfying getting the old place looking good again, and Mother's happy to have us back.'

I nodded, unable to think of a suitable reply. We'd reached the end of the path now anyway, which had delivered us into the square courtyard of the stable block. Arranged in a U-shape, it was built in the same soft red brick as the house and had been converted into four nice-looking cottages.

'Ooh, these look nice!' Elena said enthusiastically.

'Yes, and they'll definitely be ready for August,' Julian said. 'Unfortunately, I don't have the key or I'd show you inside, but you can see through the window that they're pretty roomy. The roof was high enough for us to put in a mezzanine floor so there are three bedrooms. One to the side and two in the roof. See, plenty of room for your guests. Well, some of them, at least.'

'Oh, yes! They're great!' Elena pressed her nose to the newly glazed window of the first cottage while I stood looking around. The stables looked very grand and I wondered how often they were used when Anthony and Julian were children. Anthony had never mentioned a love of horses or anything like that. But even with the stable doors removed and replaced with windows and proper wooden doors, you could see this had once been an impressive stable block. I imagined all the staff that would have been employed here; the grooms preparing the horses to be ridden by the lady of the manor. The amount of history in this place blew my mind.

'Did you have horses when you were growing up?' I asked.

'No. Just a couple of fat Shetlands when we were small, but they weren't kept in here. It's been used for storage for years.' Anthony stood with his hands on his hips, his blue shirt pulling tight at his shoulders. 'This is the bit I've enjoyed. Renovating buildings that have been doing nothing for years.'

'Overseeing it, you mean.' Julian laughed. 'It's not like you did any of the work yourself.'

'Well, no. But I was involved in the planning.' He turned, his foot scraping on the gravel, and I retrieved my sunglasses from my bag and put them on. Despite the tall surrounding trees, the courtyard was a real suntrap and I had to squint in the bright sunshine. Elena put her head back, tipping her face up to the sun.

'It's so lovely here. I think I could stay for ever.'

Julian laughed. 'It's the obvious choice for your wedding then, isn't it? Come on, you know you want to.'

Elena smiled. 'I know *I* want to, but it's not just about what I want. I'll check with Daniel and let you know.'

'Okay.' Julian shrugged. 'Well, I've done my best. You can vouch for me, can't you, Anthony? That means I won't get in trouble with my wife.'

Elena laughed. 'When will you need to know by?'

Julian shrugged. 'As soon as possible really. How about you, Rachel? Do you think you'd be able to convince Jayjay to get married here this year?'

'Err, no, I don't think so.'

'Oh, really?' Julian's face dropped. 'Don't you like it?'

'Of course I like it! It's beautiful. But…' I glanced at Elena and she shook her head slightly. 'It's complicated.'

'Okay. Well, take a business card each and just give us a call if you change your minds. Perhaps you could bring Daniel for a visit, Elena? Just give me a call and let me know when you'd like to come.'

He took a small pile of business cards from his breast pocket and handed one to me and one to Elena. Willow Hall was embossed in gold script across the top and, underneath, both Anthony and Julian's mobile telephone numbers were included. I stared at Anthony's number for a second before putting it in my handbag.

'Great! Thanks! Well, I guess we'd better get going then.' Elena checked her watch. 'Thank you for showing us round. It's been wonderful.'

'It's our pleasure. Lovely to meet you, Elena. And to see you again, Rachel.' Julian smiled. 'Right, I suppose I'd better get back to the pavilion and see if anyone wants to book a wedding!'

Anthony nodded. 'I'll be along in a minute. I'll walk Rachel and Elena back to their car.'

'Great! Bye, ladies.' Julian kissed us both before walking off with a wave. We watched him go before turning back towards the shady path. Anthony walked between us, looking thoughtfully at the floor.

'Julian's very enthusiastic, isn't he?' Elena said. 'He's a natural born salesman.'

'I don't know about that. He's a solicitor, really.' Anthony laughed. 'He's determined to make this work, though. We both are. He's just better at it than I am.'

'Oh, I don't know. You did all right.' Elena smiled at him. 'How are you, anyway? Are you fully recovered from the car crash?'

'Yes. I'm fine now, thank you.'

'Back at work? Busy being a detective.'

He nodded. 'Yes. I went back after Christmas.'

'Only after Christmas? Wow! That's a long time off.'

'Yes. I'm okay now, though.' He shrugged. 'I had lots of physio to get me walking again. I still limp if I get tired but I'm lucky really.'

'Are you back driving?'

'Oh, yes. I work in Manchester so I have to.'

'Still? Can't you get transferred somewhere closer?'

'It's okay. You get used to it. Ah, here's the car park,' he said as the path grew lighter. 'Well, it's lovely to see you both again.' He stopped walking and looked at us both. 'I hope we'll see you again soon, but if not, good luck with your weddings.'

'Thank you.'

He bent to kiss Elena before turning to me. It was the briefest of kisses. A faint brush of his lips against my cheek, a warm hand on my arm, and it was over. For one fleeting moment, our eyes caught and my heart jolted as though an electric current had passed through me. But I was already turning to go, saying goodbye, thanking him for his time. I didn't even look back over my shoulder as I walked over to Elena's car, my jaw rigid.

'Well, that was nice,' Elena said as she opened up the car. The warm air inside seemed to warp and pulsate as I lowered myself into the passenger seat.

'Blimey, it's hot in here!' I fanned myself with my hand and blew a strand of hair from in front of my face. 'I don't want to close the door.'

'I know, it's boiling. I'll get the air con going. That should sort it.' She closed her door and started the engine. 'Are you all right? That must have been a bit of a shock for you.'

'You could say that,' I said, wrapping the seatbelt around me. 'That will teach me to go snooping around ex-boyfriends' stately homes.'

Elena laughed. 'He didn't seem to mind, though. I think he was quite pleased to see you. Look, he's still watching.'

'Hmm.' It hadn't escaped my notice that Anthony was still standing where we'd left him, watching us go. He raised a hand as the car moved off and Elena and I waved back. Even at this distance, his eyes seemed to rest on mine. Goose bumps sprang up on my arms and the blood fizzed in my veins.

'I can't believe how beautiful Willow Hall is,' Elena said as we drove out of the car park and down the drive. 'Ohhhh, I'd love to get married there.'

'Do you think Daniel would go for it, though?' I said, doubtfully. 'I mean, you've got everything organised already. Wouldn't it be stressful to change everything?'

Elena shrugged. 'I don't think it would be a huge problem in terms of organising everything, but I'll have to discuss it with Daniel and our parents. How do you feel about it? Would you mind if I got married there?'

'I don't mind at all. Why should I? You know I'll be there, whatever, and we'll sort getting the flowers here somehow. It shouldn't be a problem.'

'Yes, but what about the Anthony situation?'

'What about it? I've seen him now. The worst part is over.' I looked out of the window, trying to pretend I was unaffected by the afternoon.

'How did you feel seeing him again? I mean, I know it was a shock when you first saw him, but how did you feel walking round the house with him? Did it feel awkward?'

'Errr… well… Not awkward, exactly. It was more surreal than anything else.'

'I kept thinking maybe I should tell him off for treating you so badly, but he was so pleasant today it was hard to summon up any negative feelings towards him at all. Especially with Julian there too.'

'Of course.' I shrugged. 'It wasn't like he treated me badly when we were together. I was just hurt when he didn't want to be with me any more, but that's his right. And like you say, he was perfectly polite and civil today. It wouldn't have been right to be rude to him. I mean, a whole year has passed since then. What's done is done. There's no point dwelling on the past, is there?'

'No, of course not. Especially as you're engaged now.' She looked over at me with a sly smile. I rolled my eyes at her.

'I wish you hadn't said that, Elena,' I said indignantly. 'Or rather, I wish I hadn't gone along with it! I feel bad for lying. Especially about Bobbi's boyfriend.'

Elena laughed wickedly. 'Don't be daft. He's never going to know, is he?'

It was like a slap. The thought of Anthony never finding out I wasn't engaged depressed me immeasurably, but Elena was right; he probably never would know I'd lied. 'Oh. Well, I suppose not.' I stared out of the window at the passing fields, my throat aching with the effort of not crying.

'What?' Elena looked across at me in surprise. 'What's wrong? Have I upset you?'

'No!'

'What then? Surely you want him to think you've moved on and are happy with someone else? You don't want him to think you're pining for him, do you?'

'Of course not, but… I don't know. I suppose the fact that he won't ever find out means I won't see him again. It just underlines the fact that I'm not part of his life and he's not part of mine.'

Elena blinked at me before looking back at the road. 'But he hasn't been part of your life for the past year.'

I sniffed and rummaged in my bag for a tissue. 'I know. I'm just being silly. Ignore me.'

'Do you still have feelings for Anthony?'

'Of course I still have feelings for Anthony. Wasn't it blatantly obvious?'

'Oh, Rachel, not at all! You held it together beautifully.'

'Really? I was a bag of nerves.'

'Well, it didn't show. You were composed and gracious. The perfect lady, in fact. He's mad to have finished with you. I bet he realised that too. I bet he's kicking himself right now, if he wasn't already. What was he talking to you about on the way to the stable yard?'

'Nothing much. He just apologised for being so shocked when he first saw me, that's all.'

Elena laughed. 'It must have been a surprise. Especially with you in a bridal gown.'

'I know.' I smiled and played with my tissue, stretching the fragile soft paper over my fingertip.

'So, would it make it better or worse if we moved the wedding to Willow Hall?'

'Either is fine. Honestly, it makes no difference either way. It's over. I know it's over and I just need to get over him. Who knows, maybe it will be easier now I've seen him. I know where he is, I know what he's doing, I know that he's well…'

Elena laughed. 'That sounds like a line from some stalker thriller… *I know where he is…*'

'You know what I mean,' I chuckled. 'He's doing okay. I just need to move on and leave him behind.'

Elena nodded but didn't look convinced. I wasn't convinced myself. The further we got from Willow Hall, the more I wanted to go back. The hollow feeling in my stomach seemed to grow and grow until I felt sick. Everything felt wrong and out of place and, beneath it all, I had a renewed conviction that I really did belong with Anthony.

The problem was, he thought he didn't belong with me.

Anthony,

I came to the hospital today but they wouldn't let me see you. Do you know how humiliating it is to be turned away from a hospital ward when you've driven an hour to get there? I know what you said in your letter, but I couldn't believe it was true. I have no words to express how hurt and angry I am right now. I needed to see you, Anthony, because I love you and I want to know you're all right. I want to be there for you, to support you during your recovery. You must know you need as much support as possible at this time. Why would you push me away when you know I want to be with you? I can't stand the thought of you lying in that hospital bed, so many miles away from me. I would stay with you every minute of every day if I could. I can't stand not seeing you and not knowing what's going on.

Please, I'm begging you, don't shut me out. I need you and I know you need me too.

I love you.

Rachel

Chapter Three

We never said I love you, Anthony and I. The only time I said it was in that final letter to him and I'd regretted it ever since. Maybe if I hadn't told him that, maybe if I hadn't sounded so desperate, then maybe he would have replied with more than just a curt: it's over.

Maybe.

But why shouldn't I have said it? It was true. I was in love with him. Head over heels, full-on obsessed, completely in love with everything about him. I loved him so much I wanted to shout it from the rooftops. But I knew how panicky he felt about the whole serious relationship thing. He hated the thought of being tied down. He didn't want a long-term relationship, and I was at pains to keep things casual and fun so as not to frighten him off.

When I received that terrible phone call saying he'd had a car accident and been taken to hospital, my mask slipped and I could no longer hide how I felt. He'd seen it and panicked. Shut me out. I don't know why I thought expressing my love for him in a letter was a good thing to do. I suppose I was too angry and sad and shocked to think clearly at the time, but there wasn't a moment that went by that I didn't wish I hadn't said all those things and sent it to him.

It had been just over a week since Elena and I visited Willow Hall, and I'd thought of nothing but Anthony ever since. I was haunted by his voice and kept replaying everything he'd said over and over in my mind, analysing every moment, every look, every move. I was driving myself mad. Even though Anthony hadn't been far from my thoughts all year, I'd learned to live without him. He was a constant niggle I couldn't quite shake off, but I'd managed to function well enough. Now, though, that niggle was a full-on itch that dominated everything. I couldn't eat, I couldn't sleep, I was distracted at work.

I didn't know what to do. It felt pathetic to be yearning for him a year after he'd dumped me, but I couldn't help it. It was like I'd peeled off a bandage, thinking the wound beneath had almost healed, only to find a huge, gaping gash pumping out blood.

It wasn't even like I was going to be seeing him again. Elena hadn't managed to convince Daniel to move the wedding to Willow Hall after all. I hadn't let her see how disappointed I was; I'd just agreed it was a big thing to rearrange everything at this stage and said I didn't blame them. But I'd cried when I put the phone down. Which was stupid, because I didn't want to see Anthony again if I felt like this afterwards. It was better all round.

Even so, I was plagued with irrational thoughts and madcap ideas about how I could get back to Willow Hall. Who did I know that was getting married and might choose it as their wedding venue? Could I convince my parents to renew their vows? Maybe I could carry on pretending I was getting married and go back for a second look. Hmm, no… too dishonest and much too desperate.

Sighing heavily, I filled a jug of water and started topping up the vases of flowers around the shop. I felt so tired and hopeless that even the cheery spring blooms couldn't perk me up. The shelves of our florist shop, The Birdcage, were filled with beautiful multicoloured tulips, jaunty yellow daffodils, pink fluffy peonies, purple irises and white calla lilies. We had roses of every colour, gerberas, lilies, lisianthus and anemones. Potted primroses and hyacinths, which filled the shop with their own sweet scent. Usually just the sight of the flowers in our lovely shop cheered me up, but today, for some reason, I only felt like going home. But what would I do there? Just mope?

The water I was pouring into a vase of yellow roses overflowed and puddled on the shelf before dripping on to the floor. Groaning, I set my jug down and went to get a paper towel to mop up the spillage. It was only water, but at that moment it felt like the end of the world. Tears pricked my eyes and I couldn't help thinking everything would be better if Anthony were here. The water wouldn't have spilled, the flowers would smell sweeter, the shop would look prettier, and I wouldn't feel so bloody wretched.

I sighed again as I looked round at the flower-filled vintage birdcages hanging from the ceiling; the shabby chic dresser displaying scented candles; the twinkling white fairy lights I kept on all year round. It was just the same as it had been last year when Anthony had been around. It was depressing to realise that virtually nothing had changed in that time, including my feelings for him. Where would I be this time next year? Still standing here in the same spot, looking at the same shop and pining for him? I couldn't see anything changing any time soon.

The bell above the shop door tinkled and someone stepped into the shop behind me.

'Hello, Rachel.'

I froze at the sound of his voice before slowly turning my head to look over my shoulder. Anthony smiled awkwardly and shut the shop door with a clunk.

'I'm sorry to call in so unexpectedly,' he said, clearing his throat. 'I just wondered if I could have Elena's phone number.'

I couldn't speak for a moment. I just stared at him, disbelieving my own eyes. Anthony raised both eyebrows and I suddenly realised I had to say something.

'Oh.' I turned towards him then retreated to the other side of the shop, putting the counter between us. I didn't trust myself to stand so close to him and not do something desperate and humiliating. It wasn't fair of him to show up today of all days, when I was feeling so weak and emotionally raw. 'Why?'

He shrugged. 'We'd like to know if she's thought any more about having her wedding at Willow Hall.'

'She has but she hasn't been able to convince Daniel, I'm afraid.'

'Oh, really? That is disappointing.' He walked slowly across the shop towards me, his boots clicking on the stone quarry tiles. He was more casually dressed today. Dark jeans and a navy rugby shirt, white T-shirt showing beneath. 'Any idea why?'

'They just think it would be too much effort to rearrange.' I smoothed my trembling hands over the flat sheets of wrapping paper on the counter and drew in a deep, calming breath.

Anthony frowned. 'But they'd get a really good deal.'

'I know they would. Elena knows that too. But it's only four months until their wedding and the invitations have gone out already.'

'So what? It's just a venue change. No big deal.'

'Well, they obviously think it is.'

'Can't you convince them otherwise?'

'Me? It's nothing to do with me. I'm just the bridesmaid. Besides, you saw for yourself how much she loved Willow Hall. If she can't convince Daniel, no one can.'

'Will he not come to the hall for a look himself?'

'I don't know. You'll have to ask Daniel, not me. I can give you his number if you like?'

'Yes, please.' Anthony nodded and then turned to gaze around at the shop as I nipped into the back room for my mobile phone. My heart was beating in my throat and I felt short of breath as I opened my contacts to find Daniel's number. I scrolled past his name three times before finally focusing enough to remember who I was searching for. My head was spinning so much I felt dizzy. I couldn't believe Anthony was here in the shop when I'd been telling myself I'd never see him again. 'Do you want me to give you my number and you can just send it through to me?' Anthony called.

'Erm, it's okay. I'll just write it down.'

'It'd probably be easier. No chance of mistakes.' His voice got louder suddenly and he appeared in the archway to the back room. Producing his phone from the back pocket of his jeans, he proceeded to read out his phone number. Flustered, I fumbled with my phone and managed to input his number. I could only hope he didn't notice how shaky I was. 'There, you can forward the contact to me now.'

'Okay.' It was a straightforward task, but my mind went blank as I gazed at my phone, trying to work out how to forward the number to him. The only thing in my head was the fact I now had Anthony's number in my phone, and how was I going to stop myself from calling him in the middle of the night? The business card Julian had given me was sitting on my kitchen windowsill at home, proudly propped up against an orchid. I'd been proud of myself for not inputting it into my phone straight away, but now Anthony had scuppered that.

'It hasn't changed in here, has it?' Anthony said, looking around him.

'No, nothing's changed,' I said, a slightly bitter edge to my voice.

'It's like stepping back in time.' He smiled and I felt a little glow of happiness. I was glad he had good memories of this place, even if he had ultimately dumped me. 'Who's living upstairs now?'

'Erm, a family.' I glanced up at him. I wasn't sure I wanted to talk about when we lived together in the apartment above the shop. Everything was broken and wrong now. It made me feel sad to think about it. 'My parents no longer own the flat. They sold it last year.'

'Oh, really? That's a shame.'

'Hmm... it was getting too much for them. Dad decided he didn't want the stress of dealing with tenants.'

'Were we such bad tenants?' he joked. A wide smile spread

42

across his face and his eyes sparkled mischievously. I wondered what he was playing at, coming here and joking about our relationship when it was still so painful to me. But then, I suppose he didn't know that. Most normal women would have moved on and been over him by now.

'The worst,' I replied. At last my brain slotted into gear and I managed to send Daniel's number to Anthony. His phone gave a beep and he glanced down at it in his hand.

'You're still on the same number?' He seemed surprised.

I shrugged. 'There was no reason to change it. I still have the same phone.'

There was an awkward pause and he hovered in the archway between the shop and the back room as though he was about to leave. I was caught in a kind of panicky limbo where I couldn't tell if I wanted him to go so I could calm my nerves and have a good cry, or stay so I could be with him for longer.

He seemed undecided himself for a moment, but then he leaned back against the wall, seemingly in no hurry to leave. 'Where's Bobbi?'

'On her lunch.' It was on the tip of my tongue to mention she was out with her boyfriend, until I remembered I was supposed to be engaged to Jayjay myself. Bobbi had been hugely amused when I'd told her what had happened at Willow Hall and hadn't seemed to mind me hijacking her boyfriend's name.

'Is she well?'

'She's good, thank you. Her mum's a lot better and back at work so Bobbi's not shouldering all of the responsibility any more.' Bobbi was only nineteen and had had a tough time last year, struggling to support her family on her wages after her mother fell ill. Anthony had been particularly kind and supportive towards her.

'That's good to hear.'

'Yep.'

Another pause.

'And how are your parents?'

'They're fine, thank you. Dad's slowing down a bit, which is why he sold the apartment. He's seventy this year.'

'Really?'

I nodded. My goodness, this was painful. Without the subject of Willow Hall or Elena's wedding, we were just trying to make small talk, with neither of us mentioning his accident or the fact that he'd dumped me and banned me from the hospital. What I really wanted to ask was why? What had I done that was so wrong? Why had he pushed me away at such a crucial time? I'd been so upset by him being injured. I'd been desperate to know how he was, and yet he'd shut me out. Cath had kept me updated for a while, but I felt guilty phoning her when she had so much to deal with herself.

'What about the shop? He's not selling that I take it?'

'Oh, err…' I had to wrench my head back from reliving the moment I'd shown up at the hospital only to be told he didn't want to see me. 'No, well, not right now, anyway.'

'But they might in the future?'

I swallowed. 'Perhaps.'

His brow furrowed and he gave me a searching look. 'So what will that mean for you?'

'I don't know right now. We haven't really talked about it.'

'But surely as their only daughter you stand to inherit this place?'

'Yes, but it… it depends if it's profitable.' I sighed. I really didn't want to be discussing this with Anthony of all people. Besides, this was business I'd been putting off thinking about for months now. There had been a vague suggestion around the time they'd sold the flat that they might look into selling the shop if it didn't make a profit this year, but we were doing pretty well so I wasn't too worried. 'And I think it is profitable, so it will be all right.'

'Are you still doing wedding flowers?'

'Of course.'

'Would you like for us to put you forward as one of our

44

recommended florists? You could come and exhibit at our next open day.'

'Oh! Really?' I frowned slightly, confused by the offer. 'Aren't I a bit too far away?'

Anthony shrugged. 'It's only an hour's drive.'

'I suppose.' I frowned, confused about why he would want to promote his ex-girlfriend's business when he hadn't seen me in so long. I opened my mouth to say something gracious, then changed my mind and decided to say what was actually on my mind instead. 'But that would mean you'd see me more often, Anthony. And forgive me for bringing it up when we're going to such pains to avoid it, but you actually banned me from your hospital room because you didn't want to see me again.'

I didn't know what kind of reaction I'd expected from him, but the slight shrug of his shoulders took me by surprise. Was he really so oblivious to how much he'd hurt me?

'This is business,' he said. 'We're trying to get Willow Hall known as a great wedding venue, and you're an experienced wedding florist with lots of contacts. I think we could be very useful to each other.'

'Really?'

'Yes, of course. Why not? The past is the past. You've moved on, haven't you? You've got this… Jojo…?'

'Jayjay.'

'Right, that's what I said. Anyway, we're both adults, aren't we? I don't see why we can't work together. Besides, you probably wouldn't be seeing a lot of me anyway. I'm planning on taking a backseat in all of this. Weddings aren't my favourite thing, as you well know.' He grimaced and straightened up slightly. 'How are your wedding plans, anyway?'

'Errr…' I shook my head. 'Nothing yet.'

'No ring, I see.' He nodded at my empty left hand.

'Not yet.'

Unable to stop myself, I shoved my hands in the pockets of

my cardigan. I was rubbish at lying and convinced Anthony would see straight through me. He was a detective, after all, and trained in reading people's body language.

The bell above the shop door jingled and I heard Bobbi's laugh ring out as she entered the shop. Did that mean she was with Jayjay? Oh no, this just got worse.

'Anthony!' I heard her say in surprise. 'Oh, my God! I can't believe it.' She appeared in the archway and threw her arms around him. 'It's so lovely to see you! Isn't it lovely, Rachel?'

'Yes,' I said, far more cheerfully than I felt.

Bobbi widened her eyes meaningfully at me. 'Ooh, guess who I found walking back from lunch? Jayjay.'

'Oh, is he here?' I said.

'Yes. Jayjay, your fiancée's in the back.'

'Huh?' I heard him say, confused.

'Rachel's through here, in the back.' Bobbi was talking to Jayjay like he was a reluctant toddler. 'Come through. Come on.'

My heart thudded with dread and I had to fight hard not to cringe as Jayjay appeared through the archway, pausing to shake Anthony's hand as Bobbi introduced them to each other. To my relief, Jayjay looked fairly tidy today and a bit older than his twenty-two years, so we didn't look quite as mismatched as I feared. As I was twenty-six, I didn't want to look like some kind of cradle snatcher, especially when Anthony was ten years older than me.

'All right, love?' he said, smiling cheekily at me.

'Hi,' I replied cheerfully. 'How are you?'

'Fine, thanks.'

There was an awkward pause during which Jayjay, Bobbi and I all stared at each other with frozen smiles.

'Well, I'd better go,' Anthony said. 'Lovely to see you again, Bobbi. Nice to meet you, Jojo.' And then he was gone. The door slammed shut behind him and Bobbi and I looked at each other.

'Oh, my God! Are you all right?' Bobbi asked as she peeled off her denim jacket.

I nodded mutely and sat down on the wooden chair next to me. 'Bit of a shock.'

'I bet it was.'

Jayjay looked confused. 'Not being funny, but what was all that fiancé stuff about?'

'Elena told Anthony that Rachel was engaged to someone called Jayjay, so you've got to pretend to be her fiancé every time Anthony's around.'

'Oh.' A frown appeared on his face and he ran a hand through his dark hair. 'Why?'

I opened my mouth to respond, then shut it again. I wasn't sure why either. Luckily, Bobbi seemed to understand everything perfectly.

'Because Rachel's still in love with Anthony but she doesn't want him to know that so she's pretending to have moved on.'

'Hey!' I protested.

'Oh.' Jayjay's face cleared and he laughed. 'So I'm like a stunt double?'

'Erm… if you like.' Bobbi laughed and rolled her eyes at me.

'Cool.' Jayjay laughed. 'Right, I'd better get going.' He leaned over to kiss Bobbi. 'I'll pick you up later, okay?'

'Okay. Bye.' Bobbi watched him go, her face slightly flushed and her eyes bright. I smiled at her.

'Thank you for that. I never thought we'd ever actually have to pretend.'

Bobbi laughed. 'I think it's funny. I can't believe Anthony was here. What did he want? Just to see you?'

'No, he wanted Daniel and Elena's number so he could call and pester them about the wedding.'

'Really? Like a pushy salesman?'

'Pretty much.'

Bobbi winced. 'Still, it was nice to see him again. He looked well.'

'Hmm, he did.' I gnawed at a fingernail and stared at the rough brick of the wall opposite. Now Anthony had gone, I missed him desperately.

'Anyway,' Bobbi continued, 'do you want to go for your lunch now I'm back? You look like you need a break.'

'Do I look that bad?' I laughed as I stood up and reached for my coat.

'Not *bad*. Just a bit shell-shocked, that's all. It must be difficult seeing him again after the way he finished with you. I must say, you've been very restrained about it all. I think I would have punched him in the nuts.'

I laughed, picturing the scene. 'Tempting, but not very dignified.'

'But ultimately very satisfying. See you later.'

I went out on to the street and turned right to go down to the river. The busy city centre with its tourists, shoppers and office workers rushing to get their lunch held no appeal for me today. My nerves were too frayed and the only thing I needed was some fresh air and space to think. The blustery wind had goose bumps racing across my flesh and my skirt billowing around my legs. It was a lot colder than it had been last week at Willow Hall.

But as I was walking, it occurred to me Anthony might still be around somewhere, getting a bite to eat in a café or simply looking around the shops. I stopped suddenly as an overwhelming urge to find him took hold. The woman walking behind tutted loudly and cast an irritated look over her shoulder as she scooted around me.

'Sorry,' I muttered, before forcing myself to carry on towards the river. What was I thinking? I'd been almost relieved when he left the shop just now. The conversation had been so awkward and stilted, and so much remained unsaid between us, that it had been almost painful. And yet, I still had some kind of masochistic urge to see and speak to him again. It wouldn't do. I needed to get some control over my emotions. Anthony wasn't interested in me. He'd only come to the shop to find out about Elena's wedding. He didn't even care that I was engaged – or, rather, pretending to be engaged. All he cared about was drumming up business for Willow Hall.

I couldn't blame him. It was he who had finished it, after all, and that was more than a year ago. Any normal person would be able to move on with their life, and he obviously had. It was only me clinging to the past, trying to hold on to something that had long since died. I couldn't even understand why I was still so attached to him. I'd had plenty of boyfriends in the past who had meant nothing to me. They'd come and gone from my life and I'd given them barely a second thought. Okay, so he was the only man I'd ever lived with, but that was only because my house had been flooded by a burst boiler so he'd offered to let me stay. It wasn't like we'd bought a house together, chosen furniture, shared dreams. We hadn't even been together that long. Just four months. Maybe that was why I couldn't get over him. It had all felt so new and exciting, and then he'd had the accident and shut me out when I was agonised with worry.

The river was only at the bottom of the street. Cars trundled past and, spotting a break in the traffic as the lights turned red, I nipped across the road. A stiff breeze was stripping pink blossom from the trees and blowing it up the street, where it nestled in pavement cracks and gathered in gutters. Spring was a time of new life and fresh starts, but I always felt sorry for the blossom that ended its short life soiled and damaged on the ground.

The riverfront was surprisingly busy for a weekday. I paused by the weir to watch a cormorant fish in the rushing water, its thin black neck emerging triumphant from the white foam, clutching its wriggling silver prize in its beak. Although the sun was shining, the fresh breeze carried flecks of rain, and I shivered as one splattered inside my ear. Pulling my coat around me, I left the roar of the weir and rumble of traffic from the bridge behind me and headed down to the riverfront. I'd intended to sit on one of the benches but they were all taken, so I walked slowly along the front instead, enjoying the fresh air and smell of the water. The trees were all in blossom and pink petals fluttered to the floor with each gust of wind. One of the big white show boats was docked next to the wooden jetty, waiting to take people on a sightseeing cruise upstream. Shielding my eyes from the sun, I watched a young couple take a seat together on the top deck, remembering when Anthony and I had done the same thing in happier times. We'd been more interested in kissing than watching the view slide past, but it had been a lovely day, warm for March. I remembered the sun sparkling on the water in the same way I'd seen a thousand times before, but because I was with Anthony it seemed magical somehow.

The couple on the top deck were kissing now, oblivious to me watching below. With a silent wish that their relationship would last longer than mine and Anthony's, I walked on towards the bandstand.

Further on, a toddler girl and her grandfather were throwing bread for a family of swans while seagulls wheeled above, their shrill cries slicing the air. The girl looked so adorable in her bright-red coat and red wellingtons that I couldn't help but smile. Her dark hair was tied up in stubby pigtails and she kept shouting at the gulls and waving her little arms around while her grandfather knelt beside her, laughing. I looked around to see if anyone else was watching them and my heart lurched as I spotted Anthony sitting on a bench a few rows back.

He hadn't seen me yet. He was hunched over with his elbows on his knees, staring at the space between his feet. I hesitated, suddenly terrified and unsure whether to pretend not to have seen him and walk on. After all, he'd just been introduced to my pretend fiancé. I wasn't sure I was ready to talk to him right now, especially if he was going to ask me questions about Jayjay.

But there was something about his posture that made me carry on staring. He looked sad, somehow. Dejected. Why did he look like that? What was happening in his life?

So I found myself walking slowly over to him, my red mary-janes making a satisfying clop-clopping noise on the concrete until I was standing directly in front of him. He stared at my shoes for a moment before slowly straightening up and looking at me.

'Oh.'

I experienced a flutter of panic. What did *oh* mean? Did he think I'd followed him here? Maybe I should have just walked on after all.

'I was just out for some fresh air.' I pointed behind me at the river, as though it wasn't obvious where we were. 'I thought you'd gone.'

He shrugged. 'I thought I'd come down here. Relive some old memories.' He smiled up at me, his eyes on mine, and I felt my heart shift in my chest. Had he really been thinking about me? Us? Before I could say anything, he looked around him. 'I've missed this place. I forgot how pretty Chester is.'

'Yeah, I guess I forget to look because I live here.' I opened my mouth to ask if he remembered going on the boat cruise, then quickly changed my mind. I didn't want him to say no, or say yes, it was boring, or something that might ruin my precious memories of a perfect day. 'You live in a pretty place anyway, don't you? Willow Hall is beautiful.'

He grunted and shrugged. 'I suppose so. But… ah, never mind.' He sighed heavily and ran a hand over his face. 'Would you like to sit down?' He indicated the bench next to him and I sat down at the far end, leaving a generous gap between us.

'So what's up? Are you not happy living there?'

'It's not that. I like it better than I ever thought I would. It's just a lot of pressure, you know. We need to make it work or we'll lose it. We've only got one wedding booked for next year.'

'Well, even one wedding's a good start, isn't it? And you have more open days coming up, don't you? You're bound to get something from those.'

'Let's hope so. The renovations have cost us a fortune. We need

51

to start making some money somehow. Julian and I have put this off for far too long.'

'I don't understand how your mother's kept it going for so long without your support. How did she cope?'

Anthony shrugged. 'We rent out land to farmers, so that's provided some income. But if we're going to keep the hall, we need to increase our revenue.'

I stared thoughtfully up at the branches of the tree above us. 'Why don't you put on some other events this year if you can't get weddings? Corporate events? Dog shows? Horse shows? Flower shows? Craft fairs?'

'It's a bit late to organise it all now.'

'Why? They don't have to be huge events. Start off small and well organised and invite the local press to get coverage.'

Anthony stared thoughtfully at the river. A group of teenagers had hired a bright-orange pedalo and were laughing raucously as they tried to pedal against the current.

'Hmm, that's an idea.'

'Do you know any rock stars that would put on a concert for you?'

'Sadly not.'

'Shame.'

He chuckled and rubbed his face again. 'Jayjay seems like a nice lad. Why aren't you with him?'

'He had to get back to work.' I kept my eyes on the pedalo. Anthony's use of the word lad hadn't escaped me; he'd obviously noticed that Jayjay was younger than me. I hoped he wasn't going to ask me questions I couldn't answer. I was no good at lying.

'What does he do?'

'He's a roofer.' *I think*, I added silently to myself. I was pretty sure Bobbi had told me that, anyway.

'He didn't seem dressed for work.'

'He had an appointment this morning, but he's going back to work this afternoon.'

'Ah, okay. So this flower show thing, how would we set that up?'

I hesitated. Why was he asking my advice? 'Err, well, you could advertise your own, although that might take a lot of organising and you might not be able to attract enough interest this year. Unless you contact your local horticultural society to see if they have any events planned that they might like to move to your hall?'

Anthony pulled a face. 'I doubt that would encourage any interest in our wedding business, though.'

'Maybe. Maybe not. I don't really know. How about a craft fair? That might be easier and could attract a broader range of people. Are the house and gardens open to visitors during the week?'

'Not at the moment. We talked about it, but Mother's not interested.'

'But you wouldn't have to open every day. You might not even get any visitors at first.'

'Well, then, that begs the question of whether it would even be worth the effort.'

'I suppose.'

There was a pause in conversation as a couple of ducks waddled up to investigate us for food. Quacking gently, they stared at us with their shiny black eyes and pecked hopefully at the floor by our feet.

'Hello, ducks,' Anthony said mildly. 'We have no bread. Try the little girl over there.' He nodded towards the toddler in the red coat who was now walking away, hand in hand with her grandfather. The swans were already gliding off down the river.

'She's so cute!' I said wistfully.

Anthony laughed. 'She is, isn't she. You should see Julian's kids. They're lovely. Grace is such a little chatterbox. She never stops talking. She's amazing, she really is. And Charlie is growing so fast! I can't get over him. Every day he seems to have grown another inch. He's great.'

'Aw, bless!' I stared at Anthony in amazement. He'd always

been fond of his niece and nephew, but he never used to gush about them like this.

'Liz is expecting again too. Did Julian tell you that on Sunday?'

'No! That's wonderful news. When is she due?'

'September, I think.' He grimaced. 'Don't quote me on that, though. I might have got it wrong.'

I laughed. 'Well, that's lovely. Tell them congratulations from me. I bet your mum's pleased.'

'Yes, she can't wait. She loves having the little ones around. They seem to make everything better.'

'I can imagine. Can I ask you something, though? Why did you move out? There must be plenty of room at the hall for everyone.'

He shrugged. 'You know what I'm like; I need my own space.'

'Don't you get lonely? I mean, I haven't seen where you're living, but I can imagine it must be pretty remote.'

'It's only a short walk from the main house. I'm all right. I like living on my own, away from all the nagging.'

'Nagging?' I felt a surge of indignation. 'I didn't nag, did I?'

'Not you!' he laughed. 'My mother. She's great but she does go on at me, checking I've done this and that. It's like I'm a kid again. No, I liked living with you.'

'Really?' I blinked in surprise.

'Of course. We got on all right, didn't we? You were easy to live with.'

'Oh.' I cleared my throat, my flush of happiness floating away with the blossom being stripped from the trees around us. Easy? Hmm, easy was convenient and unremarkable. It wasn't exciting or passionate or fun. No wonder he'd found it so easy to say goodbye. It was painful to think that while I counted the days I'd spent living with Anthony as some of the happiest of my life, to him they had just been pleasant and... *easy*. Still, what did I expect? I knew he didn't love me. He'd told me in his letter. *You know I don't love you.* Those words haunted me. They popped

54

into my head when I least expected them, leaving me with a burning pain deep in my gut. I sighed. It was well and truly time I got over him.

'I'd better go.' I stood up, pulling my bag over my shoulder. 'Good luck with everything. I hope Willow Hall turns into a roaring success.'

Anthony looked up at me in surprise. 'Where are you going?'

'Back to work.'

'Why? You're not that busy, are you? You used to take an hour for lunch.' He nodded towards the show boat. 'How about we take a trip on that? Come on, for old time's sake.' He stood up and his eyes twinkled as he looked down at me. 'I don't remember much about our last trip.'

I blushed and looked down at the floor, my resolve weakening. It would be nice to go on the boat. It would certainly make a change from being in the shop all afternoon, and I'd been so bored all morning. 'Well… all right then. It's only a half-hour trip, isn't it?'

'I think so, yes. Come on, I think it's about to leave.'

We hurried down the river and boarded the boat. Anthony paid for us both before leading the way up the stairs to the top deck. Our feet clattered against the wooden boards and we found a seat towards the back. I was thankful the seat we'd sat in last time was taken by two elderly ladies, otherwise I had the strangest feeling Anthony would have sat there.

'Jayjay won't mind you coming on this with me, will he?' he said as he slipped his wallet back into his pocket.

'Why should he?' I shrugged and looked away. 'It's just a boat trip.'

I pulled my coat tighter around me, an act that was less about being cold and more a nervous gesture. Now I was here, the memories of last time were too close to the surface, too raw. I folded my hands primly in my lap and did my best to look serene as the boat moved slowly away from the jetty, leaving the Victorian bandstand and people sitting on benches behind.

Anthony was quiet at first. We let the commentary fill the silence and sat silently, gazing in different directions as the view slipped past. We passed under the white suspension bridge from which people waved and took photographs.

I couldn't believe this was happening. It seemed so surreal to be sitting here with Anthony after so long apart, on the boat trip that held some of the happiest memories for me. I hoped this silent, separate trip wouldn't override them. Or perhaps that was what was needed. Perhaps I could reprogramme my memory by going back to all our old haunts and replacing happy memories with slightly strange ones, like today.

Anthony nudged my leg with his knee. It made me jump, although the feeling of warm, rough denim against my bare skin wasn't altogether unpleasant. Not seeming to notice my reaction, he kept his knee pressed to mine as he pointed out a kingfisher sitting on a branch.

'Oh, wow! You must have great eyesight!' I leaned closer to get a better look at the small blue bird with its orange chest. 'I've never seen one before. Not in real life, anyway.'

'They're beautiful. We've got a couple living on the estate, down by the river. They've always been there. I used to lie in the grass for ages as a kid, just watching them.'

I looked at Anthony in surprise. He'd never told me that before. Despite knowing he'd grown up on a country estate, I'd always pictured him in urban settings, wearing a suit and driving a sleek car. This new image of him as a bird-watching child was unexpected and really quite endearing. I pictured him as a little boy, blond and cute, lying in tall grass by a lake. He'd always painted his childhood as a miserable time, trapped in a house that was more mausoleum than home. In fact, he'd hardly spoken about his childhood at all, overshadowed as it was by his father's death. I wondered if moving back to Willow Hall had made him remember a happier time before his father died. How wonderful if it had.

He looked around and caught me watching him instead of

the bird. He smiled and my breath caught. *Oh, Lord, this was such a mistake. How will I ever get over him like this?*

'I never had you down as a bird-watcher,' I said, to cover my embarrassment.

He shrugged. 'It's hard not to be in a place like Willow Hall. It's weird, but I think I forgot about it in the years I spent away from the place. It's like I couldn't see anything good about it at all.'

'Do you think you could stay there for ever? You know, for the rest of your life?'

He looked thoughtful for a moment. 'Yes. Providing it doesn't all go wrong and we have to sell. But yes, I really do feel like I've come home. Well, literally I have. I'm done with moving around from place to place. I like the quiet of the countryside, and I like being with my family.'

'Wow! That's quite a change.'

He laughed. 'I know. If you'd told me last year I'd be living back at Willow Hall and loving it, I'd have said you were mad. But here we are.'

I smiled at him. 'I'm really pleased for you. I think it's wonderful. It's great to see you happy and settled, and I'm so pleased you've recovered so well from the accident.'

He looked uncomfortable for a moment before nodding. 'Thank you.' He opened his mouth to say something and then changed his mind and closed it again. I looked away, wanting to ask but not wanting to pry. There was so much left unsaid between us, but perhaps it was better that way. There was no point being bitter and unpleasant. It wasn't like I hated him. I just missed him. And while it might not have been the best idea to spend time with him when I was trying to get over him, I liked being in his company again.

Hopefully, he'd reveal something really unpleasant about himself that would make me go off him for good.

'So, tell me about the shop then,' he said after a few minutes of silence. 'You were quite vague before about the reasons why your parents might sell up. Is the business in trouble?'

'Not really trouble, no. Not yet, anyway. It's just that we don't get many people actually coming into the shop and buying flowers any more. We still get orders through the website, and the wedding and funeral side of things is going well, but if we don't get people coming into the shop, how do we justify keeping it open?' I sighed and looked away. 'I'm in denial about it, to be honest. I just keep telling myself it's all going to be okay. I put signs out and run promotions, but I can't force customers to come in.'

'What will you do if it does close?'

'I'd have to find cheaper premises. It's bizarre really. I'm telling you about this now, but really I can't get my head around it. How can we close it when so much of our family history is wrapped up in that shop? Just this morning I was thinking how bored I was and how my life was never going to change; that I'd live and die in Chester, working in the same shop and living in the same house. But that's not a given at all.'

Anthony looked puzzled. 'Why were you thinking like that? I thought you loved your shop.'

'I do. I was just feeling low. Silly really, when the thought of losing it fills me with such dread.'

'You never know what's round the corner,' Anthony said. 'I mean, look at me. I thought moving back to Willow Hall was the end of the world, but it's actually been good for me. You never know, if the shop does close, you could find something better. Besides, you're getting married to the boy-child, aren't you?'

'Boy-child?' I laughed. 'He's the same age as me! It's just that you're so old you think everyone below the age of thirty must still be at school.'

Anthony looked disbelieving. 'Are you sure? He looked younger. And besides, I'm only thirty-six.'

'Nearly thirty-seven.'

He rolled his eyes, pretending to be offended, and looked away. 'So, I'm ten years older than you. Big deal.'

'I never said it was a big deal, did I? I'm just stating a fact.'

He laughed good-naturedly. 'You can try to make me feel bad about my age, but these days I just feel lucky to be alive.'

'I'm not trying to make you feel bad,' I protested, laughing. 'I'm just making a point.'

'Yes, that I'm old.'

'*Older*, not old! Anyway, you started it by calling Jayjay a boy-child. Did people say that to you about me when we were together? Did they think I was too young?'

'No, they just thought you were mad for being with me.'

'Yeah? They were right.'

He laughed. 'They were.' He shook his head and looked away from me. The boat trip was nearly over and we were gliding back towards the jetty. The weather had worsened and most of the benches were now empty. I stared out of the rain-specked window as the bandstand slid past, feeling sad my time with Anthony was coming to an end. This would probably be the last time I'd see him. If Elena and Daniel decided not to move the wedding, there would be no reason for us to see each other again. I didn't hold out much hope for the wedding flowers thing.

I sighed as the boat docked next to the jetty. 'Thank you for that. It was lovely.'

'Yeah, it was.' Anthony stretched before getting to his feet. 'I think I preferred it last time, though.'

It took me a moment to process what he meant. Had he really said that? That was such a strange thing to say when he was the one who'd dumped me. Was he just trying to be funny? I stared at the back of his head as I followed him downstairs to the bottom deck, my eyes drawn to the nape of his neck, which I'd always had a thing for. It looked so pink and vulnerable compared to the rest of him. I longed to touch it; to feel the smooth, warm skin and the soft bristles of the back of his hair. How could he be so close, and yet not be mine to touch?

I was so distracted and flustered that I missed my footing on the bottom step and stumbled into the back of him. Grabbing his waist to keep myself upright, I face-planted into the space between his shoulder blades.

'Steady on! Are you all right?'

'Sorry!' I said, righting myself, my cheeks hot with embarrassment. 'I'm not sure what happened. I think I lost my footing.'

Anthony laughed. 'And I thought I was meant to be the old one. Come on, old girl. Take my hand, I'll make sure you don't fall.'

I couldn't have planned it better if I'd tried. Anthony's fingers wrapped around mine and we walked hand in hand off the boat. I expected him to drop my hand as soon as we were back on dry land, but he kept on holding it as we walked up towards the road, huddled together slightly as the wind splattered us with rain. Blossom fluttered in the wind, blown this way and that, and my hair whipped around my face so that I had to hold it back with one hand.

'Oh, my goodness!' I said, breathless and laughing as we reached the road. 'Where did that wind come from? It wasn't that bad before! Have you parked in town?'

'No. Near your house, actually.'

'Oh, okay. So… I guess I leave you here then.' I smiled up at him, feeling suddenly awkward. 'Goodbye. It's been lovely to see you again.'

Smiling, he reached out a hand and plucked a pink petal from my hair. He showed it to me before gently smoothing my hair down and tucking it behind my ear. 'Yes, it's been lovely to see you too.' Leaning down, he planted a lingering kiss to the right of my mouth. 'Goodbye, Rachel.'

And then he was gone, striding across the bridge in the direction of my house.

Chapter Four

'Are you okay?' Bobbi looked up as I closed the shop door and leaned back against it.

'I don't know.'

She gave me an odd look. 'Why? What's happened?'

'I just went on a boat trip with Anthony.'

'Really? Why?' She straightened up.

'I don't know. I saw him sitting down by the river and I was talking to him and then he said shall we go on the boat, so we did.'

'Oh! Was it good?'

I nodded. 'Yes. It was nice.'

'Great!' Bobbi smiled. 'So why do you look like that?'

'Like what?'

'Like you've just been kissed by the most gorgeous man in the world?'

'Because I have.'

Bobbi gasped. 'What!?' She came out from behind the counter, her eyes as round as saucers. 'What happened? Tell me?'

I laughed. 'Oh, nothing really. Not like that. It was strange because it was nothing and everything at once.' I pushed off from the door and went into the back room to hang up my coat.

'What?' Bobbi said, following me. 'Have you been taking drugs or something? You're making absolutely no sense at all.'

'Nothing happened that I can explain. We just talked about things. It was nice, and nothing really happened, it was just feelings and... I don't know. I probably just imagined it. But it was nice to be with him again, that's all.'

'But there was a kiss? He kissed you?'

'Just goodbye. On the cheek. Nothing passionate.' I felt my cheeks flush at the memory and turned away before Bobbi saw. 'I doubt I'll see him again now. Not unless Elena and Daniel move their wedding, and I doubt that's going to happen.'

'Oh.' Bobbi looked sad for a moment. 'It's probably for the best, though. You've got Jayjay to think about now, you big hussy!'

'Oh, ha ha, very funny! Poor Jayjay. What must he think?'

'He didn't mind. You know what he's like. He just thought it was funny.'

'Anthony noticed how young he was too. He called him the boy-child. I told him he was the same age as me, but obviously he's younger. Poor lad.'

Bobbi laughed. 'He does look young. He's always getting ID'd in pubs.' She stared at me for a moment. 'You look awfully happy considering you've no plans to see Anthony again.'

I shrugged. 'It's over. I know it's over. It was just nice to see him again.'

'Hmm.' Bobbi put her hands on her hips and looked at me through narrowed eyes. 'Now, why don't I believe you?'

'I don't know, Bobbi.' I laughed and crossed the room to make a cup of tea.

'Hmm, maybe because I haven't seen you look this happy for an entire year?'

I shrugged. 'Well, maybe this is the closure I needed. A proper goodbye where we part on good terms.'

'Like hell it is. We haven't seen the back of Anthony Bascombe. No way.'

I gave her a look over my shoulder. 'Why do you say that? You only saw him for five minutes.'

The kettle bubbled to the boil, steam erupting from its spout. I took down two multicoloured spotty mugs from the cupboard above the sink and added a teabag to each.

'Because I saw his face when he looked at Jayjay. He was jealous,' Bobbi said.

'He was not jealous!' I scoffed, my heart beating faster.

'Oh, yeah? What was all that Jojo stuff about then? He clearly knew his name.'

I shook my head as I opened the fridge and took out the milk. 'I don't think so, Bobbi.'

'Well, I do! I could see it in his eyes and the way he was standing all tall and straight like he had a steel rod up his backside.'

'He always stands like that.'

Bobbi laughed. 'He does not! I remember him being quite laid-back actually. He was always really kind to me.'

'I know,' I conceded. 'I feel bad about lying to him. I don't know why. It just feels so wrong.'

Bobbi raised an eyebrow. 'Maybe it's because you want to be free if he asks you to get back with him?'

'No!' I protested, heat creeping up my neck. I knew she was right.

'Well, would you?'

'Would I what?' I passed her one of the mugs of tea and took a sip of mine.

'Get back with him if he asked, silly.'

'No, of course not!'

'Really?' Bobbi gave me a look that said she didn't believe a word of it.

'Why would I? It's over. If he didn't love me then, why would he love me now?' As I said the words, a trickle of sadness entered my heart and I was suddenly certain that everything I'd felt beside the river this afternoon had been in my head.

Bobbi shrugged. 'He probably wasn't in the best place. Think about it. When he wrote that letter, the doctors still weren't sure what damage he'd done to his spine and were wondering if he'd ever walk again. They must have been really dark days for him. Now he's made a full recovery, he might be wondering if he made a mistake.'

'Hmm, a year's a long time to wait, isn't it?'

'Well, you know what he's like with all his commitment issues. Maybe he was too proud to say he made a mistake. Or maybe he'd managed to live with it until he saw you again last week.'

I sighed heavily. 'I really doubt that, Bobbi.'

'Well, there must be some reason you looked so happy when you came back into the shop.' The bell above the shop door tinkled and Bobbi rose to her feet. 'Ooh, customer! I'll serve them. You just sit here and think about Anthony.'

Think about Anthony? Ha! Did I have a choice? My head was full of him. With a groan, I put my head in my hands. What was I going to do? How would I ever get over him?

Chapter Five

'We're going to look around Willow Hall again!' Elena practically shouted down the phone later that evening.

'Really?' I held my phone away from my ear slightly. 'So, Anthony phoned Daniel then? I hope he didn't mind me giving him his number?'

'Not at all. He said he already had it anyway. You know they used to get on really well. They were talking for ages. I couldn't believe it!'

'Oh, good,' I said, lamely. I was sat on my bed surrounded by tear-sodden tissues, rereading the letter he'd sent me from the hospital. 'When are you going?'

'Sunday. Do you want to come too?'

'Oh, no, I don't think so.'

'Go on, it will be fun. Anthony told Daniel you're going to be their Preferred Wedding Flower Supplier.' She said it proudly, stressing each word as though it was a very grand, prestigious thing.

'Well, not their only one, I'm sure,' I muttered. 'Anthony said they'd put my name forward to potential clients, that's all.'

'Are you all right?' she asked. 'You don't sound very happy?'

'I've got a cold,' I said, reaching for a tissue and blowing my nose loudly. The happiness I'd felt before at seeing Anthony had slowly dissolved through the course of the afternoon, leaving me with a sort of Anthony-hangover. All I wanted to do was lie down and cry. He didn't love me. I had the proof in the letter, written in his own scrawly handwriting.

'Oh no! Daniel said Anthony told him you'd been on a boat trip this afternoon.'

'Yes. It came on this afternoon. So what did Anthony say to get Daniel to agree to see Willow Hall?'

'I think just by reminding him of how well they used to get on. I was a bit miffed with Daniel to be honest. He was really mad at Anthony when he dumped you, and yet he just rolled over after one phone call. Mind you, you and Anthony are friends now, aren't you? He told Daniel you'd had a nice time.'

'He said that?'

'Yes.'

'Oh.' I reached for my glass of water from the bedside stand and took a sip. It tasted stale and warm and I grimaced as I swallowed. 'Yes, it was nice. We just talked about stuff.'

'Did you ask him why he broke up with you?'

'I know why he broke up with me. He didn't love me.'

'You'd only been together a few months. He could've at least given it a chance. Besides, banning you from the hospital wasn't exactly fair, was it? You should ask him about that.'

'Mmm, I don't know. It should be left in the past, I think.' I squeezed my eyes shut as another tear escaped and rubbed my nose roughly with a tissue. 'It doesn't matter any more.'

There was silence from the other end of the phone. 'Clearly it does.'

'No, it doesn't,' I said, forcing my voice to sound less feeble. 'What matters is that we're on good terms so that if you and Daniel do move your wedding to Willow Hall, there's no problem between us.'

I'd already decided this must be Anthony's motivation for being so charming today. He obviously wanted to get me onside so he could convince Elena and Daniel to change their plans. I'd been silly to read anything into it at all.

'Hmm, well, that doesn't sound very healthy to me and I don't think he should be allowed to get away with it.'

'Oh, Elena, he was in hospital. I think he was punished enough.'

'Not by you!'

I laughed, in spite of my misery. 'So, do you think Daniel will go for it once he looks around? He's not one to be swayed by fancy nonsense, is he?'

'I really don't know to be honest. That's why I want you to come and help me convince him.'

'You don't need me there too. Besides, if I still feel like this on Sunday, I won't be going anywhere.'

'Take some paracetamol and drink lots of fluids.'

'Yes, Mum.'

'And have a bath! They always help.'

I said goodbye to Elena and ran myself a bath, just like she'd advised me to. I tried to think about anything else other than Anthony, but as I slipped into the warm, bubbly water, random, tiny details kept popping unbidden into my head. The tan-coloured mole just above his collar. The exact shape of his soft pink earlobe. The crinkles around his eyes when he smiled. The curve of his lips. I thought about the feel of his hand in mine and felt my heart flutter. Closing my eyes, I fought to remember the exact details of the wedding bouquet I was making on Saturday morning.

Pale-pink ranunculus, slightly darker-pink roses, white muscari, rosemary and eucalyptus.

It was going to look so pretty. I'd already done a mock-up for the bride and it had looked gorgeous. There would be a smaller basket for her five-year-old daughter who was to be the flower girl, and another hand-tied bouquet for the maid of honour. I smiled when I thought about the little girl. She'd been so cute when she'd come in with her mother and helped choose the wedding flowers. She'd told me all about how pretty her brides-maid outfit was and I could just picture her in her little white dress.

It made me think of the little girl I'd seen at lunchtime, feeding the ducks. Anthony agreeing she was cute had taken me by surprise. And the way he talked about Grace and Charlie. He never used to talk about children like that. He sounded almost broody.

I stretched out my leg as I soaped it, admiring the red nail polish on my toenails in the flickering candlelight. I loved having baths. That was the great thing about being single; I could have as many as I liked when I liked. When I'd lived with Anthony, he'd always wanted to get in the bath with me. The memory made me miss him even more than I already did and brought on a fresh wave of tears. If seeing him made me feel this miser-able, I was better off not seeing him at all.

***

Elena tried a couple more times to get me to go with her to Willow Hall, but each time I refused. It wasn't until Saturday night that I changed my mind and agreed to go, and that was because Anthony himself phoned me. My heart nearly jumped out of my chest when I saw his name flash up on my mobile phone screen, and I stared at it, violently vibrating on my kitchen table, until it stopped and the screen went black. Almost immediately, a noti-fication came through to say he'd left me a voicemail message. Unable to stop myself, I snatched up my phone to listen to it.

'Answer your phone, Miss Jones,' he drawled.

He'd always had that cockiness.

I placed my phone back on the table, my heart beating too fast and too hard. What did he want? Should I call him back? Definitely not. It was half past eight on a Saturday night and, as far as Anthony was concerned, I was in a relationship with someone else. Why would he expect me to answer my phone? Surely he'd expect me to be out for a meal somewhere, or else in some busy pub, surrounded by chattering voices and loud music. I should definitely not be sat at my kitchen table in my pyjamas, updating our shop's website and drinking wine alone.

When he rang again, I jumped so violently that I sloshed wine over my wrist. I took a moment to catch my breath before deciding to answer it.

'Hello?'

'Ah, Rachel, how are you?' His voice, warm and pleasantly deep, made goose bumps break out along my arm.

'Fine, thank you. How are you?'

'Good, thank you. I hope I'm not disturbing your Saturday evening, but we're just putting a pack together for prospective clients and I was wondering if you could bring some of your business cards and flyers with you tomorrow so we could include them.'

'Oh!' I said, surprised he was expecting me to visit Willow Hall with Elena and Daniel. 'I'm not actually coming tomorrow, but I could give them to Elena to bring with her.'

'You're not coming?' He sounded shocked. 'Why not?'

'It's just for Elena and Daniel to look around really, isn't it? It's not really my business.'

'It quite literally is your business if you're going to be doing flowers for us. We've had two more weddings booked in for next year so it would be really helpful if you could bring us some information.'

'Like I said, that's no problem. I'll just pass them to Elena and she can bring them.'

There was a heavy pause. 'That's a shame. My mother was looking forward to seeing you again. And Liz.'

I narrowed my eyes at the wall. Was this some kind of emotional blackmail tactic? But then, I had got on quite well with Cath and Liz. It would be lovely to see them again. 'Well…'

'Well?'

'I'm quite busy tomorrow.'

'With Jayjay? Bring him too! You might be able to convince him to get married here. We could cut you the same deal as Elena and Daniel if you do it quick.'

I scowled and reached for my wine, annoyed he didn't seem bothered at all that I was engaged to someone else and was trying to marry me off as quickly as possible. 'Thanks, I might just do that.'

'Great! We'll see you tomorrow then. Don't forget your business cards!'

'I won't. Goodbye.'

I put my head in my hands and groaned. Oh, God, I really didn't need this. Downing the rest of my glass of wine, I rang Elena to tell her I was coming with her.

***

Daniel drove us in his big black truck and I sat in the backseat, staring out as the fields blurred past. Elena and Daniel laughed, talked and sang all the way there, and they were both so happy and positive that I was almost certain Anthony and Julian would be able to convince them to move their wedding to Willow Hall before we left this evening. Daniel was such a pushover where Elena was concerned. I couldn't imagine him denying her anything. I was surprised he hadn't agreed straight away.

The closer we got to Willow Hall, the more nervous I felt. As we swept into the pretty village and turned right at the church, my heart started thumping so hard I felt sick.

What was I doing here? I didn't want to see Anthony again. Could I just stay in the truck?

But as Daniel made his way up the long, tree-lined drive and parked in front of Willow Hall, both Julian and Anthony came spilling out from the studded oak door followed by Julian's two children, Grace and Charlie. My heart crashed in my chest as I tried not to look at Anthony.

Elena opened her door and jumped down. 'Hello! Who do we have here then?' she said, talking to the children.

'This is Charlie and this is Grace. Say hello to Elena.'

'Hello, Elena.'

'Hello, Charlie. Hello, Grace.' Elena solemnly shook each child by their hand before introducing Daniel. 'This is Daniel.'

'Hello, Daniel,' they chorused.

'Hi, kids!' he said with a wave.

Slowly, I unclipped my seatbelt, delaying the moment I had to get out of the truck. It was probably best if I let them get the introductions out of the way first. I wondered if Charlie and Grace would remember me. I hoped they would, but there was no reason why they should. A year was a long time to a child and they'd both changed so much since I'd last seen them. I listened to Charlie's high-pitched voice telling Daniel about his new football as I fumbled with the folder of business cards.

'Come on, Rachel!' The door was suddenly snatched open and Anthony stood grinning at me. I gave a start and stared at him stupidly. He seemed to sparkle in the sunlight: his blue eyes, his teeth, his hair. Even the golden hairs on his arms appeared to shimmer. What the hell was happening to me? Had Elena slipped me some LSD or something? Maybe I shouldn't have finished off that bottle of wine last night. 'What's taking you so long? Out you get. What, no Jayjay? Now there's a surprise.'

'Oh, he's err…'

'Busy. Yes, yes, come on.' He took my arm to steady me as I stepped down from the truck, and I thanked him weakly. 'No doubt he's busily doing the thing you were meant to be busy doing together.'

I glanced at him suspiciously. Did he know I'd lied? But he was already leading the way back round to join the others.

'Hello!' I said cheerfully.

'It's Auntie Rachel!' Grace said joyfully. And she ran and put her arms around my legs.

71

'Hello, Grace!' I put my hand on the back of her head, unbelievably touched that she'd remembered me. Not to be outdone, Charlie hugged my legs too from the other side, so that I felt like a sort of Grace-and-Charlie sandwich. 'Aw, hi, Charlie. It's so lovely to see you both again and you've grown so much! You both look so grown-up I hardly recognised you. And you're living here now, in this big house with your granny. Are you enjoying it?'

Grace nodded as she let go of my legs. Her dark hair was tied up in a high ponytail and she grinned up at me, showing a gap in her two front teeth. Charlie let go too, and I stroked his fair curly hair back from his freckled face. He looked so like his father and Anthony that it took my breath away.

'I'm getting a pony!' Grace told me.

'Wow! Lucky you!'

'Right, you two, are you going to help me show Elena and Daniel around or are you going back to sit with Mummy?'

'We're helping you, silly Daddy!' Grace said, catching hold of his hand. 'I'm going to convince them to get married here.'

'Excellent! I was kind of hoping the hall would sell itself, but any help is welcome. Right, Daniel, where do you want to start? The pavilion?'

'Err, yeah, sounds good.' Daniel smiled amiably and shrugged.

'Great. We'll walk this way round the back of the house. Follow me.' He started to lead the way to the left-hand side of the house.

'He's like a scout leader, isn't he?' Anthony grinned, swinging Charlie up on to his shoulders. Charlie squealed with laughter and gripped Anthony's hair to steady himself. 'Ouch!'

'Careful, Charlie!' Julian laughed. 'Don't pull any of Uncle Anthony's hair out – he'll be losing it soon enough as it is!'

'Hey! Don't be cheeky. You're not far behind me, you know.'

'Don't I know it. I found a grey hair the other day. I swear it's the kids.'

Anthony laughed and, reaching up to steady Charlie, spun

around, making him scream in delight and curl over Anthony's head, holding on even tighter.

'Careful! You'll make him sick. He's just had his lunch.'

'Oops, sorry!'

Julian laughed. 'It's you who'll be wearing carrots, not me!' He turned to Elena and Daniel. 'Anthony pretends to hate kids but he really doesn't. He's always coming over to play with Charlie and Grace. They think he's fantastic!'

'I *am* fantastic!' Anthony laughed as he turned to face us, walking backwards a few steps with Charlie grinning from his shoulders. 'Isn't that right, Rachel?'

I raised an eyebrow. 'That's a matter of opinion!'

He laughed and turned to face forward again. I was angry he'd asked me like that. What did he want me to say? That I was still in love with him? I'd sooner tell him I hated him than give him the satisfaction of knowing that. I glared at his back through narrowed eyes as we rounded the corner of the house and the pavilion appeared.

'Wow! That's impressive!' Daniel's eyebrows shot up in surprise. 'How many guests can you get in there then?'

'One hundred. Here, have a look inside.' Julian indicated the entrance and Daniel and Elena disappeared inside. Everyone else followed them in but I lingered outside, looking around at the large garden. It was bordered by shrubs and trees on one side, stretching out towards a line of willow trees at the far end. The air was full of birdsong and the sweet smell of hay.

'Rachel?' I turned as I heard my name called and saw Anthony and Julian's mother, Cath, emerging from the back door.

'Hi, Cath!' Smiling, I walked towards her. I was fond of Cath. She'd been quite distressed when Anthony had banned me from the hospital and had phoned me a couple of times afterwards to keep me updated on his progress. Contact gradually stopped when it became clear Anthony was going to make a full recovery. 'How lovely to see you.'

'It's lovely to see you too!' Her bright-blue eyes, so similar to those of both her sons, were full of warmth as she held out her arms to embrace me. 'I'm so glad you're here. How are you?'

'I'm very well, thank you. How are you?' I was touched by how pleased she seemed to see me.

'Oh, I'm fine. A few aches and pains but we carry on. Where is everyone else? Are they in the tent?'

'Yes.' I laughed at her use of the word tent. 'I was just looking at the view. It's glorious here! And you have so many gorgeous shrubs and trees and flowers growing.'

'Ah, thank you! It helps that the sun is shining, of course. It's not quite so glorious when the wind's whistling and the rain's lashing the house. Why don't you come inside for a cup of tea? It's your friends who need to look around, isn't it?'

'Yes, I suppose so.' I looked back over my shoulder. 'I'll just let them know.'

Five minutes later, I was sitting at a large oak table in the middle of a huge kitchen that smelt of baking cakes while Cath set the kettle to boil on the Aga. Doris Day was playing on the radio and sunlight flooded in through the large window, lighting on a large earthenware mixing bowl in the centre of the worktop.

'It smells nice in here.' I sniffed the air appreciatively. 'What are you baking?'

'A batch of scones, a lemon drizzle cake and a Victoria sponge. It's for the WI cake sale in the village hall later on this afternoon. I've left it a bit late, really, but I think they'll be ready in time. So, tell me how you really are. I hear you're engaged to be married?'

'Err, well…' I hesitated, not wanting to take the lie further than I already had. To my relief the door opened and Julian's wife, Liz, appeared holding an empty washing basket against her hip. Her long dark hair was tied back from her face and a large baby bump protruded from her floral dress.

'Rachel! Hello!' she said, a wide smile spreading across her face. 'Julian said you might come today. How are you?' Putting the basket down on the table, she came over and hugged me. Her large, hard belly felt strange pushing against me and I laughed.

'I'm fine, thank you. How are you? I see you're having another baby! Congratulations!'

'Thanks!'

'When are you due?'

'End of September.' She smiled and ran her hands over her tummy. 'As you can see, I'm huge already! Julian's worried that we're having twins, but the scans only show one baby.'

'Perhaps the other one's hiding.' Cath chuckled. 'I've just put the kettle on, Liz. Would you like a drink too?'

'Ooh, yes, please!' Liz sat down heavily on the chair next to mine. 'It's so good to see you again! Cath and I were so angry with Anthony for pushing you away like that. We couldn't believe he'd done it. We told him, didn't we, Cath?'

'We did.' Cath tapped a teaspoon on the edge of a cup with a dink-dink.

'We knew he'd made a massive mistake and would regret it. Still, it can't have worked out too badly for you. You've met someone else, I hear?'

I smiled politely, silently willing her not to ask any more questions.

'Julian was saying he was trying to convince you to get married here. Any chance?'

I laughed and shook my head. 'I don't think so.'

Liz tipped her head to one side and looked at me curiously. Realising I wasn't going to get away with leaving it like that, I expanded a bit more.

'I mean, it would be a bit awkward, wouldn't it? With Anthony... you know...'

'No reason why it should be. It's been over a year, after all.'

I laughed lightly and accepted a steaming mug of tea from Cath. 'Thank you. Well, let's see what Elena and Daniel decide. Julian and Anthony are showing them round now.'

'I heard their voices coming from the pavilion. Grace and Charlie were telling them all about the stars on the ceiling.'

'Aw, it's beautiful in there. It's perfect for a wedding. This whole place is perfect, in fact.'

'Thank you.' Cath looked pleased as she scraped back her chair and sat down at the table with us. 'I've been saying so for years, but the boys have taken until now to realise it.' She rolled her eyes and sighed heavily. 'Of course, we have to make this wedding thing work or else we'll have to sell. Not that I really want strangers traipsing all over my property, of course, but I can see it's what we need to do if we're going to keep Willow Hall in the family.'

'You never know, you might enjoy it.' Liz reached over and squeezed her mother-in-law's hand. 'Weddings are happy occasions, after all.'

'How did you like the open day last week?' I asked. 'Were you here in the kitchen or did you get caterers in?'

'Well, both really. I made the cakes and we hired a few waiters and waitresses to do the serving.'

'You made all those cakes? Wow! You must have been baking for days.'

Cath shrugged. 'I enjoy it. We made a little bit of money from all those afternoon teas, too, didn't we, Liz? Even if we only have three wedding bookings for next year.' She rolled her eyes.

'Yes, we did. I'm not too worried about the wedding bookings at the moment. It was only our first open day and it was more about getting the word out than anything else. Hopefully our next one will attract a bit more attention. How did you and Elena find out about it, Rachel?'

'I spotted it in the back of one of Elena's wedding magazines. You need to have one of those full-colour, glossy, full-page adverts to really catch people's attention.'

Liz sighed. 'I know. I think we might have to invest in something like that, but Julian and Anthony nearly choked when I told them how much they cost.'

'Or, you need a celebrity to get married here. Everybody would want to get married here then. Do you know anyone?'

'No, we've already considered this. I don't suppose you do either, do you?' Liz looked hopeful for a moment.

I shook my head. 'Sorry.'

Liz sagged in disappointment. 'You don't get any celebrities in your shop?'

'Not that I know of. I had a *Hollyoaks* actress in one day, but I don't think she's been in since. I've put your brochure in my shop in case anyone's interested, but I think most people choose their venue before they book their florist, so I don't know if it will be very effective.'

'Any publicity like that is useful. Thank you.'

'My pleasure. I'm happy to do whatever, although I'm not sure if I'm a little bit too far away to be useful. It's like the florist thing. People will probably prefer a florist that's a bit more local to the area.'

'Well, you never know. Chester's only an hour away.'

'I was saying to Anthony, perhaps you could put on some different events over the summer to get your name out there – you know, as an event venue.'

'Oh, yes, Anthony was saying about that.' Cath pulled a face. 'I'm not sure I could cope with a rock concert or anything.'

'You don't have to put on a rock concert, but you could host a craft fair or flower show and advertise in local towns.'

Cath sighed. 'It all sounds rather exhausting to me.'

'It doesn't have to be. I doubt it would be more trouble than the wedding open days you're going to be doing already.'

'Could you organise a flower show?' Liz asked.

I blinked in surprise. 'Me?'

'Well, yes, you're a florist, aren't you? You could do it.'

'Oh, I don't think so. How about a craft fair? They'd be pretty simple. Exhibitors could pay to have a stall and you could perhaps charge people a small entrance fee. You can make cakes and sell them. You probably wouldn't make a huge amount but it would bring in a little bit of money and possibly get people talking about Willow Hall.'

'It's a good idea,' Liz said thoughtfully. 'I think we should organise one soon.'

Cath nodded vaguely. 'Yes, that does sound more reasonable than a rock concert. I was a bit worried when Anthony was talking about it.' She sighed and took a sip of her tea.

Liz laughed. 'We'll put it to the boys when they come in. It sounds good, though.' She sighed. 'Of course, a wedding would be even better. Do you think your friends will move their wedding to here?'

'I don't know.' I shrugged. 'It all depends on what Daniel thinks, but he sounded positive when he arrived.'

'It's hard changing your plans when everything is already organised,' Cath said doubtfully. 'I'm not sure I'd want to.'

'We'll have to see. I think it could work, though.'

There was a lull in the conversation as both women stared worriedly into their tea. Part of me wished I *was* engaged so I could have my wedding here and give them a bit of a push.

'So…' I said, after a moment of silence. 'It must be lovely having all your family living here again, Cath! I bet you can't believe it, can you?'

Cath brightened. 'I know. It's just been me and Arthur on our own for years and suddenly we have two sons and two, soon-to-be-three, grandchildren living with us. It's wonderful, really.'

Liz laughed. 'I don't think poor Arthur knew what had hit him when we first moved in. He didn't know what to do with himself, bless him.'

I smiled. 'I suppose the house is big enough for everyone, isn't it? It's not like you're living on top of each other.'

'No, of course not. Julian and Liz are renovating one of the cottages on the estate so it's not for ever anyway. I'll miss them when they're gone, though. It won't be the same without them!'

'We'll only be a short walk away. It's not like you'll never see us. Then, if the wedding business takes off, we'll have more bedrooms to convert into guestrooms.'

'That's true. Always a silver lining.'

'I can't believe Anthony isn't living here with you all,' I said. 'I mean, the house is huge. Surely he could live here and still have his own space.'

Liz glanced across at her mother-in-law. 'After the accident he withdrew, didn't he, Cath?'

'Hmm, yes. He was really quite hard to live with. Very angry and uncommunicative. But recently he seems happier and has been spending more time up here with us. I don't know if it's since he returned to work, or perhaps it's because the wedding business looks like it's finally going to take off, or maybe just spending time around the children makes him happy. He's good with them, isn't he, Liz?'

'He is. They love him.'

'I suppose you weren't living here when he first came out of hospital. It was probably a bit boring for him living here with me and Arthur.' She looked across at me. 'I don't suppose you know about me and Arthur, do you, Rachel? He's my partner, but he used to be our gardener. Anthony was a bit sniffy about it when he found out, but he's come round to the idea now. They get on rather well, in fact. Hopefully you'll get to meet him before you go.'

We sat chatting for a while longer, while the cakes baked and the sun streamed in through the window. Despite the house being so huge and imposing, the kitchen felt homely and warm and I felt comfortable with Cath and Liz. After a while, when the tea had been drunk and Cath had taken the last of the cakes from the Aga, the back door opened and Julian came in with Elena and Daniel. I could tell by their flushed, excited faces that it had gone well. Julian introduced them to Cath and Liz and then told them to sit at the table while he made another cup of tea.

'We're going to do it,' Elena said eagerly as she sat down across the table from me. 'We're getting married here!'

'Really? Oh, that's amazing! Have you been down to the church and asked about availability?'

'Yes, that's why we've been so long. We've just been talking to the vicar now. He says he'd be happy to marry us, but he'd like us to attend Sunday services before the wedding.'

'That shouldn't be a problem, should it?'

'Not at all. And he seemed like a really lovely man.'

Cath laughed. 'You'll be the only ones there! The congregation's been dwindling in recent years.'

'I said we'd go too.' Julian gave Liz an apologetic look. 'I think we should go really, especially if he's willing to let people from other parishes marry in his church because they've booked their wedding with us.'

'Of course. Makes sense. Where are the kids?'

'Anthony took them to the park while we talked to the vicar. I thought he'd be back by now.' Julian peered out of the kitchen window then shrugged. 'I'm sure he's okay.'

Liz frowned slightly. 'Do you mean Anthony or Charlie?'

'Anthony.' Julian laughed and sat down at the table. 'The kids will be fine.'

'Julian!' Liz rose from her chair and crossed to the window to look outside. 'Did you see him in the park when you left the church?'

'No. They've probably gone for a walk to see the lambs. Grace was asking about them before. Anyway,' he said, turning to Elena and Daniel, 'shall we fill in some forms? I'm quite excited. You're our first guests!'

'Okay! I'm excited too!' Elena said.

'Liz, do you know where our forms are?'

'In the study, I expect.'

'Well, can you get them then? There's no need to fret about the children. They're with their uncle.'

'I know, but what if they run off?'

'He can run after them.'

'But he still gets so tired.'

Julian rolled his eyes and got up from his seat. 'Excuse me,' he said to Elena and Daniel. 'I'll just get the forms.'

He came back a moment later while Liz was still watching anxiously from the window for her children. I wondered why she was so worried about them when they were with Anthony. Had he lost them in the past? And what did she mean about him still being so tired? I thought he'd made a full recovery.

Cath was asking Elena about her wedding dress and seemed unconcerned about Liz's worry. I watched her rubbing her swollen stomach in a soothing motion and got up from my chair. 'Would you like me to go and look for them?' I asked her. 'They can't have gone far.'

'Oh, would you mind? I think they'll just be looking at the sheep along the driveway, like Julian said.'

'Okay, fine.'

I went outside and took the path round the side of the house to the front lawn. I wasn't sure why I'd volunteered to find Anthony when I'd made up my mind to avoid him. Besides, I hardly knew the estate at all. They'd probably end up having to send someone out to find me if I got lost.

Luckily, Anthony, Grace and Charlie were clearly visible when I got to the top of the drive. They were standing by the fence, watching a particularly bouncy pair of lambs playing around their mother.

'Hello!' I called as I got nearer.

Anthony turned to look at me and smiled, his eyes half-closed against the sun. 'Oh, hi. Is Mummy getting worried?'

'A little.' I smiled and stopped a few feet away, torn between joining them and hurrying them back up to the house. Everything seemed so fresh and bright out here, like a Technicolor film. The bright-blue sky, the emerald-green grass, the fluffy white lambs and the jaunty yellow daffodils waving by the gatepost – it was all so pretty. 'Julian said you'd be watching the lambs. They're cute. Do they belong to you?'

'No, we rent the fields to a farmer. Grace and Charlie enjoy watching them, though.' He squatted down next to Charlie and peered through the fence with him, pointing out another sheep a bit further on. I watched, fascinated by the sight of him taking such an interest in the children. 'We watched a lamb being born last week, didn't we, Grace?'

'Yes. It was all wet and slimy and then it fell to the floor with a splat!' Grace informed me.

'Oh! Nice.'

'And then the mummy sheep licked it all over and it stood up.'

'Wow! Amazing!' I walked a bit closer and leaned on the fence next to her. She was standing with her feet on the bottom rung, her chin on the top, burgundy dress billowing in the breeze. 'Do you like animals?'

'Yes. I'm going to be a vet when I grow up.'

'Excellent.'

'And I'm getting a pony soon.'

'Yes, you said! That'll be nice.'

She nodded, her brown ponytail bobbing behind her. 'Uncle Anthony's going to teach me to ride.'

'Is he? I didn't even know Uncle Anthony could ride.'

'Uncle Anthony can't ride.' Anthony straightened up and laughed. 'I told you, Grace, you'll have to go to a proper riding stables and learn to ride there.'

'But that will be boring.'

'No, it won't!' I told her. 'I used to have horse riding lessons when I was little and it was my favourite thing.'

'I didn't know you could ride a horse?' Anthony looked at me with interest. 'You never told me that.'

'I probably couldn't ride a horse now. I was about ten the last time I rode one. And I'm sure you must have seen photos of me on a pony. Mum made you look through all our photo albums.'

Anthony laughed. 'Oh, well, I must have forgotten.'

The wind blew a strand of hair across my face and I pushed

it away. 'I don't blame you. You had to plough through loads of them. It must have been so boring.'

'Not at all!' Anthony looked at me in surprise. 'I loved your parents, you know that.'

Ha! Loved? Loved my parents, maybe, but certainly not me. I swallowed hard and kept my eyes on the lambs jumping around in the grass while their mother grazed placidly nearby.

'I'm cold,' Charlie complained. 'Can we go back now?'

'Okay.' Anthony took his hand and held his other one out to Grace.

'I don't want to go back now!' she complained. 'Can't Auntie Rachel stay with me?'

'No, I think we must go back now, Grace. We can come and say hello to the lambs later on if you like?'

'Okay.' Relenting, she jumped down from the fence and took Anthony's hand before reaching for mine with her other hand. My heart swelled as I felt her little fingers wrap around my own. 'We haven't seen you for ages. Where have you been? Have you been to hospital like Uncle Anthony?'

'Me? No. Oh, no, I'm not allowed in the hospital, am I, Uncle Anthony?' I said sweetly.

'Why not?' Grace demanded. 'Everyone's allowed in hospital, aren't they?'

'Of course she is, Grace. Auntie Rachel's only joking. And she hasn't been in the hospital, she's been busy running her flower shop in Chester and getting on with her lovely, happy life. Right, who wants a race? Last one back at the house is a rotten egg.' Scooping Charlie up, Anthony ran off up ahead while Grace sprinted after them, complaining loudly that it wasn't fair on her if Charlie got carried everywhere like a big baby. I lagged behind, not sure I should be racing back to the house with my ex-boyfriend. When they got closer, Anthony slowed down, letting Grace catch up and then win.

'Ha ha! You two are the rotten eggs!' Grace screamed triumphantly.

'No, we're not.' Anthony stopped and looked back at me. 'Old Auntie Rachel's the rotten egg. Look how far behind she is! Come on, slow coach!'

'Well, that's a charming way to treat a guest,' I said, mock serious, as I caught up with them. 'Surely I should be exempt from being a rotten egg.'

'No. You don't get special treatment. And you're an even smellier rotten egg because you didn't even try.'

'Oh, right. Thanks.'

'You're welcome.'

Grace smiled up at me and took my hand. 'Next time you can hold my hand and we'll run together.'

'Okay, Grace. Thank you.'

We rounded the corner of the house and Anthony opened the back door to let the children inside. I went to step inside too, but he put a hand out to stop me and closed the door on us, keeping me outside. I looked up at him, surprised by the serious look on his face.

'Why did you do that?'

'What?' I blinked, confused.

'Have a dig at me in front of the kids about the hospital. Don't bring them into it.'

'Oh.' I felt winded all of a sudden, a hollow feeling in my gut. He was right, of course. It was hardly the time to bring that up. 'I'm sorry. It was just a throwaway comment and I really didn't think.'

He blinked, obviously still annoyed. 'It's obviously on your mind if it just came out like that.'

I felt my cheeks flush. 'Well...'

'Do you want to talk about it?'

Laughter floated out of the kitchen window and I heard Charlie's voice asking for some cake. 'I guess it just still hurts that you shut me out like that.'

He sighed. 'I know I hurt you and I'm sorry. It's not my proudest moment, but it was a dark time for me. I didn't know

84

if I'd ever walk again and I thought my life was over. You can't imagine how low I felt. I hated life and I hated everyone around me. I didn't want to inflict that on you.'

I dropped my gaze to the floor and nodded. I wanted to tell him that the heartbreak and suffering he'd inflicted had been much worse than that. 'I never thought it would be easy, but I would have stuck by you and supported you because that's what you do when you lo—' I stopped abruptly. 'I just wanted to be there for you. It was horrible getting the news about your accident and I was so relieved when they said you were going to pull through and survive. But when you stopped me from coming, it was almost like you'd died. I don't know. It's hard to explain, but it was like one day we were happy and together, and the next you were hurt and I wasn't allowed to see you.' Tears burned behind my eyes at the memory and I dropped my gaze to the flagstone step. I rubbed my tingling nose hard and sucked in a deep breath. 'Still, that's in the past now,' I said, making my voice sound stronger and more cheerful. 'You're fully recovered and that's all that matters. It's lovely to see you looking so well.'

He scratched his head. 'You have every right to be angry with me about what happened, Rachel. I'm so sorry. If I could change things, I would. But like I said, I was in a bad place and I didn't want to inflict that on you.' He smiled sadly and I tried to smile back, but it wobbled and twisted on my face. A cool breeze stirred my hair, bringing with it the scent of hyacinths from a nearby tub. More laughter from inside drowned out the birdsong from a nearby tree.

'Well, it's done now. Shall we go in then?'

He nodded and went to open the door, but before he could do so the handle turned and Elena and Daniel appeared.

'We'd better be going, Rachel,' Elena said, her eyes flicking curiously between me and Anthony. 'Mum's making us a Sunday roast and I told her we'd be back by four.'

'Okay, then.' A mixture of relief and regret flowed through me and I braced myself to leave Anthony once more. Cath came out and hugged me.

'Bye, Rachel. Hope to see you soon.'

'Yes, lovely to see you again, Cath. Bye, Liz. Bye, Julian.'

To a chorus of goodbyes and lots of cheerful waving, we walked back around the side of the house to Daniel's truck.

'Wow! Aren't they lovely!' Daniel said, as soon as we were out of earshot. 'It was like leaving family or something. I expected them to be all snobby and snooty, but they're seriously lovely people.'

'They are,' Elena agreed happily. 'And the house is just perfect.' She turned back to look at it and sighed happily. 'I feel like this is all a dream and I'll wake up and it won't be real at all.'

There was a general air of happy excitement in the truck on the way back to Chester. Elena phoned her mum to tell her what had been decided, while Daniel sang along with the radio, one elbow sticking out of his window. I sat in the back thinking about Anthony. I hated that he'd felt so low while he was in hospital. It was horrible to imagine him lying there in a black pit of despair.

'Are you okay?' Elena asked, turning to look at me as she ended the phone call to her mother. 'What were you and Anthony talking about?'

'He was just explaining about the hospital thing.'

'What did he say?'

'Just that he felt so depressed and low he didn't want to see anyone really.'

'And what about your feelings? Didn't they matter?'

I sighed unhappily. 'I don't think he was capable of thinking about anything but what he was going through.'

'Well, you deserved more than to be cast aside like that.'

'I suppose at least I got an explanation. It doesn't matter any more. What's done is done. So, tell me about the vicar. Was he nice?'

And that was all I needed to say to turn the conversation back to the wedding. By the time they dropped me off at my little house in Chester, even I was feeling excited about their wedding plans.

Chapter Six

My house felt cold and empty after sitting in the warm, happy kitchen at Willow Hall. It was still bright outside, but the sun had moved around the side of the house so that my kitchen and living room were full of shadows. With shaking hands, I filled the kettle at the sink and leaned against the counter to wait for it to boil.

I'd been eager to get home before so I could have good cry, but now I was here I just felt kind of hollow. My bones itched with discontent and the thought of sitting inside for the rest of the afternoon when it was so lovely and sunny outside made me want to scream. But where would I go? The riverside was full of couples and families walking hand in hand. I didn't want to go down there on my own.

The kettle boiled and I made the tea, then went outside to sit in the small patch of sun that still reached the end of my scrubby back garden. I was a little embarrassed by the state of it really. It wasn't the kind of garden you'd expect a florist to have. Just a small patch of scrubby grass and a ramshackle shed filled with long since abandoned terracotta pots, unplanted bulbs and my grandfather's ancient gardening tools. There was a hoe in there that was older than me. There was also a large quota of spiders, both dead and alive, that filled me with fear. When I'd first inherited the house from my grandmother, I'd had big plans for this garden. In the first year, I'd planted up pots and pots of flowers and had them lined up all around the garden. That was five years ago now, and though I kept a pot of flowers by the front door, the only flowers in the back garden were a cluster of brave primroses that came up year after year.

Even the bench I was sitting on was half-rotten.

A robin landed on the fence and looked at me with beady eyes, as though wondering what I was doing in his territory. I couldn't blame him. It was rare for me to sit in the garden. Maybe it was time to spend more time out here and try harder to improve things. Trim the grass and plant some flowers. Lay some roots.

Tipping my head back, I lifted my face to the sun and closed my eyes. Images of Anthony crowded my mind. I could still see him with Charlie on his shoulders, could still hear his voice in my head. There was no getting away from him now Elena's wedding was moving to Willow Hall.

The doorbell rang and the robin flew off. Who could that be? Could it be Anthony? No, of course it wouldn't be Anthony! I was annoyed with myself for even thinking it. But my hands still trembled as I reached for the door catch.

'Hello, Rachel.'

It was only my parents. 'Hello! What are you doing here? Are you out for a walk?'

'No, we've come to talk to you about the shop.' Dad stepped into my hallway, wiping his feet on the mat.

'That sounds ominous,' I said as he kissed me on the cheek. Mum stepped in behind him and I kissed her too before shutting the front door. 'Have you been going through the accounts?' My legs had gone rubbery with fear.

'Yes.' Dad sat down heavily on the settee and set down a blue foolscap file on my coffee table. 'It's not good news, I'm afraid.'

'Oh, no, really?' I said, dismayed. I sat down on the armchair and stared at my parents. Mum looked sad and anxious, dark circles beneath her pale-blue eyes.

Dad peered at me from over his glasses. 'Well, we're doing okay, but we're not doing great. You remember we talked about this before?'

'Yes, of course. I know the number of people that actually come in and buy flowers has fallen off dramatically. But won't the wedding and Internet orders cover the shortfall?'

'Not really, love. They're still not enough to cover the running of the shop. With the business rates, and energy bills, and your and Bobbi's wages we're only just breaking even. We can't afford to keep the shop open for sentimental reasons. I really feel like it's time to call it a day.'

I stared at him sadly, hardly daring to believe my own ears. It wasn't a complete surprise, of course. We'd talked about it and I wasn't a fool. Customer footfall had fallen sharply in the past year, and had got even worse since Christmas, so I knew it wasn't good. Dad was right: we couldn't afford to keep the shop open for sentimental reasons. The overheads were too great.

It still hurt, though.

'I know it's sad, love. Your mum's upset too. We have a lot of memories wrapped up in that shop. But at the end of the day, it's just a building, and if it's not working for us any more we have to let it go. I really feel like it's at the wrong end of the city centre, away from all the main shops and the places most people go.'

'So are you saying move closer to the city centre?'

'No, it's not worth the risk. I'm saying, find somewhere cheaper and build up the Internet business. Keep doing the weddings. Run flower-arranging workshops. You love doing them, don't you?'

I nodded, my hand over my mouth, trying to control my emotions. Mum looked distraught. How was I going to tell Bobbi?

'When do we close?'

Dad sighed. 'Well, I say we start looking for cheaper premises now.'

I nodded. He was right, but it still seemed inconceivable that we were going to lose the shop. It was part of our family history. Our little empire. Some of my earliest memories were in that shop, playing with my dolls in the back while my mum served customers in the front, or making up my own little bouquets from offcuts of flowers. And now it had been passed to me and I'd lost it.

'Don't feel bad,' my mum said, reaching for my hand as though she knew what I was thinking. 'It's not your fault, it's just the way things are now. The shop's getting more and more expensive to run. We'd need to increase our prices drastically to survive, but then we'd price ourselves out of the market.'

I nodded. I understood perfectly but it was still devastating.

Mum made us all a cup of tea and we went through the accounts together. I looked and listened and nodded but said very little. There wasn't anything to say. We were losing the shop.

Mum patted my hand. 'Don't worry, love. We'll find somewhere else and you can make it just as nice.'

'But we have so many memories wrapped up in that place.'

'Nothing can take those away, can it? They're our memories and we can make more new ones somewhere else. Look at this as an opportunity, not a disaster. A fresh start. You could rebrand and put more of your own stamp on it. Change the name. Call it Rachel's or whatever you like. You needn't stick with The Birdcage.'

'I like The Birdcage. We'll need to keep our brand for continuity.'

'Well, that's your choice. There's plenty of time to think it over.'

Was there time? It didn't seem like it to me. It felt like time, along with everything else in my life, was trickling through my fingers.

'Anyway, let's not dwell on this. Let's go and get a carvery from somewhere,' Dad said, placing the accounts back into the folder.

'Oh, I don't know, Dad. I think I'll just go to bed.'

'Don't be silly! It's only half past six. You've got to eat, love.'

So we went out for dinner, even though I wasn't remotely interested in eating. I felt so miserable. I just wanted to lie in bed and sob, but instead I found myself in a busy country pub with my parents, telling them all about how beautiful Willow Hall was and how Elena and Daniel were going to be getting married there.

'I can't wait to see it! And how's Anthony doing now? I always liked Anthony. He was such a lovely man.' Mum always went a bit pink when she talked about him. I exchanged a look with my dad who rolled his eyes at me.

'He's fine.'

'Really? No aftereffects from the surgery?'

'Not that I know of. He looks fine to me and he's back at work, apparently.'

'Do you think you'll get back together?'

'No!' Picking up my glass, I took a large gulp of red wine. 'Why would I get back together with my commitment-phobic ex-boyfriend, who dumped me by letter and banned me from the hospital?'

'Oh, well, when you put it like that…' Mum sighed. 'It's a shame, though. He was lovely.'

'Well, yes, he's still lovely. But we both want different things so there's no point.'

'Plenty more fish in the sea,' Dad said cheerfully, cutting into his roast beef. I'd barely eaten and had merely pushed my food around the plate so that the potatoes, gravy and broccoli resembled an unappetising, congealed mess. I reached for my wine again.

'Not for me,' I said miserably.

'Nonsense! A pretty girl like you should have no problem finding a man.'

My lip curled as I thought about some of the men I'd dated over the past year. There had only been a couple and I'd only gone out with them after being badgered by Bobbi and Elena. They'd been nice guys, but the spark wasn't there. Not like it was with Anthony. There was no one quite like Anthony.

Sighing, I took a giant slug of wine, closely followed by another.

'Would you like another one, love?' Dad asked, getting up and patting his pockets for his wallet.

'Oh, go on. Thank you.'

Wine always made me sleepy, so, despite all the upset, I had no problem getting to sleep that night. I awoke the next morning feeling half-dead and dragged myself into work. It was another beautiful morning, and the sun sparkled on the river as I crossed the bridge to get to the shop. It was only a short walk from my house. I doubted that our new premises, wherever they might be, would be quite so convenient to get to. I used to drive to work, but since investing in a van to deliver the flowers to our clients, there was nowhere to park. I paused to watch a heron swoop in and land on the riverbank. It was still only half past six, so there weren't many people around, just the odd delivery truck rumbling across the bridge. I walked on up the road to my shop, passing the fifteenth-century timber-framed pub with its hanging baskets full of flowers. Should I tell Bobbi today? I supposed she should know as soon as possible. I was dreading telling her.

The bell tinkled as I opened the door and I stood for a moment, just savouring the sound in the early morning silence. How many times had I heard that bell? Thousands upon thousands, no doubt. Gently, I closed the door behind me and removed my dark sunglasses to look around, trying to commit every last detail to memory. The flowers on the shelves in their cast-iron vases, the birdcages full of trailing ivy and flowers, the scented candles on the whitewashed Welsh dresser and potted orchids behind the till. The pale sunlight slanting through the windows cast a magical glow over it all and my heart ached that it was going to end.

How could I have lost this beautiful shop? I wanted to weep.

But I couldn't weep. I had work to do and weeping wasn't going to solve anything. I had to be practical and businesslike, and we needed to move to somewhere more cost-effective. Positive thinking, that was what was needed. Especially when I had to break the news to Bobbi.

Walking through to the back, I hung up my jacket on the hook and fired up the computer to check for online orders.

The tinkle of the door opening sent me rushing back into the front of the shop. Why hadn't I locked it? Who on earth was in the shop at this time in the morning?

'Anthony?'

'Morning!' he said cheerfully, closing the door behind him. He was holding two takeaway cups of coffee and held one out to me as he walked slowly towards me.

'Thank you. But what are you doing here?'

He shrugged. 'I was working in Chester and thought I'd pop in and say hello.'

'At this time in the morning?' I could barely look at him. He looked too handsome in his navy suit and pale-blue tie. His hair was combed neatly to one side and he was all clean-shaven and neat.

'Well…' He looked around him as though he was going to choose a bunch of flowers. 'I thought you might need a coffee. You sounded quite drunk on that phone call you made to me last night.'

'Phone call? What phone call?'

'The phone call you made to me at…' He pulled his mobile phone from his jacket pocket and glanced at the screen. 'Ten fifty-seven p.m.'

'What? I didn't phone you last night.' My voice trailed off as he turned his phone to face me so I could see my name clearly displayed in the received phone calls list. 'Oh!'

'You did sound quite drunk.'

I frowned. 'Did I just leave a message or did I speak to you?'

'Oh, no, you spoke to me all right. We had quite the conversation.'

'Err?' I shuffled backwards away from him as fragments of last night started to come back to me. I'd had a couple of glasses of wine when eating dinner with my parents, but when I'd got home, I'd carried on drinking and I couldn't actually remember going to bed. Oh, no, what did I say? Should I ask or should I just try to bluff my way out of it?

'I'm sorry you're losing the shop.' He looked around him at the rows of flowers.

'Did I tell you that?'

'Yes. Are you all right this morning? You were very upset on the phone.'

Oh, no, had I cried down the phone at him? My stomach turned over and I felt sick. 'I'm okay. Just a bit of a headache, that's all. I went out with my mum and dad and…'

'I always said those two were bad influences!'

I laughed awkwardly. 'Yes, they're terrible. Plying me with drink all night.'

'I was concerned because it wasn't even that late. I thought you must have been drinking on your own.'

'No. We'd been out for a carvery.' I didn't mention the bottle of wine I'd drunk after they'd dropped me off. Christ, I couldn't believe I'd phoned him and had no recollection of it this morning. How drunk had I been last night? 'What did I say?'

Anthony's eyebrows shot up. 'You really don't remember?'

I shook my head, feeling hot and panicky. I had a horrible feeling I might have poured my heart out to him and told him things I didn't want him to know.

'You said you were closing the shop, but I didn't catch why. I presume you'll just move premises like you said last week on the boat rather than go out of business altogether?'

'Yes.' I scratched my head, sighing heavily. 'I haven't even told Bobbi yet.'

'Are you sure you didn't phone her last night?'

I winced. 'Hope not. She deserves better than me phoning her up drunk. How bad would that be?'

Anthony laughed. 'I should check your phone if I were you.'

I laughed weakly and sipped the hot coffee. I couldn't believe I'd phoned him. Why would I do that? Anthony was looking at me closely, as though trying to figure something out.

'What? Do I have something on my face?'

'No. Why?'

'You're staring at me strangely.'

'Sorry. You've gone a funny colour, that's all. Kind of... puce.'

'Oh, great!' I backed away and slid behind the counter.

'Are you sure you're feeling all right?'

'I'm fine. Just horrified by the thought of phoning you, that's all.' Flustered, I put the coffee down and started rearranging the cards on the rotating rack next to the till. He laughed as he leaned one hand on the counter, slipping his phone into his inside breast pocket with the other. As his jacket parted, my eyes were involuntarily drawn to the body harness beneath. I tore them away and tried to concentrate on the cards.

'It's not a problem. I just didn't like to hear you so upset.'

I shook my head. 'Honestly, I'm fine. It's sad but it has to be done. I'm sure I'll find somewhere cheaper and be just as happy there. I thought I might check out some rental properties on the Internet today.'

'I was thinking, actually... we've got an old Brew House in our grounds that we were thinking of converting into offices. You could use that as a base if you thought it would work.'

'Brew House?' I stared at him, astonished. 'Oh, err, thank you, but it's... a bit far? I don't know.'

He smiled. 'You don't have to decide anything now. I just

thought it might be an option, that's all.' He checked his watch. 'Right, I'd better go. I'll see you soon.'

'Okay, bye. Thanks for the coffee and sorry again for phoning you last night.' I ran a hand through my hair self-consciously. 'I don't know why I did that.'

'No problem. It's always nice to hear someone loves you.' He flashed a grin as he opened the door and stepped outside. 'See you soon.'

The door banged shut behind him and I stared after him in horror. What? Surely not! I would never have betrayed myself like that, even paralytic. No, he must have been trying to wind me up. He'd succeeded too. All day I wracked my brain, trying to remember what I'd said to him on the phone, but nothing would come. The most worrying thing of all was that when I checked my own phone, it had logged the duration of the call as ten minutes.

Ten minutes!

What could I have been talking about for that length of time?

I was definitely never drinking again.

***

'So, what do you think this Brew House would be like?' Mum asked later that day, when I called round after work.

'I have no idea. I didn't see it when he showed us round.' I opened up the newspaper and turned to the property section. 'He said it needed renovating, so it probably wouldn't be ready for ages. Besides, it's too far away.'

'Well, if a lot of the wedding flower business is generated by Willow Hall, then maybe it makes sense to move down there anyway.'

I gave her a look. 'And what if their wedding business doesn't take off? They only have four weddings booked in so far, and one of them is Elena and Daniel's.'

'I bet they'll get more, though.' Mum sat down on the sofa next to me. 'From what you said, it sounds like a magical place.'

'Well, it is lovely, but it's not Narnia! It's down to Anthony and Julian but they're hardly experts. I suppose Liz has a background in event management, but I still think it's going to be difficult for them.'

'Oh, well, I do hope they succeed. It would be terrible if they had to sell their family home.' She glanced fondly at the framed photograph of me and Anthony that sat on the fireplace.

I shook my head. 'I can't believe you've still got that photograph up.' It had been a source of contention between us since Anthony and I had broken up. She'd refused to take it down, saying it wouldn't be right when he was so poorly in hospital. It had then stayed up all year, pride of place, as though we were still together. I was sick of complaining about it. She never took any notice anyway. All she said was that it was a lovely photograph of me, when I knew it was because it was a lovely photograph of Anthony. I thought it very disloyal of her.

'I'd love to see him again,' she said, ignoring me completely. 'Such a charming man. Ooh, perhaps we could go and look at this Brew House together? That would be exciting.'

I rolled my eyes. 'How would being stuck in the middle of the countryside help our business? There would be no passing trade. No one would be able to find us.'

'But passing trade is dying off anyway. You could concentrate on Internet orders and wedding flowers and flower-arranging workshops. How much would our overheads be? Did he talk about the financial side?'

'No. He only mentioned it in passing. I doubt he's even serious.'

I sighed heavily, wishing he'd never mentioned it at all. Now my head was full of all kinds of possibilities about working at Willow Hall and seeing Anthony every day, but I knew it wasn't practical. I had to prepare myself for disappointment. 'I was thinking about a little shop just outside of Chester, in a village somewhere. We could look in North Wales too.'

'Have you seen anything in the paper?'

'No.' I folded it back up and placed it on the side table next to me. 'I had a look on the Internet too, but the only thing I found were industrial units.' I shuddered. 'I hate the thought of working in one of them after our lovely shop.'

'I know, but beggars can't be choosers.'

I rolled my eyes again. 'Well, it's worth waiting for the right place, surely. It's not like we're going bankrupt.'

'Well, not yet, but it makes good business sense to move now before we do start to struggle. Come on, Rachel. We went through this last night.'

'I know, I know! But like I said, we need to find the right place.'

The door opened and my dad came in, dressed in his golfing gear. 'Hi, Dad.'

'Hello, love.'

'Rachel's seen Anthony this morning,' Mum blurted before he'd even taken off his jacket. 'And he's got a Brew House he says might be suitable for the flower business.'

'Really?' Dad scratched his chin thoughtfully before shrugging off his jacket and hanging it on a peg. 'That sounds interesting.'

My jaw dropped. I couldn't believe it! Surely my dad could see that moving to a country estate an hour's drive away wasn't the cleverest idea in the world.

'What's it like?'

'I have no idea,' I said, picking the newspaper back up and shaking it out. 'He said it needs renovating so it's probably dere-lict.'

'Do you have his number? Phone him and ask.'

I frowned. Did they even realise how insensitive they were being? 'You do realise he's my ex-boyfriend?' I snapped. 'With the emphasis on the ex! Why do you think this is a good idea?'

Dad shrugged. 'I'm not asking you to get back with him, am I? But if you're already involved in doing wedding flowers for Willow Hall, it might turn out to be a great location.'

'I've just had this conversation with Mum! What if their wedding business doesn't take off? They could fail and take me with them.' Realising I sounded horribly negative, I added: 'I hope they don't fail, obviously. I'd hate for them to lose the hall, but the fact is they're just starting out and we're in a precarious position ourselves.'

'We're not that precarious. We're making money and we have orders in the pipeline. We just need to cut our overheads as soon as possible. I'm only saying this building might be worth having a look at it.' Dad sat down in the armchair opposite and eased his feet into his slippers. 'Besides, if it doesn't work out, you'd just move on again. As simple as that. Did you tell Bobbi today? What did she say?'

'No, she phoned in sick. She's got a sickness bug.'

'Oh dear, poor Bobbi.' He rolled his eyes and sighed. 'So, have you seen anywhere else that might be suitable?'

'Not yet.'

'Well, go on then, give Anthony a ring.'

'What about a market stall?'

'Ring Anthony.'

With a stroppy sigh, I got up from my seat and went to get my phone from my bag. My face felt hot and my hands were shaking with nerves. Clearing my throat, I found his name in my contacts list and pressed the call button. Realising my parents were watching me, I walked through to the kitchen and closed the door behind me. The phone rang twice before he answered.

'Rachel.'

His voice, soft and low, sent such a flood of emotion through me my knees went weak and I sank down on to the chair next to me.

'Hello, I just mentioned your Brew House to my parents and they'd like to take a look if that's possible.' The words tumbled from my mouth too fast and I cringed at myself. Luckily, he didn't seem to have any difficulty understanding what I'd said.

'Of course. I'm heading home now if you want to come tonight?'

'Erm, I'm not sure about tonight. Dad's just come in from playing golf and Mum's got a pie in the oven.' Cringing again, I unclipped my hair and let it fall around my neck. Running my hands through it, I stood back up and went to the window to look out at the back garden. A blackbird was pulling a worm from the lawn and I could just make out the hollow wooden notes of the bamboo wind chimes hanging by the backdoor.

'Well, when would it suit you to come?'

'I'm not sure. Are you working?'

'I'm off tomorrow. But even if I'm not here, Julian would show you around.'

I laughed and lowered my voice. 'I think my mum would like to see you again, actually. Hold on, I'll see if they're free tomorrow. I'll be working, obviously, but I think they'd be able to find it on their own.'

'Hold on, don't you need to come too?'

'I already know it's unsuitable, Anthony. I thought I'd let them see for themselves.'

'How do you know it's unsuitable? You haven't seen it.'

'Well, it's an hour away, it's in the middle of nowhere, there's no shopfront, it needs renovating… oh, and it just happens to be owned by my ex.'

'Your ex's family, actually,' he corrected. 'Not just me. Well, if you feel like that I won't waste my time showing your parents round. Bye.'

'No, hold on,' I said, quickly. 'They really do want to see it. And Mum would love to see you again.'

'Why? So she can kick me in the balls?'

'Of course not.' I laughed. 'You're still on the mantelpiece, actually.'

'What, like a voodoo doll?'

'No!' I wound a strand of hair around my index finger. 'A photograph.'

'Really?' I heard the smile in his voice and felt my insides start to melt. Surely talking to him shouldn't make me this happy. 'Okay,' he went on, 'I'll show them around, but only if you come too.'

'It will have to be one evening then. Or the weekend.'

'Tomorrow evening would be fine.'

'Okay, I'll just ask.' I poked my head through the door. 'Tomorrow evening okay for you two?'

'Yes!' Mum and Dad said eagerly.

'Okay,' I said into the phone. 'About half past six?'

'Perfect. See you then.'

'Bye.'

There was a pause where neither of us hung up. I could hear him breathing and goose bumps broke out on my arms. Taking control, I ended the call and pressed my phone against my chest. Mum gave me a shrewd look.

'So what did he say?'

'Not much. We were just trying to sort out a time.' I sat back down, placing my phone on the arm of the chair. 'He said tonight, but I said Dad had only just come in and you hadn't had your tea yet.'

'Oh, okay.' Mum looked disappointed. 'We could have gone, though.'

I rolled my eyes. 'It's an hour away. And I've already told him I think it won't be suitable, so don't get your hopes up.'

Mum grunted and then got up from the chair to go into the kitchen. Pausing by the fireplace, she picked up the photograph of me and Anthony and flicked off a bit of imaginary dust.

'*Mum!*'

101

'What? I thought I saw a smear.'

I exchanged a look with my dad as she put it down with a guilty expression on her face. 'Well, I am looking forward to seeing him again. He's such a lovely man.'

Raising one eyebrow, Dad reached for the remote control and switched on the TV.

***

The following evening, Dad picked me up from work and drove us to Willow Hall in his Land Rover. My stomach had been in knots all day and I felt like I was going to hyperventilate when I finally locked up the shop and climbed into the backseat. Mum was sitting in the front, and it looked suspiciously like she'd had her hair done. I was about to say something but then decided that might be a bit hypocritical considering I'd chosen to wear a blue polka-dot tea dress Anthony had said he liked when we were together. Accepting a Mint Imperial from my mum, I settled back for the journey.

'Was Bobbi in today?' she asked.

'No, still being sick, apparently. And I didn't want to tell her about the shop when she was so poorly.'

'No, of course not. Poor thing. Do you think I should pop in tomorrow and check how she is?'

'Best stay away if it's a bug,' Dad told her. 'You don't want to catch it.'

'She thinks it might be food poisoning. Hopefully she'll feel better tomorrow.'

We chatted for the duration of the journey and I was glad of the distraction. I'd been on my own all day and felt like I'd been starved of company. If that was how I felt in a shop, how would I feel working from home or in an industrial unit?

'Ooh, this is very grand!' Mum said as we passed through the gateposts and drove through the tree tunnel leading to Willow Hall.

'I know. Wait until you see the house!'

As predicted, Mum gasped as the soft red stone of the hall came into view.

'Blimey!' Dad said mildly. 'That's a bit good.'

He parked his Land Rover outside the house and Julian appeared out of the front door. 'Hello!' he called cheerfully as we climbed out of the car. 'I saw you coming up the drive. Anthony's been a bit delayed, I'm afraid, so you'll have to make do with me.'

'Marvellous. I'm Jim and this is Birdie.' Dad held out his hand to shake Julian's.

'My goodness, you look so like your brother I thought you were Anthony!' Mum said as she greeted him.

'Everyone says that. Important to note that I'm two years younger, though.' Julian laughed.

'Where is he?' I asked, trying hard and failing to keep the note of disappointment from my voice.

'He was called into work. He should be back any minute, though.'

'Oh, okay.' I slammed the door of the Land Rover and then realised the end of my cardigan was caught in the door, which had locked. I opened my mouth to tell my dad, but he was already walking away with Julian, deep in conversation. With a tut, I shrugged it off and left it dangling from the car before running to catch them up.

'It's not in bad condition at all,' Julian was telling my dad. 'We were thinking of offices or a residential let but we hadn't settled on anything. It would be a great space for Rachel, especially if she does the wedding flowers for our weddings. It would be ideal, really, to have you on-site. And there's plenty of space for you to run flower-arranging workshops and tutorials. Anthony said you used to love doing them, Rachel. And of course, we have a two-acre walled garden where we grow all sorts of flowers, as well as vegetables. And all over the estate we have shrubs and wildflowers that I'm sure could be used in arrangements.'

I opened my mouth to say I usually bought my flowers from the flower market, but then shut it again as an idea started to form. Yes, I'd probably still use the markets for a lot of the flowers, but it would be great to use the wildflowers in the flower-arranging workshops. The students could even go and pick their own flowers and decide what type of bouquet they wanted to work on. It would be amazing.

I caught myself before I got too carried away. It was bound to be unsuitable. It would never work.

Julian led us round the other side of the house to the one I'd previously taken and we walked along a gravel path between the house and the side of the walled garden. The clank and squeak of a rusty wheelbarrow came from the other side. The stones on the gravel path dug into the thin soles of my shoes and I was glad when we reached the end and I could walk on the grass for a while.

'It's just round this side of the house. It's quite easy to get to. See, it's just there.' Julian pointed ahead and I saw a rectangular building in the same soft red brick as the house, the side and part of its roof covered with ivy. 'It's a listed building, so obviously we're limited in terms of what we can do to it. Early nineteenth century, we think.'

'It's quite big, isn't it?' Mum said, standing back to look at the two-storey building. It had windows either side of its round-arched doorway. 'It's bigger than our bungalow!'

Julian laughed and slotted the key into the panelled wooden door. It swung open with a whiny creak and we stepped inside. I'd expected it to be full of junk, but aside from a couple of old barrels in one corner, it was completely empty. Just bare stone floor and plastered white walls. It smelt pleasantly of cool brick, and I felt my skin start to tingle with excitement as soon as I walked in. I loved it.

Could this work? I imagined the empty spaces filled with our shop furniture and rows and rows of flowers. The large oak table we had in the back room of the shop could be placed in the centre, and people would come and learn how to make hand-tied bouquets and garlands and table centrepieces. It was a blank canvas, waiting for a second chance at life, and I was filled with a sudden fierce desire to provide it.

Dad started asking questions about its architecture and what it had been used for over the years, and I went up the stone steps to the first floor. Light poured in through the large sash window and I walked slowly around, my footsteps echoing on the wooden floorboards. Unlike downstairs, which was one large, open space, upstairs had been divided into two separate rooms and looked like it had been lived in at some point. I could live up here, I thought to myself, excitement stirring within me. Crossing to the window, I looked out at the beautiful view across the lake and woodland. The water sparkled in the evening sunlight. Imagine waking up to that every morning! It was beautiful.

There was the crunch of approaching footsteps and I stepped back as Anthony's blond head came into view. My heart speeded up as I watched him walk purposefully up the path. He paused in front of the door and straightened his tie before being almost knocked off his feet by my mother, who seemed to virtually throw herself into his arms. I was equal parts annoyed by her lack of loyalty to me, jealous she was doing something I'd like to do, and amused because she looked a bit like Miss Piggy throwing herself at Kermit the frog.

'Oof! Hi, Birdie, how are you?' Bending down to my mother's height, he kissed her on the cheek before reaching out to shake my father's hand. 'Sorry I wasn't here when you arrived. I was meant to be off today but I got called into work. Still, Julian's the man you need to talk to about all this.'

'I was just telling Julian how very alike you both are,' Mum said, tucking her hair behind her ears.

'I know.' Anthony laughed. 'So, what do you think about this place? Do you think it will work?'

'I think so!' Mum said enthusiastically. 'It's an amazing space. And look at that view down to the river. Beautiful.'

'There's certainly plenty of space,' Dad said. 'Whether we'd need all of it or not is another matter.'

Anthony shrugged. 'It's up to you. No pressure. Where's Rachel?'

'Upstairs, I think.' Dad stepped back into the building and shouted upstairs as though it were three storeys high or something. 'Rachel?'

'Yes. Coming.' I backed away from the window, just as Anthony looked up and caught me watching. With my heart galloping, I went back down the stairs and joined them by the front door.

'Hi,' I said coolly, noticing that Anthony had lipstick on his cheek from my mum.

'Hello.' He straightened up slightly and jerked his chin at the Brew House. 'What do you think then? Too big?'

'Not really. I was just thinking I could live upstairs.' Suddenly shy under his gaze, I turned and looked up at the upstairs window, which was reflecting the leaves from the tree opposite. A pigeon cooed from the roof. 'It's beautiful.'

'Live? In there?' Anthony raised an eyebrow. 'Rather you than me. Besides, what about Jayjay? Doesn't he get a say?'

'What does Jayjay have to do with it?' Mum said, confused. 'He's Bobbi's boyfriend.'

Hardly registering what she'd said, I carried on staring up at the upstairs window before moving round the side of the building. It was quite overgrown, and clusters of nettles and brambles prevented me from going much further. A sparrow peered at me from a spiky branch and a white butterfly fluttered past my face. Withdrawing, I went back to the front and followed the path round to the other side of the building. A garage had been joined to the side. It was obviously a later addition, built in a similar shade of red brick and with a white wooden door. I peered through the dusty window, trying to get a look inside, but it seemed to be piled high with old junk.

'It's full of old rubbish, I'm afraid,' Anthony said, coming up behind me. 'I have no idea what's in there, to be honest. It probably all needs throwing away.' He peered through the glass next to me, his arm against mine and the smell of his aftershave filling my nose. 'I think there might even be a car buried under there.'

'Really?' I stepped away and walked to the end of the path where it joined a wider driveway, flanked on both sides by woodland. 'Where does this go?'

'It's another entrance to the hall.' He came and stood next to me and pointed at a white cottage further down. 'That's where I live. Gatehouse Lodge.'

'Really?'

'Yes. So, if you really did feel the need to live here, we would be neighbours. Why did you lie to me about Jayjay?'

'Oh!' It suddenly occurred to me what Mum had said. I shook my head. 'I'm sorry about that. It was just silly really. You saw me trying on that wedding dress and I didn't want to look like an idiot so I lied. Well, Elena lied. And then Bobbi panicked when she saw you at the shop and lied for me too. Bless her. Jayjay's a lovely lad but most definitely Bobbi's boyfriend, not mine. They're very well suited.'

'Good.'

I glanced up at him. 'Yes, I'm glad she's found someone nice. She deserves it.'

I went to walk away, but he caught my arm and pulled me back. 'I didn't mean that. I meant I'm glad you're not engaged.'

'Oh!' I looked up into his fierce gaze and swallowed. 'Why?'

I wanted him to say he loved me. That he wanted us to get back together and try again. But whatever it was that had been burning in his eyes just a moment ago had simmered down, to be replaced by uncertainty. His grip on my arm loosened. 'I... I don't know. I just am.'

Disappointment withered the hope that had surged within me. I looked down at his fingers still wrapped around my arm. Goose bumps had broken out across my flesh, but whether it was from cold or from his touch I wasn't sure.

'You're cold,' he said. 'Here, take my jacket.'

'Oh, no, I'm fine.' I started to protest, but he was already shrugging it off to reveal his white shirt.

'Here.' He draped it over my shoulders and smiled. My heart shifted in my chest as the jacket, still warm from his body and smelling of his cologne, enveloped me.

'Thank you.' I pulled it closer around me and smiled shyly back up at him.

'Anthony?' Julian called. 'Can you come here for a minute.'

'Okay.' He raised his eyebrows at me before disappearing back round to the front of the Brew House. I stayed where I was for a moment, savouring the feel of his jacket against my bare arms. It smelt so good I wanted to wear it for ever.

Mum appeared. 'Oh, there you are!' she said. 'What are you doing back here?'

'Just looking around.'

'Do you really think you'd want to live here?' she asked. 'I don't think you should. You might be lonely.'

I shrugged. 'It's a bit far to come every morning.'

'Well, if you don't have a shop to open, maybe you don't have to keep to shop hours. You could start later or work from home some days. Besides, Anthony's commuting to Manchester at the moment. Think how he feels.' She lowered her voice. 'And he had a serious car accident last year. I think that's very brave.'

'True.'

Her eyes rested on his jacket. 'And a gentleman too.'

I sighed. 'I wish you'd stop trying to sell him to me like I don't already know how great he is. He dumped me, remember. He doesn't want me.'

'I think perhaps he just needs a bit of convincing.' Mum's eyes twinkled kindly. 'Men are stupid. Most of them don't know what they want or need. They have to be shown.'

I rolled my eyes at her. 'And how do I do that?'

'I don't know, but I'm sure you'll think of something.' She patted my arm. 'Come on, let's go back inside.'

The sun had started its descent towards the horizon, staining the sky pink and orange. Anthony, Julian and my father were inside the Brew House now, discussing what would need to be done to make it suitable for use. It would need an electricity and water supply before we could think of doing anything.

'How long would that take?' I asked, taking out a notebook and pen from my bag. 'And more importantly, how much would it all cost?'

Julian glanced across at Anthony. 'You wouldn't need to worry about the cost of doing it up. It's up to us to make this place suitable for you to rent. We have builders working on various parts of the estate at the moment, so we could send them over here and get the work done pretty quickly. I'd have to talk to them about timeframes but I reckon it could be done within a month or so? Maybe less. I don't know – it's not really my area of expertise. How soon are you looking to move?'

'We're fairly flexible, although the sooner the better really. How much would the rent be?'

Julian looked across at Anthony and sucked in his bottom lip. 'We were discussing this last night, weren't we, Anthony? We figure you'd be doing us a favour by being here really, so we'd only charge you a small amount, much less than the going rate. We'd ask you to pay for your utilities, of course, and perhaps if you would make the odd display for the house and hall...'

'Why would I be doing you a favour?' I interrupted, genuinely confused. 'You need to make money, remember.'

'We know, but prospective clients are bound to be impressed if we have a florist already on-site. Especially one as experienced and talented as you.'

I laughed. 'Well, I don't know about that. But I can see this place could be perfect, and if it's not too expensive, well, it's a no-brainer really.' I turned a slow arc, looking around at the walls again. 'I can't believe I love it so much. When Anthony said you had a building I thought it couldn't possibly work, but now my head is full of all these ideas and possibilities.'

I went back upstairs and watched the reflection of the sun setting on the lake below. Would I be lonely living here? I wasn't sure. It was cooler now and I pulled Anthony's jacket on properly, slipping my arms into his sleeves and inadvertently putting my hand into his pocket as I did so. My fingers closed around a smooth leather pouch and, thinking it was his ID badge, I took it out and flipped it open, only to realise it was a wallet. I went to shut it again before the protruding edge of a photograph caught my eye. It couldn't be…

Glancing behind me to check I was alone, I eased it out from behind his driver's licence. My stomach swooped. It was a strip of four photographs we'd had taken in a photo booth. I was sitting on his lap and we were both pulling faces in the first one, laughing in the second, and full-on kissing in the third and fourth. We never could keep our hands off each other. But why was he carrying these around with him?

'Rachel?' I heard Anthony's footsteps on the stairs and quickly stuffed his wallet back into his jacket pocket. His head appeared and he smiled.

'Shall we go up to the hall to discuss details? You don't have to sign anything now if you don't want to, but Julian's got contracts we can go through to see if you're happy.'

'Sounds good.' I followed him downstairs, my heart thudding guiltily. What was I meant to do with this information now? I couldn't tell him I'd been looking through his wallet, and yet how was I supposed to live with the knowledge that he carried photographs of me without saying anything?

Julian closed the door to the Brew House and we walked back

up the path to the hall. The shadows had lengthened and the birds were singing loudly in their nests as they settled down for the night. Bats flitted across in front of us, chasing insects, and Mum clutched my dad's hand nervously; she'd always hated bats.

'There's no way I'll be visiting you after dark if you do move here,' Mum told me. 'It's a beautiful place but I can't stand bats.'

'They're fine!' I laughed. 'Just think about them as flying hamsters.'

'Oh, stop! That makes them even worse!'

We reached the hall and Julian let us in through the kitchen door. 'Mother?' he called. 'We have visitors.'

Switching on the lights, he directed us to sit down at the kitchen table. Cath appeared through a door at the opposite end of the kitchen, smiling and smoothing down her hair.

'Hello!' she said warmly. 'I do apologise. I fell asleep on the sofa. It's been such a warm day. You must be Rachel's parents.'

'Yes, I'm Birdie and this is my husband, Jim.'

'Lovely to meet you both,' Cath said as she shook hands with them. 'Do you like the Brew House? Do you think it might be suitable?'

'Yes,' I said, giving her a big hug. 'I love it.'

'Really?' Cath looked delighted. 'Anthony said you weren't sure when he first mentioned it.'

'No, I wasn't, but now I've seen it I really think I could make a go of it here. If you'll have me, of course!'

'Don't be silly. We'd love to have you working here.'

'We're just about to talk about the financial side of it all,' Julian said, sitting down at the table and opening up a file. 'Of course, there's no obligation to sign anything tonight. You can take a copy away with you and mull it over for a few days if you wish. There's no rush from our point of view, anyway. I just thought laying it all out like this would make everything clearer for everybody concerned.'

'Great.' I took the contract he was holding out to me and

started reading through it. I couldn't believe how low the rent would be. I glanced up at Anthony, wondering if he'd had anything to do with this. He was across the kitchen, helping Cath make the tea. He'd loosened his tie and undone the top button of his shirt, just like he used to when he came home from work when we lived together.

Julian cleared his throat and said in a low voice: 'I understand you'll have to think carefully about committing to this. I know you have a complicated relationship with my brother so it may not be quite as straightforward as it appears to everybody else.'

I glanced at him, surprised by his grave tone. He held my gaze, his eyes suddenly serious. Was he warning me off? Or just being extra cautious? He made a good point, of course. It was all right getting carried away with the wonderful setting and the possibilities the building offered, but perhaps I should think about it a little more. Moving my business to Willow Hall would mean I'd see Anthony day in and day out. He might carry photos of me around in his wallet, but what did that actually mean in practical terms? Probably not very much at all. It certainly didn't mean he wanted to get back with me, no matter how friendly he was being at the moment. And even if he did, what then? I wanted him, but I knew I also wanted marriage and children. Anthony had made it clear in the past that he didn't want that, so was I just heading for more heartbreak by signing up for this?

A thousand different scenarios played out in my head. I suddenly foresaw a future where I'd resigned myself to a life of unrequited love, watching Anthony longingly from the sidelines while he went about his life as usual, being charming and lovely but offering nothing in the way of a romantic relationship. Even as my father was urging me to go for it, I was imagining the horror of watching Anthony turn up with a new girlfriend, introducing her to me like I was his sister or something. Could I bear that? I wasn't sure I could.

Julian was right; I really did need to take a few days to mull this over. Dad was only seeing this in terms of reduced overheads, but I understood it was my heart on the line.

'Okay, well, I'm going to take a few days to think about it. I might look around, just to see if there is anything a bit closer to home.'

'Whaaaaat?!' Dad said, his voice rising in disbelief. 'Are you mad? You'll never find a deal as good as this! You were all for it ten minutes ago.'

'I know it's a great deal,' I said reasonably. 'And I do love it. I just want to make sure it's the right decision, that's all.' I glanced at Anthony again, who was now glaring at his brother across the kitchen. There seemed to be some kind of silent communication going on between them. 'We've only just decided to move out of the shop, after all. There's no point rushing into something immediately. I just need a few days, that's all.'

'That's fine by me,' Julian said supportively. 'Honestly, we have no one else lined up for it so it's yours if you want it, but no hard feelings if you don't. It would be marvellous, of course, if you did want it. You know you're always more than welcome at Willow Hall.' He smiled warmly at me as Cath brought over a tray of tea and scones and set it down in the centre of the table.

'It's too dark now,' she said, scraping back a chair and sitting down next to my mum, 'but next time you come I'll get Arthur to show you around the walled garden. It's mostly vegetables, but over the past few years he's started growing more and more cut flowers too. He picks some for me, but mostly they're just left for the bees. I don't know if you could use any of those in your bouquets, Rachel? I hear most florists use imported flowers these days.'

'That's really interesting, actually. There's a real movement towards using British-grown flowers recently. I use them where I can, but the arrangements I do at the moment do contain a lot of imports. Bobbi, the girl who works with me, is really into the idea of making more unstructured bouquets with wild, British-grown flowers. She's really creative and makes some beautiful arrangements. I'd love to have a look next time I'm here. Even the wildflowers and flowering shrubs you have everywhere would make amazing arrangements. And the range of foliage available is never-ending. I pay a fortune for some of the stuff you've got growing here.'

'Really?'

I nodded. 'Even if I don't end up moving here, you should maybe look into selling some of your flowers to the floristry markets. It might well earn you more cash.'

We stayed for a while longer, drinking tea and chatting about business rates and taxes. Anthony was very quiet. He stayed over the other side of the kitchen, leaning against the counter. I could feel his eyes on me, but each time I looked over, he looked away again.

'Well, I suppose we ought to get going,' Mum said, getting to her feet. 'It's been a lovely evening. I'm sure Rachel will be in touch soon.'

'I will,' I promised, as I slipped off Anthony's jacket and hung it on the back of the chair. Julian led us through the house to the front door to show us out and we said our goodbyes in the hallway. 'Thanks for lending me your jacket,' I said as I kissed Anthony's cheek.

'You're welcome.' He caught my hand and squeezed it before letting me go. He still seemed quiet, standing slightly apart from his mother and brother as they waved us off from the top of the steps, as though he were in a mood. I wasn't daft. I knew it was because he wanted me to rent the Brew House, but what I didn't understand was why. Why was he trying to draw me into his world when he'd pushed me away twelve months ago?

Chapter Seven

Bobbi arrived at work at eight, looking pale and peaky. 'Hello! How are you feeling?' I said cheerfully. 'You still look rough!'

'Thanks,' she said weakly. Taking off her denim jacket, she hung it on the coat hook by the door then immediately sat down at the table with her head in her hands.

'Oh, dear!' I said, thinking how poorly she still looked. I needed to tell her about the shop, but I didn't want to when she was looking so ill. Her bleached-blonde hair, dyed pink at the ends, fell over her face in lank strands. 'Maybe you should just go home? I can manage here.'

'No. I'll be okay in a little while.'

'Really?' I pulled a face. 'If it's a bug, you should be home in bed.'

'It's not a bug. It's food poisoning. I was better last night. I don't know why it's come back this morning. Maybe I have an allergy or something.'

'What have you eaten?'

'Toast. Maybe I have gluten intolerance?'

'Maybe. And maybe you should just go home.'

She put her head on the table and groaned. 'But I've just got here. I can't face getting back on the bus now.'

'I'll pay for a taxi.'

'No, just let me whimper here for a while. I'll be all right.'

I watched her doubtfully for a moment. 'Well, if you're sure.' Checking my watch, I realised it was time to open up the shop. The sun warmed my back as I set up the pot plants and flowers on the table outside. Cars rumbled past, their tyres hissing in the puddles left by the rain shower we'd had first thing this morning. I paused to look at the window display. Was it good enough? Was that why people weren't coming in? Perhaps I should introduce some brighter-coloured flowers. Maybe some sunflowers. As it was, it was full of pinks and purples, but perhaps some yellow would set it off nicely. Bobbi could do that today if she was feeling up to it.

I'd spent all night thinking about the Brew House and weighing up the pros and cons of moving there. It seemed to make perfect sense from a business point of view, but from an emotional one I wasn't so sure. The only way I could see of moving forward was to go and speak with Anthony himself and tell him how I was feeling. He'd always been straight with me in the past, so I thought I could trust him to be honest with me this time too.

Bobbi perked up a little over the course of the day and by the end of the afternoon I felt she was strong enough to take the news about the shop.

'What? But why?' she said, looking horrified.

'Because we're not getting enough customers.' I sat down at the table opposite her and reached for her hand. 'I know it's sad about the shop, but we're not closing, we're just moving. Your job's safe, I promise.'

'But this shop's been in your family for years! How can you bear to let it go?'

I shrugged sadly. 'We can't afford to be sentimental about it. As much as I'd love to stay here, we're not making enough money to justify it so we're going to have to find somewhere cheaper.'

'Have you found anywhere yet?'

I hesitated. I didn't know whether to tell her about the Brew House or not. 'Not yet, no,' I said, deciding against it. I assumed she would jump at the chance to work at Willow Hall and I didn't need anyone else telling me what to do. 'I don't suppose you know of any units to let, do you? Any lovely little shops in a pretty village somewhere?'

'No,' she huffed. 'Surely they'd be just as expensive and attract just as few customers as this place.'

'Maybe you're right.' I sighed. 'I don't know. We've only just started looking.'

Bobbi sat looking dejected and I felt sorry that I'd ruined her mood when she was just starting to look better. I couldn't blame her for being upset. 'You can go home early if you want to?' I told her. 'I can finish up here.'

'Are you sure?'

'Of course. You still don't look well. Go and get some rest.'

She nodded and got to her feet. 'Thank you. I'll see you in the morning.'

Once she'd gone I sat for a while, just looking around the shop and committing small details to memory. It didn't feel right to give Bobbi the news that we'd be moving, but not give her any details about where we'd be moving to. I'd hate to lose her, but I wouldn't blame her if she started to look for another job. I wondered if what she'd said was true; would another shop in a village be just as expensive? If I turned down the Brew House, would the only cost-effective alternative be some soulless commercial unit? The thought made me want to cry.

I needed to talk to Anthony. As far as I could see, he was the only negative thing about the Brew House.

***

The sun was already low in the sky by the time I arrived at Gatehouse Lodge. I'd driven through the village, past the main

117

entrance to Willow Hall, and turned right into a country lane, thinking it would be a more direct way to get there. I was right. The small cottage had come into view about a mile after the turning and, though it was partially shielded from the road by a line of tall green conifers, I was driving slowly enough to recognise it and turn into the driveway, only to be greeted by a pair of electric wrought-iron gates. I eyed the intercom system attached to the gatepost before pressing the call button. As soon as I pressed it, I wished I hadn't. I wanted to turn and run away. Did I really want to do this now? Maybe I should have left it for another day.

Hopefully, he would be out. I peered through the gate at the cottage. It was so pretty. Honeysuckle clung to the wooden porch and a climbing rose grew up and over the front window. There was no sign of life from the windows.

The intercom crackled into life.

'Yes?' he barked.

I was taken aback by his unwelcoming tone. Perhaps I should have phoned first. Yes, phoning would have been a far better idea. 'It's me,' I said, hesitantly. 'Could I have a word?'

'Rachel?' His voice immediately got much warmer. 'Yes, of course. I'll buzz you in.'

The gate swung slowly open and I parked next to his BMW. 'Jesus!' I murmured a moment later when Anthony appeared at his garden gate. He was shirtless and holding an axe, a thin veil of sweat glistening on his forehead. I tried not to stare as I got out of the car, telling myself it wasn't anything I hadn't seen before when I lived with him. 'Hi,' I called cheerfully. 'Sorry to disturb you. I just needed to talk to you about something.'

'Okay, no problem. I'm just chopping firewood to make myself feel manly. Come and sit in my garden.'

I smiled, aware that the tone of this visit was wrong already. Following him through the garden gate, I stepped into a rectangular garden bordered by conifers and sat down on the bench in the corner.

'I've only got these last two to do, then I'm all yours,' he said, placing another chunk of wood on top of a stump. Narrowing my eyes slightly at his choice of words, I watched his muscles ripple as he swung the axe down on to the wood. As it splintered and split in two I had the weirdest sense of déjà vu. I was pretty sure I'd dreamt about this at some point over the last year.

'What did you want to talk to me about?' he asked, as he got ready to chop the last piece of wood.

'The Brew House.'

'Oh, what about it?'

'Whether I should take it or not.'

'Of course you should take it. It makes perfect sense. Why wouldn't you take it?' Resting the axe on the floor, he looked at me, perplexed.

'Because of you.'

'Me?' His eyebrows shot up. 'What's it got to do with me?'

I sighed. Now the time had come for me to say it, I was finding it harder than I thought. I had it all planned out. Nothing too emotional or sentimental. No tears. But in all the times I'd imagined making this speech, it was never with Anthony shirtless, nor with a couple of pigeons crashing about in the tree above me.

'Can I use your toilet?'

'Of course – up the stairs on the right.'

'Thanks.' I bolted into the house and up the stairs. I knew I was being a coward but I needed some space away from Anthony's biceps to remember what I was supposed to say. I sat on the toilet and screwed my eyes shut. I couldn't for the life of me remember what it was. What was it again? I love you and I want your babies? No, no, it was about the Brew House. That was it. How could I rent it when I still had feelings for him and he had none for me? I drew in a deep breath. I wasn't sure why I'd thought coming here was a good idea. I could never think straight when Anthony was around.

I washed my hands in the sink and went out on to the landing.

Anthony's bedroom door was open and I paused at the top of the stairs, my eyes drawn to the rumpled grey covers on his unmade bed. A blue suit jacket hung on his wardrobe door and his watch lay on his bedside table. It brought back so many memories of our time living together that it brought a lump to my throat. I missed him. Even when I was with him, I missed him.

I could hear Anthony clanking cups in the kitchen below. Tearing my eyes away, I went downstairs and lingered in the doorway. He'd put his T-shirt back on and was pouring water out of a filter jug into a glass.

'So, go on then, what's the problem?' He poured a second glass of water and pushed it towards me.

'This,' I said, producing the letter he'd sent me from the hospital and placing it on the counter.

He stared at it for a moment before crunching it up in his fist and throwing it into the bin. 'There, problem solved.'

I wasn't sure what reaction I'd expected, but it certainly wasn't that. I hadn't even intended to show him the letter. It was just meant to be in my pocket, reminding me I wasn't what he wanted.

'It doesn't solve anything. I still know what you wrote.'

He gave me a look like he thought I was mad and put his hands on his hips. 'Didn't we go through this the other day? I was really angry and low when I wrote that letter. I was a selfish bastard, pushing everyone away. Lashing out. I hated everyone, myself especially.'

I sighed and scratched my head. This was it now: the part where I jumped in with both feet. 'But you didn't love me, did you? You *don't* love me. The problem is, I still love you.' Heat rushed through me and the air seemed to warp. There was no going back now.

Anthony stared at me, long and hard, and I braced myself for whatever came next. 'Who says I don't love you?'

'You.'

'Forget about the letter. The letter's gone.' He took a step towards me and held out his hand. I looked at it for a moment before taking it, feeling his fingers wrap around mine, warm and strong. 'I'm ashamed to admit that I deliberately chose words that would inflict the most pain and keep you away from me. I never expected you to show up at the hospital after that and be turned away. Even at my most spiteful and mean-spirited, I felt bad about that.'

I stared at him, not speaking, disbelieving my own ears. Was he saying he loved me? He couldn't possibly be saying that, could he?

'There's not a day goes by that I don't regret what I did,' he went on. 'The thing is, I didn't think I was in love with you. Not really. We got together so fast I thought it was just infatuation and the feeling would disappear over time.'

'But you never said you loved me when we were together.'

'You never said you loved me either.'

'That's because I didn't want to scare you away. You were always so adamant you didn't want a long-term relationship. I just wanted to keep you as long as possible.'

He smiled sadly, his thumb moving in circular motions over the back of my hand. 'You always did scare me. You made me feel things I'd never felt before. I've been telling myself all year we're better off apart, but I couldn't get you out of my head. You're always there. Always. I couldn't believe it when I saw you in that wedding dress. The thought of you marrying someone else was horrible and I knew for sure I wasn't over you at all.'

I didn't know what to say. This was too good to be true. Was I going to wake up any minute and find it was all a dream? But when he pulled me into a hug and crushed me hard against him, I knew it couldn't be. This was really happening. Anthony loved me.

'I'm sorry I pretended to be getting married.'

'Don't be. I deserve everything you throw at me. In fact, I'm amazed you've been so nice to me considering what I did to you.'

'Well, that is true,' I admitted. 'There have been a couple of times when I wondered what I was doing being so polite. I don't know whether it's because I'm a lady or because I didn't want to jeopardise Elena's chances of having her wedding here.'

He laughed. 'Trust me, we're so desperate for anyone to get married here, it wouldn't have mattered. In fact, my family would probably have applauded you.'

'I doubt that very much.'

'So, come on then, what's the problem with the Brew House? You said I was the problem.'

I withdrew slightly. Was it still a problem or did this fix things? 'I didn't want to sign a contract and move into your building without telling you how I felt. It felt dishonest and I didn't want to consign myself to a life of unrequited love, being treated like part of the furniture and having to endure watching you with other women. I got really scared I was going to be stuck here, loving you for ever without ever telling you how I felt.'

Anthony stroked my hair back from my face. 'But what did you think I was doing when I kept showing up at your shop and finding reasons to contact you?'

'Trying to get Elena to have her wedding at Willow Hall?'

He laughed. 'I already had Daniel's number. I could have phoned him any time.'

'Oh.' I laughed too, embarrassed I'd been so gullible. 'Sorry.'

'Don't be sorry.' He kissed me softly and I felt like I was melting into him. It was heaven to feel his lean, hard body against mine after so long apart. I still couldn't believe this was happening.

'So how are we going to play this?' he asked, pulling away slightly.

'What do you mean?' I blinked up at him, my eyes unfocused and hazy.

He smiled. 'Well, on the one hand, I'd like nothing better than to take you to bed right now. But I know I've treated you badly and that I need to work harder to earn your trust, so I think perhaps we should take things a little more slowly this time.'

I nodded. It made sense despite the fact that I wanted to go as fast as possible. 'Okay.'

'So, can I take you out tomorrow night?'

'Yes. Do you want me to come here?'

'No, I'll come and pick you up about eight, if that works for you?'

'Perfect.' I smiled up into his eyes as I disentangled myself from his arms. 'I suppose I'd better go home then.'

'What? Now? It feels like you've only just got here!'

'Oh! I thought when you were telling me we should take it slowly that you were telling me to go.'

'No. Come on, we shouldn't be doing this in my kitchen.' He took my hand and led me towards the front door. 'Let's go for a walk down to the lake.'

We left his cottage and walked up the drive in the direction of the Brew House. I felt excitement stir inside me as I spotted its dark shape ahead of us. We stopped to look at it in the moonlight, and Anthony hugged me to him. I felt like I'd come home.

Turning off the path, we cut across the grass, through the trees, and down the edge of the lake. The light was almost gone and a pale moon was rising above the trees on the opposite bank and reflecting in the rippling water. Further along, a small rowing boat bobbed next to a wooden jetty.

'Do you want to go for another boat trip?' Anthony asked.

'Not in the dark, no.' I laughed. 'Do you actually go out on it?'

'Of course I do. I love it.'

'I tell you what, you can take me out on a nice sunny day sometime.'

'Deal.'

We sat at the end of the jetty, our bare feet dangling in the black water. It was so cold that it made my skin sting and I squealed at first, making Anthony laugh. The breeze rustled the leaves in the branches above us and the row boat bumped gently against the jetty, making it shudder slightly. Now my feet had gone numb, the water didn't feel too bad. I moved them around, making the water splash further up my calves, soaking the hem of my skirt.

'I come here a lot, just to think,' he told me. 'I've thought a lot about you here. It's like a dream come true to have you here with me now.'

I could hardly believe these words were coming out of Anthony's mouth. When I'd left home earlier, I'd convinced myself he would reject me and I'd be driving home in tears within half an hour. To be sitting here in the moonlight with him was more than a dream come true. It was a miracle.

Chapter Eight

'Two rules,' I said when I opened the door to Anthony the following evening.

'Which are?' He leaned on the doorframe and looked down at me, his eyes sparkling with amusement.

'We don't talk about the past. And we don't talk about the future.'

'Oh! Okay.' He looked surprised but he smiled.

'Yes, I thought you'd like that.' I laughed as I closed the door behind me. 'Tonight is about enjoying ourselves. You look nice.' I passed an appreciative eye over his dark-grey shirt and blue-black jeans. 'But then you always do.'

'Thank you. You look beautiful. But then you always do, too.'

I smiled at him and then stood on tiptoe and kissed his cheek. 'Guess what?'

'What?' He took my hand as we walked down the path.

'I got tickets for the Moonlight Flicks in the Roman Gardens.'

'The what?' he laughed.

'The open-air cinema. It's in the Roman Gardens and you sit on deckchairs and wear headphones. I went last summer with Bobbi. It's great.'

'Are you joking?' He looked up at the grey sky. 'It's going to rain.'

'It's okay. I've got my big golf umbrella and a blanket each.' I showed him the straw beach basket I was carrying on my shoulder.

'Can we get something to eat? I'm starving.'

'We could get a pizza and take it in with us.'

'Okay. Anything. I just need to be fed.' It started to spit with rain and Anthony took the umbrella out of my hand and put it up over our heads. I waited for him to put his arm around me, but he kept a disappointingly polite distance between us. Cars rumbled past as we crossed the bridge over the river to get into the city centre, and we walked up past The Birdcage. Anthony paused as we passed by, putting his nose up to the window. 'It's a shame you have to lose it.'

'I know.' I pulled a sad face. 'Bobbi's gutted but I told her about the Brew House today and that's cheered her up. She's excited to see Willow Hall too.'

'Oh, good. Do she and Jayjay want to get married there?' Anthony said mildly.

I laughed. 'Nice try but I don't think so. Not yet, anyway.'

'Shame. We could do with another one this summer.' He sighed heavily and I glanced up at him, concerned.

'What's wrong?'

'Oh, nothing. I just feel the weight of everything sometimes, that's all. The hall's such a huge responsibility. My mother can't understand what my problem is, but being responsible for such a huge building terrifies me. It's not even the amount of land that comes with it. Most of that's rented and managed by farmers anyway. But the house itself is protected and so many people love it and care about it. It's hugely expensive and everything needs to be carefully restored. I'm just glad Julian's onboard. He's so enthusiastic about it all and is really excited about the wedding business. Has he shown you the house he and Liz are doing up?'

I shook my head.

'It's going to be amazing. I don't expect they'll move in until after the new baby, but their future is all sewn up and he's really happy and settled.' He looked off into the distance, his brows drawn together into a frown.

I looked up at him thoughtfully. For someone who didn't want to settle down and have a family, he seemed rather envious of his brother's life. I opened my mouth to ask him about it and then shut it again. He would only get defensive and it would probably count as breaking my own rules about not discussing the future.

'Are you looking forward to the new baby?'

'Yes.' He smiled. 'I lived miles away when the other two were born so it will be good to get to hold this one.'

'You like babies?'

He raised an eyebrow and looked at me. 'I like other people's babies.'

I laughed and opened the door to the pizza shop. We ordered a large farmhouse pizza and leaned against the yellow-tiled wall to wait for it. The rain was getting heavier and I started to worry that perhaps this wouldn't be quite the romantic date I'd planned. Anthony didn't even have a waterproof coat, though I'd brought one of my dad's old cagoules for him if he needed one. I doubted he'd really want to wear a fifteen-year-old sheet of plastic, but never mind.

I'd been wondering what to do for our date all afternoon. The obvious choice was to go to a restaurant, but that seemed too boring and formal after our moonlit date by the lake last night. Plus, I was conscious that I didn't want him to call all the shots. I needed to keep a little bit of control.

Anthony seemed quite happy, though. I knew he'd be okay as long as he had food. Besides, it was quite nice to be just standing in a brightly lit pizza shop, waiting for our food. This was the sort of normal stuff we'd done when we were together. It couldn't all be fancy restaurants and stately homes.

'You've gone very quiet. Are you okay?' He tucked a strand of hair behind my ear and ran a finger over my cheek. His eyes were soft and my knees went weak. I blushed.

'Yes.' I nodded at the rain running down the window. 'I'm just worrying about the weather.'

Bending his knees, he peered up towards the sky. 'Ah, don't worry. Look, there's a break in the clouds up there.' He pointed to a tiny patch of blue in the opposite direction to where we were going. 'It'll be fine. Besides, I'm a country boy, aren't I? Skin's waterproof.'

We collected our pizza and walked the short distance to the Roman Gardens, sheltering beneath the umbrella. The air was full of misty, spitty rain, but there were already about twenty people sitting in deckchairs on the grass, waiting for the film to start. We collected our chairs and set them close together on the grass; then I pulled out the bright-yellow cagoule and offered it to Anthony.

'What the hell's that?' he laughed, opening it out and looking at it.

'An old waterproof coat that belongs to my dad. Or, I have an old poncho from a theme park. You can have that if you'd rather.'

'Err…' He glanced up at the grey sky. 'No, it's all right,' he said, dubiously. 'I'll wear this.'

I put on my raincoat and sat down with a blanket on my lap.

'Do I get a blanket too?' Anthony put up his hood and then pulled the drawstring so tight only his nose could be seen. I laughed.

'Yes, of course you do. Sit down.' I covered his legs with the blanket and then positioned the umbrella so it was covering both of us.

'Do you know what this reminds me of?' Anthony asked, opening the pizza box.

'What?'

'Fishing with my dad.'

'Aww.'

'Don't say "Aww". I hated it.'

'Oh! Well, I'm sure you won't hate this.' I bit into a slice of pizza and closed my eyes as I chewed it. 'I know it's a bit damp but at least it's something different. And this pizza's divine.'

'Mmm, I know. Have we got anything to drink?'

Rummaging in my bag, I took out two bottles of beer. 'I've got water and Coke too if you want something soft.'

'Jesus! How big is that bag?' He peered at it with renewed respect. 'It must weigh a ton. You should have let me carry it.'

'It's fine.'

'Well, thank you.' He leaned across and kissed me on the lips. 'I wasn't sure if you'd be drinking?'

'I can't if I'm driving.'

'You could always stay on the sofa.'

He frowned. 'If it's the same pink sofa I remember, there's no way I'm sleeping on that thing. A park bench would be more comfortable.'

'No, that went after the flood. I've got your old sofa actually. When Dad sold the apartment, he let me have it.'

'You always did have your eye on that.'

'I know I did. So you see, it's very comfortable and I have spare bedding.'

He reached for a bottle of beer. 'Okay then. I'm not in work tomorrow so that works.'

I didn't usually drink beer, but it was just what I needed with the pizza. The garden filled up around us and the air was filled with the rising buzz of chatter and laughter as people settled down to wait for the film to start. Oddly, the more people that arrived, the closer I felt to Anthony. It was like we had our own little private oasis, huddled together beneath the umbrella, with the rain dripping from the trees and pattering around us. The Roman remains looked like hulking dark figures in the dusky twilight and the silver moon sailed high in the starlit sky.

We finished the pizza and stowed the box beneath the seat. The beer made me sleepy and I laid my head on Anthony's shoulder.

'The film hasn't even started yet,' he murmured against my hair.

'Mmm, I'm not used to beer.'

'But you can drink a whole bottle of Prosecco?'

I giggled. 'No!'

He kissed my head. 'Maybe I'm just boring you.'

'Don't be silly.' I opened my eyes and he lowered his face and kissed me softly. His lips were cold from the beer and made chills run up and down my spine. I put my hand on his face, stroking the hollow beneath his cheekbone and running my fingers through his hair. How had I lived without this for a full year? I felt like I'd come home at last. I wasn't even going to question how long it might last. I'd decided to live in the present.

When it was dark enough, the cinema screen flickered into life. Reluctantly, I pulled away from Anthony and we put our headphones on. I'd completely forgotten what film I'd booked to see, but it didn't really matter. All that mattered was that I was with Anthony, and I felt happy and relaxed. The hum of conversation around us died down as the opening credits rolled, and Anthony slipped his hand around mine and squeezed it.

'Was it okay?' I asked after the film had finished. I was fairly certain he'd fallen asleep somewhere in the middle, but I wasn't complaining because he'd held my hand throughout.

'Of course. It was great.' He looked amazed I'd even asked. Getting up, he stretched, making my dad's plastic jacket crackle noisily. The rain had stopped and the air smelt fresh and earthy. 'Did you enjoy it?' he asked.

'Yes! I loved it.' I didn't say that I was slightly disappointed to be going home; that I wished we could have sat there for ever. With movement comes change, and I didn't want the feeling of closeness to disappear as we walked home. I folded up the blankets and put them in my bag while Anthony sorted out the deckchairs, then we walked home through the park and over the river.

'You're very quiet,' Anthony said, swinging my hand. Huge oak trees rose up around us and, apart from the occasional call of a night bird, everything around us was quiet. 'Are you okay?'

'I'm fine.' I smiled at him, squeezing his hand. 'I really enjoyed tonight.'

'Me too.' He stopped and looked at me. 'It feels magical to be spending time with you again.'

I laughed nervously, my heart stuttering to a stop. 'Are you sure that wasn't just the cinema?'

'Of course not!' He smiled down at me. 'It was lovely, though. We need to do more stuff like that. Create new memories and leave the past behind.'

We stared at each other in the moonlight and then I reached up and kissed him.

'Speaking of the past...' I said, as I continued walking. He groaned and I laughed. 'It's nothing bad, don't worry, but you always used to be dancing. Do you still dance?'

'Not really. My leg gets stiff.'

'Oh, no, really? That's a shame. You were a great dancer.'

'I know, but a guy's got to slow down sometime.'

I laughed at him. 'You poor old arthritic man! You look all right to me.'

'Yeah, well, appearances can be deceptive.' I must have looked stricken because he laughed. 'I'm all right. Don't worry. Here...' He lifted my arm and spun me round before pulling me against his body. 'Maybe I've just had no one to dance with. And no reason to dance.'

He kissed me harder and deeper this time, making my head spin with lust. The trees above us rustled in the breeze, showering us with droplets of water, but it didn't matter. Nothing mattered except Anthony and the feel of his lips on mine. Eventually, we started walking again, but kept having to stop to kiss every few minutes. It must have taken us an hour to do the ten-minute walk home.

'Wow! It looks a bit different in here, doesn't it?' Anthony said, looking round at my hallway as I let him in through the front door. I laughed, remembering his horror-struck face the first time

131

he'd laid eyes on my pink flowery house. It wasn't like that any more. My boiler had burst and flooded the whole place, so I'd repainted everything in pastel tones. It was still pink and girly with vintage touches, but the effect was more Laura Ashley than tart's boudoir. I could tell by Anthony's face that he approved.

'The last time you saw it, it was dripping water, wasn't it?' I said. 'Do you want a cup of coffee?'

'Tea, please.'

There was lots of rustling as he peeled off the cagoule and went into the lounge. 'Ah, old friend,' he said, sitting down on the sofa and giving its arm a pat. 'How I missed you.'

'You only want me for my sofa,' I said lightly.

He laughed and patted the cushion next to him. 'Come here, wench.'

I laughed and practically threw myself on top of him. He felt so good, pressed up against me. His hand sneaked around the back of my neck and he kissed me softly, his tongue slipping past my lips and into my mouth. Any other thoughts in my head slipped into oblivion, and all I could think about was the taste of his lips, the smell of his skin, and the heat emanating from his body.

We'd always had this passion for each other. I'd felt an animalistic pull towards him the moment I first laid eyes on him. We'd kissed that first night, almost forgetting we were in a public bar as we got lost in the moment. And when we'd lived together, we could hardly take our hands off each other. I felt the same pull now. Nothing had changed between us. The past year melted away as we kissed and stroked and pressed against each other. He was mine. And he was back. That was all I needed to know at that moment.

'I'm supposed to be making you tea,' I said, pulling away from him and standing up. 'And I'll get you some bedding.'

I expected some kind of protest but he just nodded, accepting that he wasn't going to be sleeping in my bed tonight.

I switched the kettle back on and went upstairs to get the spare duvet and a pillow from my bed. He was taking off his shirt when I came back down. I stopped in the doorway, suddenly unsure if I should be giving him more privacy.

'Come in, don't be daft,' he said, draping it over the back of the armchair.

'Okay.' I placed the duvet and pillow on the sofa ready for him, feeling flustered by the sight of his body. He wasn't exactly ripped, but he was nicely defined. Broad shoulders tapering to a narrow waist. My eyes were drawn to him over and over again, remembering the feel of his skin beneath my hands. 'Right, I'll make that tea.'

'About time. I've been waiting for ages.'

'Cheeky!'

I went through to the kitchen, and when I came back with the tea, he was beneath the covers with his head on the pillow.

'Right.' I kissed him on the head and placed his drink on the coffee table next to him. 'Goodnight.'

'Where are you going?'

'To bed.'

'Not yet. Get in here with me.'

'Err…'

'Just for a minute. Come on, come and give me a cuddle.'

'Just for a minute?'

'Of course.'

I put my drink next to his and slipped under the covers, nestling into his arms. 'Mmm. Now, this would be much better if you were naked.'

I tutted. 'Not on our first date, Anthony.'

He chuckled. 'Of course. Silly me. Sorry.'

'I should think so.'

He nuzzled the back of my neck and kissed my shoulder. It felt so good to be snuggled up with him like this. Closing my eyes, I drifted off to sleep.

Chapter Nine

Anthony was still fast asleep when I woke up at six the following morning. The early morning sunshine filtered through the living-room blinds, casting stripy shadows across the walls. He still had his arms around me, and I was so warm and comfortable that I didn't want to move, but I had to get up and open the shop.

Careful not to wake him, I slipped out from beneath the covers and went upstairs to shower. I felt rested and happy. It was nice to have just slept together rather than having sex. Somehow, it made me feel closer to him. Last night had been about being together and enjoying each other's company, and it was nice to know it wasn't just about the physical side of things.

I made breakfast and left a cup of tea and a note on the coffee table for Anthony when he woke up. I was surprised he wasn't awake yet. In the old days, he'd be up and out running by now. It was nice to watch him sleep, though. He looked so peaceful I wanted to continue watching him, but I had to get to work.

He showed up at the shop about ten o'clock. Even though it had only been a few hours since I'd last seen him, my heart soared and I reached up and hugged him.

'You should have woken me up,' he said, kissing my neck.

'Well, you're not in work, are you? I thought it was best to let you sleep. How are you feeling?'

He looked surprised by my question. His eyebrows shot up and then he frowned. 'Good. Why?'

'Oh!' I was slightly bewildered by his defensive tone. 'I just wondered if you were comfortable on the sofa. You didn't wake up with a crick in your neck or a dead arm?'

'No. I feel good.' His smile returned and I noticed how his eyes were the same blue as the sky above us. 'How about you?'

'I feel great.' Reaching up, I kissed his cheek. 'Bobbi's not, though. She's come into work but she's still not well.'

'That's no good. Do you want me to take her home? I've walked up but I can get the car.'

'Maybe. Let me ask.'

'Bobbi?' I called, going back into the shop. 'Anthony said he'll take you home if you want?'

'Anthony?' She straightened up, looking confused. 'Wait! Are you two back together?'

'Errrrr…' I went bright red, embarrassed to be having this conversation in front of Anthony. 'Sort of.'

Bobbi sprang up from her seat. 'Yes!' she said, enthusiastically. 'I knew you would! I knew it! I knew it! How many times have I told you that you and Anthony are made for each other? Oh, this is wonderful. You're going to get married and have babies and be together for ever.'

'Bobbi!' I hissed, going an even brighter shade of red.

'Steady on!' Anthony said with a nervous laugh. 'We're taking things slowly, okay? Now, do you want a lift home?'

'No, I'm going to stay. I'm feeling a bit better all of a sudden.'

'Are you sure?' I said doubtfully. 'You were at death's door a minute ago.'

'It sort of comes in waves. And you two have cheered me right up.'

'Oh, good,' I said. 'I'll make a cup of tea. Do you want one, Anthony?'

'No, I'd better go. I just came to say goodbye. I've got things to do at home.'

'Okay.' I'd been hoping he might stay all day. I wanted to ask when I could see him again, but I didn't want to scare him off by being too needy. 'Bye then.'

His eyes flickered and he pushed his hands into the pockets of his jeans. 'When can I see you again?'

I beamed at him. 'When are you free?'

'Tonight?'

That soon? My heart swelled. 'Fine by me.'

'Will you come to me?'

'If you like. What time?'

He shook his head. 'As soon as you can.'

'Oh. Okay!' I laughed in disbelief. 'I'll see you about six then.'

'Great.' He kissed me firmly on the lips. 'I'll cook. See you later.'

I gazed after him with a soppy smile on my face, then realised Bobbi was watching me.

'Rachel's in love! Rachel's in love!'

'Oh, get lost, Bobbi!' I said, my cheeks glowing bright red.

'You are! And he feels the same way about you too. Anyone can see it.'

A slow smile spread across my face and I felt so joyful I wanted to dance around the shop. Instead I asked her how she was getting on with Jayjay.

'We're good, thanks!' She smiled. 'We're thinking of getting our own place together but I'm not sure how my mum will take it.'

'Why? You're twenty now. She can't keep you by her side for ever.'

'I know, but she's been doing so well recently I don't want to change anything in case it upsets her again.'

'But what's the alternative? Wait until she's low again?'

Bobbi sighed. 'Yeah, I know. It's just hard. I think it's me more than her, really. She loves Jayjay so I can't see her having a problem with it at all. It's a big thing moving in with someone, though, isn't it? What if it doesn't work out?'

I shrugged. 'That's the chance you take, I suppose. Has Jayjay been looking after you while you've been sick?'

'No, I told him to stay away in case he caught it.' She swallowed hard and turned in her seat. Standing up suddenly, she rushed to the toilet and threw up.

'Oh! Errm, perhaps I should close up and take you home?' I suggested, feeling a bit alarmed. I liked how she'd told Jayjay to stay away but was willing to share her germs with me.

'No, it's okay,' she said after a moment. The toilet flushed and I heard the sound of the toilet roll spinning as she pulled off a few sheets to wipe her mouth. 'I feel a bit better now.' Standing up, she supported herself on the doorway for a moment before coming to sit back down.

'Bobbi,' I said firmly, shaking my head at her. 'There's no way you're well enough to work. Go home.'

***

I phoned my mum at lunchtime and told her I'd decided to go ahead with the Brew House. I wasn't sure why I hadn't told her before, really.

'Really? That's wonderful news! I'm so pleased. What changed your mind?'

'Err, well, Anthony actually.'

'Yes?'

I heard the expectation in her voice and smiled.

'We're back together.'

'Oh, my goodness! That's even better than the Brew House! I'm so pleased for you, Rachel. You know how much I adore him and I have a really good feeling about you two this time.'

'We're taking things slowly, though, just seeing how it goes.'

137

'Marvellous! Can you come round tonight and tell me all about it?'

'I can't, sorry. Anthony's cooking me dinner.'

'Really? Why don't you close up early so you have plenty of time to get ready?'

'That doesn't look very professional.'

'Just this once won't matter. Go on, give yourself an hour off.'

Anthony rang just before I left and gave me the code for his gate so I could let myself in when I got there. I wrote it down with shaking hands and propped it up on my dashboard. I was too nervous and excited to memorise it.

***

I punched the code into the electronic pad and the gate swung open. The gatehouse looked even prettier than last time, now that the climbing rose was flowering red against its white walls. Anthony appeared in the doorway, looking sexy in a blue, short-sleeved shirt and jeans. My heart leapt when I saw him and I couldn't stop smiling as I parked my little car next to his big black shiny one on the gravel driveway. Anthony came over and opened my door.

'Hi,' he said, smiling down at me.

'Hello.' I stood up and kissed him. It felt so good to see him and be able to kiss him like I used to. The warm breeze whispered through the cornfield and stirred my hair.

'Dinner's nearly ready,' he said, taking my hand and leading me into the cottage. Inside it smelt wonderfully of chicken and roasting vegetables. 'I hope you're hungry. I've made loads.'

'I've missed your cooking.' I sniffed the air appreciatively. He'd always been great in the kitchen. He was the perfect man to live with. Clean, tidy and a great cook.

'You only want me for my food.'

'No, I want you for your body,' I said lightly.

He laughed and went through to the kitchen. 'What would you like to drink?'

'Have you got lemonade?'

'Yes, but I've got wine if you want some?'

'No, I'm driving.'

'Stay.' He leaned on the worktop and looked at me. 'We don't have to do anything.'

I hesitated. 'I've got to open the shop in the morning.'

He shrugged. 'I have to leave for work at six anyway.'

'Oh. Okay.'

'You don't have to if you don't want to,' he said, opening the oven door and checking on the food inside. I felt the blast of heat on my legs. 'It's just, I really enjoyed being with you last night.' He shut the oven door and straightened up. 'I miss sleeping with you and being with you. I don't mean the sex, although I miss that too, obviously. I mean, just sharing a bed and feeling close to you. Do you get what I mean?' He looked slightly embarrassed, as though he'd said too much.

'Of course I do. I was thinking the same thing actually.'

He smiled, his cheeks flushed from the oven. 'So? Wine or lemonade?'

'I'll have wine then, please.'

He poured me a glass and told me to sit down at the kitchen table while he served the food. It was a small round table and he'd covered it with a white tablecloth and placed a single red rose in a bud vase in the middle. I opened my mouth to comment and then shut it again. He was embarrassed enough as it was, and I didn't want to embarrass him further, so instead I watched him move around the kitchen, laying the food out on the plates carefully and wiping up any spills.

'You really are the perfect man,' I said, looking at the plate of food he'd laid in front of me.

He laughed and sat down in the seat opposite. 'Says the woman whose heart I so carelessly broke twelve months ago.'

139

'We're not talking about that, remember.' I picked up my knife and fork. 'But seeing as you brought it up, I'll just say that the reason *why* I was so heartbroken is because you *are* perfect.'

'Hardly!' he scoffed. 'I have plenty of faults.'

'Like what?' I cut into a new potato and popped it into my mouth.

'I'm broken.'

'Broken?' It was such a ridiculous thing to say that I almost laughed, but Anthony wasn't smiling at all. All he did was shrug. Frowning, I waited for him to explain.

'I can't have kids, for a start,' he said, reaching for his wine.

'Oh?' Can't? That was news to me. He usually said he didn't want them. 'Was that something to do with the accident?' I asked, when it became clear he wasn't going to explain.

'No. Anyway, I think this counts as talking about the future, which isn't allowed.' Anthony smiled as he reached across the table for my empty plate. 'Shall we go for a walk? I realised earlier that you haven't met Arthur yet, or seen his garden. I think you'll like it.'

We walked hand in hand up towards the house. The sun was setting over the fields, filling the sky with golden light. The land-scape was so beautiful I made Anthony stop so I could take a photograph on my phone. I took more photos of the Brew House to show Bobbi, and then we carried on to find Arthur.

The clank of a watering can behind the tall stone wall told us he was already in his garden, watering his plants. Anthony peered round the wooden door. 'Hi, Arthur, I've brought someone to meet you.' Turning to me, he beckoned me through into the garden. 'Arthur, this is Rachel; Rachel, this is Arthur.'

Arthur was a short, stocky man, with short, grey hair and a weathered, leathery look about him. He smiled warmly as he shook my hand with his large, rough one. I liked him immediately. His smile lit up his whole face and he had the kindest brown eyes.

'Hello, Rachel. Lovely to meet you at last! I've heard lots about you.'

'Hello, Arthur.'

'I thought Rachel might like to see your garden, seeing as she's a florist.'

'Of course. Come on, I'll show you around.' He placed his green watering can on the path next to a bed of potato plants and started to give us a guided tour of his garden. The vegetable beds were beautifully neat and weeded to perfection. Rows and rows of vegetables were lined up with military precision. Spring cabbages, carrots, leeks, potatoes, onions, corn. Green beans and peas grew up trellises against the wall. Arthur looked proud as he pointed them all out to me and I found myself completely absorbed by what he was saying. It all smelt so wonderfully earthy, and I found myself thinking this garden could have been just like this one hundred years ago. It was like time had stood still. From the weather vane on top of his shed, to the sundial clock in the centre of the garden, it was all so perfect.

'I'm growing some flowers too,' he said modestly, leading us over to the other side of the garden to show us his many beautiful old English roses. 'I grow all sorts of flowers all year round, not just roses. The tulips this spring came through really well. And I have hellebores in the winter. I don't know what it is about this place but everything seems to just grow here. I've got allium, stocks, foxgloves, lupins, alysum, sweet peas. Loads and loads of sweet peas.'

'But this is amazing!' I interrupted, pushing my hair back from my face. I pointed at the variety of roses. 'These roses are amazing quality and look at all the different colours you're growing.' I bent over to inspect a dusky pink one. 'This colour is so popular for weddings at the moment. Cath was telling me the other evening about your flowers, but I never expected there to be so many! Wow! You could supply florists with the volume and variety of roses you're growing here. They're beautiful.'

Arthur looked pleased. 'Really? I just grow them for Cath. I give her a bunch of flowers every Sunday, and then we take some down to the churchyard to place on Anthony's father's grave.'

'Aww, that's lovely!' I said. 'Honestly, florists pay a small fortune to get flowers like this shipped over. I would love to use flowers grown in the UK. And think of all the good you're doing for the bees. They must love it here.'

'They certainly do. They're always buzzing about. Especially the foxgloves. The poppies come up well around here too.'

'Poppies! So many people ask for poppies and they're so difficult to get hold of because they're difficult to import. Oh, my goodness! This is like a dream come true. Anthony said you grew flowers and we might be able to use them for the weddings, but I had no idea you had so many beautiful roses. This is perfect.' I gazed in awe at all the flowers that were growing. 'Would you be able to grow more?'

'I should think so. The peonies did well last year too, so hopefully we'll have some of them soon.'

'Oh, my goodness! And you wouldn't mind me using them? For floristry displays?'

'Of course not. Just as long as you leave me a few for Cath, that's fine by me. What do I want with flowers like that? I'm quite happy with my vegetables.'

I laughed. Arthur was adorable and I could see why Cath had fallen for him, even if she was the lady of the house and he was the gardener. I wondered how their relationship had developed over the years. It was all rather Lady Chatterley.

We chatted some more about the flowers and the garden, and he suggested we turn a patch of land near the Brew House into a wildflower garden too. I felt excitement stir, and I couldn't wait to tell Bobbi about it. She'd often talked about flower farming in the past and had a tutor at college who went on and on about the advantages of using British flowers, so I knew she'd be interested. It would be hard work, of course, but the possibilities seemed endless. I couldn't believe things were coming together so beautifully.

A blackbird sang loudly from the garden wall and another one answered it in the tree above. The leaves whispered in the wind and a crow cawed. It sounded like heaven.

'Shall we go in and say hello to everyone in the house?' Anthony said. 'Are you coming in now, Arthur?'

'In a minute. Just need to finish watering these last few potatoes and the beans. Tell your mother to put the kettle on.'

'Will do.'

Cath and Liz were sitting at the kitchen table, watching Grace colouring in a picture of a horse. Once more, the kitchen smelt of freshly made cakes.

'Hello, darling.' Cath greeted me with a big hug. 'How are you?'

'Good, thanks. We've just been talking to Arthur in the garden. He says he'll be in in a minute for a cup of tea.'

'Oh, good. I've hardly seen him all day. He's always in that garden.' Cath beamed at me as she bustled past to put the kettle on. 'Did he show you all the flowers?'

'Yes! Isn't he amazing? I couldn't believe how many beautiful roses he grows. I was telling him he could supply florists. Meaning me, obviously! But like he said, we could convert one of the fields and grow flowers there too and supply more. That could be another source of income for the hall.'

Anthony frowned. 'Or for you. Remember, you need to make your business work too.'

'I know, but Arthur has the expertise. I don't know how it would work realistically, but my head is so full of possibilities right now. I'm so excited.'

Liz beamed at me. 'Do you want to know something else exciting?'

'What?'

'We've booked another two weddings for next year.'

'Hurray! That's fantastic!'

'I know. They both confirmed today.' Liz smiled happily, rubbing her pregnant belly.

Cath cut us all a slice of cake and we sat around the table chatting until Arthur came in. Wearily, he took his boots off at the door and eased his feet into his slippers. A large black Labrador with a greying muzzle padded in behind him.

'Aww, who's this?' I asked, holding my hand out for the dog to sniff. He walked slowly over, his tail wagging from side to side. 'I haven't seen him before.'

'This is Oscar,' Cath said. 'He's always here, but you probably haven't noticed him. He's getting on a bit so he just lies by the Aga all day or else is in the garden with Arthur.' She smiled fondly at him. 'He's a good boy.'

'Hello, Oscar, you're lovely!' I told him, as he licked my hand with his long pink tongue. 'I love dogs.'

'Do you?' Anthony looked surprised. 'I never knew that.'

'I love dogs. I just can't have one at the moment because I'm at work all day, but I'd like one, one day.'

'You might be able to have one if you move here,' Grace piped up from her colouring. 'I'm getting a pony when our house is ready.'

'Oh, Grace, you know that's not true!' Liz scolded. 'Telling everybody you're getting a pony over and over again won't make it happen.'

'But that's my dream!' Grace protested. 'And Daddy says that everybody's dreams come true here.'

Liz laughed. 'I think he was talking about hooks for the wedding business, sweetheart,' she told her.

We stayed in the kitchen until the sky outside grew dark, and then we walked back to Anthony's cottage together. Solar-powered lights had been placed along the pathways around the hall, so it was easy to see, but once we got on the driveway to Anthony's cottage, everything went dark. He switched on the torch he'd borrowed from his mother and I clung to his arm so I wouldn't fall.

'You should get some lights up this way too,' I told him.

'I know. I keep meaning to but I haven't got round to it yet.'

'Aren't you lonely down here on your own?'

'No. I like being alone.'

'Why?'

He shrugged. 'I can always go up to the house if I get bored. I'm just used to living on my own, I suppose. I've never lived with anyone other than you.'

'Really?' I frowned. 'No other girlfriends?' I felt weirdly jealous just talking about these faceless women from his past.

'No. They stayed over, but never moved in.'

I stayed silent, not liking the mention of them staying over. It was stupid and immature, but I couldn't help it.

'Hey,' he said, squeezing my hand.

'Hey what?'

'You're not going all jealous on me, are you?'

'Me? No!'

'Good, because there's no need to be.'

We walked on through the darkness, the yellow beam of the torch bobbing along in front of us. I tried to shake it off but the jealous feeling continued to cling to my insides.

'Can I just ask?' I said, as we neared the cottage and the amber security lights lit up as though welcoming us home. 'Has there been anyone else since we broke up last year?'

His feet scraped on the gravel as he stopped and turned to look at me. I could barely see him in the darkness, the light from the torch only illuminating part of his arm and the path ahead. 'No.'

'Really? Are you sure?' I said, making sure my tone was light and jokey. 'Because I've seen how women look at you. You could have your pick of anyone.'

'And I pick you.'

I laughed. 'No, but seriously…'

'Rachel, there's been nobody else,' he said, his voice deadly serious. He squeezed my hand. 'There *is* nobody else. Only you.' Leaning down, he kissed me tenderly on the lips. 'You don't have to be jealous.'

'Okay,' I whispered. The intensity in his voice made my knees weak.

'Besides, I don't know if you've forgotten or something, but I spent a good portion of last year recovering in hospital.' He switched on the hall light and shut the door behind us. 'How about you, anyway? Did you date?'

My heart thudded with guilt. 'A couple of times, but it was always awful.'

'Really?' He stopped and looked at me as though my answer was completely unexpected. 'Who did you date?'

'No one you know. Why?'

'Because I want to beat them up.'

'Anthony!' I laughed. 'Just a few weeks ago you thought I was engaged to Jayjay. Besides, you dumped *me*, remember.'

'Are we here again?' He put his hands on my waist and pulled me against him. 'I thought the past was forbidden.'

'It is, but I'm just making sure you know that if you don't want me to date again, don't dump me!'

He smiled. 'Point taken.'

Raising myself up on to my tiptoes, I kissed him firmly on the lips. 'I love you, Anthony Bascombe.'

'I love you too, Rachel Jones.' He kissed me and I clung to him 'Do you want to go to bed?' he asked, his voice husky.

'Yes.' I wanted this. I wanted him. Taking my hand, he led me upstairs to his bedroom and switched on his bedside lamp, casting a cool, white light over his grey duvet. My whole body tingled with excitement as I closed the door, leaning back against it as Anthony unbuttoned his shirt. It all felt so familiar and right.

My dress slipped to the floor and I knelt on the bed, watching Anthony discard his trousers to reveal white jersey trunks. He smiled and climbed on to the bed, pulling me against his hard, smooth chest. I ran my hands over his shoulders and down his back, enjoying the sensation of his bare skin beneath my fingertips. He kissed down my arms, examining my skin with a reverent wonder, as though he wanted to commit each individual hair and freckle to memory. I felt the same about him. I wanted to feel and stroke and taste and explore him; check he was still the same man I remembered. He still smelt the same. A divine mix of spicy aftershave and his own musky masculine scent that excited some deep primal hunger inside me.

We made love for hours, reacquainting ourselves with each other's bodies until we fell asleep in each other's arms, legs entangled as though we were an extension of each other. Being so rudely awakened by Anthony's alarm at five o'clock the following morning was quite a shock. Outside, the sky was pale as the first rays of sun chased away the darkness. The dawn chorus was in full flow and I'd never heard one so loud or sweet. I made tea and toast while Anthony had a shower and had to spend some time hunting for cups and spoons and milk in the unfamiliar kitchen.

It was in the cupboard above the kettle that I found the tablets. The white rectangular box toppled out while I was searching for teabags. I put it back in without taking much notice and it was only when I was staring out of the window at the cornfield opposite, while waiting for the kettle to boil, that it occurred to me they might be important. Checking he wasn't about to appear in the kitchen, I took out the box again. I didn't recognise the name on the front, but reading the small print on the back, they appeared to be some kind of beta blocker. What were beta blockers prescribed for? I picked up my phone to look it up, but the sound of Anthony's footsteps on the stairs made me shove the tablets back in the cupboard.

'Hey…' He put a hand on my hip and kissed my neck. 'Do you want a shower before you go?'

'No, I don't want to hold you up.' I checked the time on the microwave clock. 'I can't believe you have to drive all that way to work.'

'Yeah, well, that's the price you pay for living in the middle of nowhere. Besides, it's not too bad once you get used to the journey.'

He wrapped his arms around me from behind and buried his face in the crook of my neck. It tickled and I giggled and tried to struggle out of his hold.

'Careful, I'm trying to make tea.'

Laughing, he squeezed me tighter and kissed my cheek. 'Mmmmm, it's so good to wake up next to you in the morning.'

'I know.' I turned in his arms and put my own over his shoulders. His hair was still slightly damp from the shower and he smelt of shower gel and toothpaste. Reaching up, I pressed my lips to his, the beta blockers forgotten.

Chapter Ten

'Do you know what beta blockers are used for?' I asked Bobbi later that day. She was pale and tired but said the vomiting had stopped. I still wasn't sure she was well enough to work, but she'd insisted she was okay and wanted to come in. She looked up from the lavender bouquet she was working on and frowned.

'I think my mum was prescribed them for anxiety once.'

'Anxiety?' I frowned. Anthony didn't appear to be anxious, but maybe that just meant the beta blockers were working.

'Why?'

'No reason.'

The door tinkled and Mum walked in, all dressed up in a pink dress, hat and heels. 'Hello!' she said cheerfully. 'It's only a quick call; your dad and I are off to the races. How are you feeling, Bobbi?'

'Okay.' Bobbi managed a wan smile and Mum frowned, concerned.

'You still don't look well. Have you seen a doctor?'

'No, it's just food poisoning. I haven't been sick since yesterday lunchtime. I'm just tired, that's all.'

'You're not pregnant, are you?' Mum laughed.

'No!' Bobbi snapped.

Mum's eyebrows shot up. 'I was only joking, Bobbi. Sorry! I was going to say, if you're feeling better we could take you down to Willow Hall so you can see the new place? But if you're still not feeling up to it we can leave it.'

'I do want to see it but I'm not sure I feel well enough today. When were you thinking?'

'Whenever suits you.'

'It might be nicer for you to see it when it's done up a bit,' I said. 'Anthony said the builders should be starting next week. Did I tell you about all the flowers they grow there? They grow so many beautiful roses and cut flowers, not to mention all the flowering shrubs, wildflowers and foliage that's everywhere. Anthony showed me around the walled garden last night, and I met Arthur. I feel like it could become a flower farm that could supply flowers to other florists, not just us. It would be hard work, but everything's there already. We just need to harness it.'

'Really?' Bobbi's eyes lit up.

'Yes, you'll be in heaven when you see it, Bobbi.'

Mum held up a piece of card. 'Sorry to interrupt, but I've got to dash. I just came to drop this off.'

'What is it?'

Without speaking, she turned it around for me to see. My heart squeezed when I realised it was a closure notice.

'Oh, no,' I said sadly.

It was fine being excited about Willow Hall, but it was still sad to have to be saying goodbye to the shop.

'I know, but it's got to be done, and the sooner the better now, really.'

'But how will that affect our wedding flower business? Surely no one will come to us if they know we're closing?'

She shrugged. 'You'll just have to tell people. We can't just close without notice; everyone will panic. You should phone the brides who've already ordered flowers too, and tell them we're not going out of business, we're just moving.'

'Shouldn't we put that on the sign? Make it clearer to people?'

'It does say that.'

'Where? In tiny writing underneath the big red letters saying we're closing?'

'Well, yes, I thought it might shock people into coming inside and buying more flowers.'

I rolled my eyes. 'Maybe I'll make another one to put alongside it then.'

'Yes, and while you're about it, update your website to tell everyone. And put photos of Willow Hall and the Brew House.'

'Already on it, thanks!' I said, slightly offended she'd think I hadn't already thought of that.

'Excellent!' She passed me the notice. 'I'd better go.'

'Oh, Mum, wait a minute. Do you know what beta blockers are used for?'

'Heart problems, usually. Why?'

'No reason.'

Mum disappeared out on to the sunny street and I frowned. Heart problems? Surely not. He was only in his thirties, didn't smoke, and seemed fit and healthy. Why would he have heart problems?

With a sigh, I found some sticky tape and fixed the closure notice to the door. Seeing it there made it feel so much more real. Pulling out the order book, I began phoning the brides who had already booked with us.

***

With so much to sort out and organise, time passed frighteningly quickly. The builders made progress on the Brew House. It was rewired and replastered, and they plumbed in a sink and a toilet. It was strange to feel so sad about the closure of the shop and yet so excited about moving to new premises. The way the business was evolving also meant I had more control. The Birdcage had always been my mum's shop, and although she'd passed the running of it over to me, in lots of ways it still felt like hers. Not that I'd ever resented that. I got to make lots of creative decisions about what flowers we stocked and the types of arrangements we created, so it wasn't like I had no control at all, but my parents oversaw the majority of the financial running of the business. That was set to change now with Dad saying this new phase should be my responsibility. I had a degree in business management, after all.

'You really should change the name too,' Mum said, as we stood back to take more photos of the Brew House. Arthur had put potted topiary Marguerite plants on each side of the door and they softened the entire look of the building. 'The Birdcage doesn't suit this place. You should think of something more wild and free.'

'But I like The Birdcage,' I protested, bending down on one knee to take a better shot. 'What would you suggest? Just The Brew House?'

'No. Wild Birds, or Wild Flowers, or Bluebells and...'

'Mum, I'm keeping The Birdcage,' I said firmly. 'It's fine, and it reminds me of you.' I put my arm around her and hugged her. 'You've done so much for me. I could never begin to thank you.'

'Oh, you!' She hugged me hard. 'There's no need to thank me. You're my daughter, aren't you! Everything I do, I do it for you.'

'Oh, gawd, don't start singing!' We both laughed and I looked back at the Brew House. 'We still need to get Bobbi here,' I said. 'Now it's looking like this, I think it's time she came to see it.'

'Is she still not well?'

'Not really. I keep telling her to go to the doctor's but she won't. She's more worried about how she's going to get to work once we move here, but I've told her I can pick her up.'

'You can't do that for ever, though, can you? It's all right if you're living in Chester, but it won't work if you stay with Anthony more and more.'

I shrugged. 'I know, but she doesn't drive and I don't want to lose her.'

'Isn't there a train she could get? Maybe you could pick her up from a local station.'

'Perhaps. We'll have to look into it.' I gnawed on my lip thoughtfully. It was something that had been worrying me for a while. I felt bad about moving Bobbi's job an hour away from where she lived.

'You and Anthony seem to be getting on well,' Mum said, interrupting my thoughts.

'Yes.' I bit my lip, suppressing a smile. I didn't want to jinx it by saying how perfect everything was, but I felt so happy I could burst. 'Elena and Daniel are coming tonight and he's cooking dinner for us all.'

'Fabulous! Tell him your dad and I will be expecting an invite too.'

I laughed. 'I will.'

***

Elena and Daniel were coming to finalise their wedding plans. Time had flown so fast that I couldn't believe their wedding was now just over a month away. My bridesmaid dress had arrived, and Elena was bringing it with her tonight. I was excited to see it.

They arrived about six and I met them at the front door with Anthony, Julian, Liz and the children. I couldn't believe I was standing on the steps of Willow Hall with everyone else, welcoming my best friend and her husband-to-be as though I lived there. It was almost as if I was part of the family.

Elena climbed out of Daniel's truck and waved before collecting a dress bag from the backseat.

'Hello!' she called, her dark hair blowing and white summer dress flapping. I ran down and hugged her.

'Are you getting married to him?' Grace demanded, pointing at Daniel.

'I am! Do you remember us from last time?'

'Yes. Are you going to wear a big white dress?'

'Yes.'

'Can I see you?'

'Yes, of course you can.'

'Can I be your bridesmaid?'

'Grace!' Liz interrupted, taking her daughter by the hand and leading her into the house. 'Sorry, Elena!'

'It's fine!' Elena said, laughing. 'Don't worry about it.'

'Grace, I told you that lots of people are going to be getting married here, and you can't be bridesmaid to them,' Liz continued.

'Why not? I've never been a bridesmaid before.' Grace's big blue eyes filled with tears.

'I know, darling.' Liz smoothed back the little girl's hair. 'But you actually have to know the people that are getting married to be in with a chance of being their bridesmaid.'

'What about Auntie Rachel and Uncle Anthony? Can I be bridesmaid for them?'

There was a sudden deathly hush and everybody seemed to freeze. Anthony became extremely interested in one of the old portraits of some distant ancestor, narrowing his eyes to read the inscription beneath. I laughed. 'We're not getting married yet, sweetheart.' I threw a wicked glance at Anthony. 'But when we do, you will definitely be a bridesmaid.'

Liz smiled gratefully. 'Is that Rachel's bridesmaid dress, Elena? You can store it upstairs if you like? You're welcome to store your bridal gown here, too, when you get it. There's no one getting married here before you so it wouldn't be a problem.'

'Oh, brilliant! Thank you.'

'Shall I take you upstairs now? The boys can wait for us in the kitchen.'

'Great.' Elena looked at me. 'Are you coming to try it on?'

'Okay.'

We climbed the big oak staircase to the room where Elena and I would be getting ready for her big day. The big sash window was open and the filmy curtains billowed in the breeze. Elena hung the dress bag on the wardrobe door and unzipped it.

'It's so pretty!' she said, as the dress emerged from its plastic cover. 'I can't wait to see you in it.'

The dress was very similar to the one I'd tried on at the wedding fair but was a delicate shade of iced blue instead of ivory. I stared at my reflection in the mirror as Elena did up the back of the dress.

'Wow!' Liz said. 'You look beautiful! Wait until Anthony sees you in that. He won't be able to resist proposing to you.'

I laughed. 'Hardly! Did you see his face when Grace asked if she could be our bridesmaid? He looked like he wanted the earth to swallow him up!'

Liz laughed. 'It's about time he grew up. He can't go through life refusing to take responsibility for things. That's what it boils down to, essentially.'

'I don't know,' I said, turning so I could see the back of the dress in the full-length mirror. 'I think it just terrifies him.'

She grunted. 'Well, it's time it didn't. Any fool can see he's in love with you. He's been so happy since you came back into his life. Last year he was really low. We were so mad with him when he sent you away. We couldn't believe it, but the heart thing really knocked him for six.'

I stopped and looked at her. 'What heart thing?'

Liz coloured. 'Oh, err… it's really not my place to say.'

I frowned. 'No, go on, tell me. What heart thing?'

'It's nothing to worry about. He's on tablets and seems absolutely fine. I really can't say much more. You'll have to ask Anthony if you want to know all the details.'

'But he's all right?' I said, fear stirring inside. 'He's not going to die?'

155

'God, no. I told you, he's on tablets and he's back at work, isn't he? They wouldn't let him go back to work if he wasn't well.'

'I think I found the tablets. Beta blockers?'

Liz nodded.

'I didn't know what they were for. Mum said heart and Bobbi said anxiety. I was hoping it was the latter.'

'I don't really know much, but I think they work by slowing the heart down.' She shrugged. 'I'm sorry, Rachel. Please don't say anything to Anthony. He'll go mad if he finds out I told you.'

'But why wouldn't he want me to know? What's the big deal?'

'Some stupid male pride thing, probably.'

I thought back to when Anthony had said he was broken and that he couldn't have children. Was that what he was alluding to? His heart?

'He said he couldn't have children,' I blurted. 'Why can't he have children?'

Liz blinked. 'I don't know anything about that. As far as I'm aware, he hasn't ever tried, so how would he know?'

'Was it something to do with the accident?'

'I have no idea. I mean, that was how they found out about his heart condition. They did an ultrasound and picked it up on that.'

'So his heart thing wasn't caused by the crash?'

'No, it's genetic. Julian was screened but he's okay at the moment. Our children will need to be checked too.'

'Oh!' I stared at her, feeling the threads of my perfect new life starting to unravel.

Liz smiled guiltily. 'Sorry, Rachel.'

'Don't be sorry. I'm glad you told me. Thank you.'

I suddenly became aware of Elena standing to one side, looking stricken. 'Sorry, Elena!' I said, gathering myself together. 'This is supposed to be a happy moment, isn't it? Sorry!'

'Don't be silly. It's important.'

'I can just picture you getting ready in here on the morning of your wedding. I'm so excited about it! It's going to be amazing.'

Elena laughed. 'I know. I can't believe that dress fits you so well, either! I don't think it will need altering.'

'It fits like a dream!' Liz said. 'At least that's one less thing to do: getting your dress altered.'

'True.'

I took a deep breath and smiled, but really all I could think about was Anthony and his heart.

'You'll have to show me your new building,' Elena said as she unzipped the back of the dress for me. 'I'm really excited about it. Though I'm sorry you're losing the shop.'

'I know.' I stepped out of the bridesmaid dress and reached for my own clothes. 'It is exciting to be doing something new, though. Especially as it's all taking shape so well. How is your house coming on, Liz? You know, I still haven't seen it.'

'Really?' Liz looked relieved the conversation had moved on and she could talk about something less controversial. 'Perhaps we could walk over and have a look later. But first, I'd appreciate it if we could discuss the fine details of your wedding, Elena. You know, the place settings and everything. I know this might seem a little bit amateur, but you know you're our first wedding, and I really want to get this right for you.'

'Of course. And it doesn't seem amateurish at all. I appreciate you asking.'

We hung the dress up inside the mahogany wardrobe and went downstairs to join everybody else in the kitchen. Cath had made another cake and was slicing it up while Anthony, Julian and Daniel stood around, practically drooling

'Maybe you should be thinking about making wedding cakes, Cath. Willow Hall could become a one-stop shop for weddings.'

'Yes!' Julian pointed at his mother, his mouth full of cake.' That's a great idea.'

'I don't know about all the icing, though,' Cath fretted.

'You made ours.'

'That was quite a simple cake. What about the people who want really fancy ones?'

'You can only offer what you can do,' I said.

'The lady that's making our wedding cake contacted me the other day to say she wasn't very well,' Elena said. 'You could make ours if it wasn't too much work for you?'

'Really?' Cath's face lit up. 'What type of cake did you want?'

'I was going for a hexagonal cake with marbled fondant icing,' Elena said, 'but I realise I won't be able to have that now.'

'So what do you want now?' Cath said, looking wary.

'Something simple and elegant.' Elena shrugged. 'I don't really mind. I feel so sorry for the cake lady. She was really sad she was having to let me down.'

'Could you show me a photograph of what you wanted?'

Elena nodded and pulled her phone out of her bag. 'I think I have one on my phone. But honestly, don't worry if you can't do it. I think I went a bit Bridezilla when I chose it. I've seen so many lovely ones that I'm sure I'd love whatever.'

Cath peered at Elena's phone then passed it to Liz. 'What do you think?'

'You could try. I'm pretty sure you could make anything if you put your mind to it.'

'Leave it with me,' Cath said thoughtfully. 'I'm not promising, but I'll have a go. Can you send that photo to my phone?'

'Of course. I'll send you the link to the website, too, so you can get a larger picture. They're all the rage now so if you could offer something like that you might get more people coming to you for cakes.'

Cath looked excited all of a sudden. 'Ooh, I like the sound of that. Maybe I'm not such a useless old bat after all.'

'You're not a useless old bat at all!' Anthony said, putting his arm around his mother and kissing her on the head. 'We all think you're amazing.'

'Aww, thank you.' She hugged him tightly around his waist.

It was sweet to watch Anthony and his mother together. This man, who swore he would never accept the responsibility of commitment and marriage, was capable of great love and affection. He caught me watching him and smiled.

We sat down at the table and went through Elena's wedding plans. She'd brought her guest list and table plans. Liz pored over them, anxious to get everything right, and made three copies of everything so nothing could get lost. We discussed everything in minute detail and Liz made extensive notes.

'Thanks so much for all this,' Liz said, her tongue poking out of the side of her mouth as she scribbled away on her pad of paper. 'I'm determined not to mess up your wedding so all this is much appreciated. I lie wake at night worrying about this stuff so to have your input is great.'

Elena laughed. 'Aww, honestly, we're both really laid-back people so please don't worry too much. I'm sure it will all go brilliantly. Just being here in this hall is such an honour. Thank you so much for letting us have our wedding here.'

When Liz had got all the details down that she needed, I went through the placement of the flowers with Elena and worked out what flowers she needed for the church.

'Are you going to show me your new place then?' Elena asked after we'd got the last of the details down. 'Come on, I'm dying to see it.'

We left the kitchen and took the path past the walled garden towards the Brew House. Charlie scampered on ahead with Oscar the dog trotting beside him and carrying a huge stick in his mouth.

'Be careful, Charlie!' Liz called.

'He's all right.' Julian slipped his arm around her. 'Try not to worry so much. You know it's not good for your blood pressure.'

Anthony caught Grace's hand and went skipping up the path with her, gravel spurting from beneath his feet. Elena laughed and slipped her arm through mine.

'You're going to be so happy here, Rachel,' she said, looking around her at the beautiful green lawns and softly swaying willow trees. 'I can feel it.'

I winced. 'Don't say it. You might jinx it.'

'Nothing's going to jinx it. You're going to be fine.' She squeezed my arm and smiled at me. 'You and Anthony both seem so settled and happy. It's really lovely to see.'

'Thank you.'

The sky was still light but a silvery moon was rising from the east. We reached the Brew House and I opened the door and proudly showed them inside.

'Oh, wow!' Daniel said enthusiastically. 'This is a great place. I'd love a place like this. I don't suppose you need a resident tree surgeon, do you?'

'Daniel! We've only just done up our house.'

He laughed. 'I'm only joking.'

'I don't suppose you do willow sculptures, do you?' Julian asked seriously. 'Only I'd love to put something in front of the hall.'

'Not me, but I'm sure I know someone who can. Leave it with me.'

Elena was looking through the window, down towards the lake. I knew she was sad about the shop closing. She'd been coming there since she was ten or eleven, and it was hard to say goodbye to those memories.

'Come and see our house then,' Liz said. 'I can't believe Anthony hasn't shown you it yet, Rachel!'

'He doesn't want her getting any ideas, that's why,' Julian laughed. 'Isn't that right, Anthony?'

'I have no idea what you mean, Julian. You need a big house for your ever-expanding family, while I do not. I'm quite content with my little cottage, thank you.'

'What about when you and Rachel start having kids?' he laughed, knowing he was touching on a difficult subject and enjoying it immensely. 'You'll need somewhere then.'

Anthony cleared his throat, looking uncomfortable. 'I guess we'd cross that bridge when we came to it.'

I felt a flicker of hope. It wasn't an out and out dismissal of a future together, although he did look pretty shifty. Taking pity on him, I slipped my hand into his and squeezed it. 'We've only just got together, Julian. We're nowhere near that stage yet.'

'Yet.' Julian winked.

Liz and Julian's house was a lot closer than I'd realised and was actually just down the road from Anthony's cottage. It backed on to the lake and the only reason I hadn't seen it from the Brew House was because of the thick summer foliage on the trees. Julian led us around the side to the front door, and I saw it had a large gravel drive and was shielded from the road by tall hedgerows.

'Wow, this is gorgeous!' I said. It was quite a grand Georgian house built in the same soft red brick as the hall, with leaded sash windows, and an arched entrance with a clear pilot light above the studded wooden door.

'A bit better than Anthony's gatehouse, isn't it?' Julian smirked.

'You're paying for it too,' Anthony said, pointedly. 'How many thousand have you spent on doing it up?'

'That's our business,' Julian said, as he opened the front door to let us in.

It was empty inside. The walls had recently been replastered and were waiting for a lick of paint and the rooms looked huge without any furniture. All the same, you could see it was going to be a lovely home. Our footsteps echoed on bare floorboards as we walked through to the kitchen and Liz lifted a dustsheet on a large sitting room with a big open fireplace and exposed beams in the ceiling.

'Wow! This will be amazing when it's finished!' Elena was saying. 'You're nearly there really, aren't you? Just lots of decorating?'

'That's right. We'll soon be in.'

161

'I thought we had a massive job on our hands when we renovated our house,' Daniel said, looking around him with his hands thrust deep into his pockets, 'but this is on a different scale altogether.'

'We've had people in,' Julian said. 'I could never have done this myself. I don't have the skill set, for a start.'

'Come and look at this,' Liz said, beckoning me and Elena over. Lifting the corner on a dustsheet covering something big and bulky in the corner of the kitchen, Liz revealed a pale-blue Aga.

'Oh, my goodness! You are so lucky!' Elena enthused. 'I really wanted a range oven but we don't have the room.'

'I've always wanted one,' Liz said. 'Though I doubt I'll be able to make food as nice as Cath's. Everything she cooks in that Aga of hers is delicious.'

'When's the rest of the kitchen getting fitted?' Anthony asked. He was holding Charlie now, and the little boy had his head laid sleepily on Anthony's shoulder, his thumb in his mouth. They looked so much alike that I could imagine this would be how Anthony's own son would look. It made my heart hurt looking at them together.

It was dark by the time we'd looked around upstairs and seen the beautiful views out of the bedroom windows. Julian locked the door behind us and we walked back along the road, past Anthony's cottage rather than cutting through the woodland next to the lake. Daniel and Elena walked hand in hand, chatting happily, and Anthony dropped back to talk to me.

'You're good with children,' I told him, looking at the sleeping child in his arms.

He smiled. 'Yeah, they're good kids.'

'Is that what you looked like when you were young?'

'Mum says so. I can see Liz in him too, though.' He shifted Charlie's weight slightly so he could take my hand. 'Are you all right? You've been very quiet this past hour or so. Was the brides-maid dress okay?'

'Yes, it's lovely.'

'So what's wrong then?'

'Nothing. I suppose I'm just a bit tired, that's all. These early mornings are killing me.'

'Sorry.'

I laughed. 'Don't be. I just need an early night, that's all.'

'Sounds good to me,' he laughed.

'Not like that!'

The bats were fluttering around between the trees and Grace and Julian stopped to look at them. Somewhere in the wood, an owl hooted.

'This place is amazing!' Daniel kept saying. 'All these trees…'

When Elena and Daniel had been waved off after dinner, Anthony and I walked back to the gatehouse. I kept trying to work up the courage to ask about his heart, but I didn't want to get Liz into trouble. The best way to do it would be to say I found the tablets and ask what they were for.

'Are you sure you're all right?' Anthony asked as he opened the door to the cottage.

'Yes,' I said, pushing past him to go into the kitchen. 'Do you want a cup of tea?'

He looked surprised as he shut the door and drew the bolt across. 'I thought you wanted an early night?'

'I'm thirsty.' I glanced back over my shoulder and found him watching me through narrowed eyes. 'Do you want one or not?'

'No.'

'Okay.' I eyed the cupboard where I'd first seen the tablets, but I had a feeling he'd moved them since.

'Rachel, what's wrong?'

I leaned my hands on the kitchen worktop and sighed. 'I could ask you the same question.'

'What does that mean?' He straightened up, looking defensive. 'Has someone said something?'

I cleared my throat. 'I found your tablets.'

He frowned. 'I hid them.'

'Oh, did you now? That's reassuring. What else are you hiding from me?'

'Rachel! I'm not hiding anything bad. Well, not really…' He heaved a sigh as he walked into the kitchen. 'Where did you find them?'

'In there.' I pointed to the cupboard where I'd first found them. 'The first morning I stayed. It's taken me this long to work out they were for your heart.'

He hung his head before pulling out a chair and sitting down at the table. 'It doesn't affect anything, does it? You still want to be with me?'

'Of course I do! I'm just upset you didn't tell me about something so important.' I sat down opposite him and took his hands. 'What's wrong? It's obviously something that can be controlled with drugs so you'll be okay, won't you?'

He shrugged. 'I have hypertrophic cardiomyopathy. When I was in hospital, they discovered I had an irregular heartbeat so they did a scan and found the muscle in my heart had enlarged and thickened. It's hereditary, apparently. My mother thinks our father probably had it. I thought he'd died in a car crash, but it was a heart attack that actually killed him. He was only my age at the time.' He raised his eyebrows and smiled sadly. 'Makes me think I was lucky to survive my crash.'

I exhaled loudly and put my head in my hands, my whole body tingling with nervous energy. 'But they've caught it in time? You're okay on the tablets?'

'For now. There might come a time when I need an implant, but for now I'm okay.' He reached out and stroked my hair. 'I told you I was broken.'

'Don't you dare say that!' I said fiercely. 'You are not broken. You are not!'

He reached for my hand again and squeezed it. 'It's taken me a while to come to terms with it,' he said. 'I suppose I'm still not completely okay with it, or else I would have told you. It doesn't seem fair really. Not when I kept myself pretty fit and healthy and I never smoked or did drugs.'

'So what happens now? Is it degenerative?'

He nodded. 'I think so. No one knows how it will go, though. I could be fine for years, or it could worsen. My doctor monitors me pretty closely.'

I nodded, trying to absorb this new information. Could he die from this? I didn't want to ask when I was so scared of the answer.

'I'm sorry, Rachel. I know this is hard to hear, and I'm sorry I didn't tell you before. I just didn't want to burst our happy bubble.' He sighed heavily. 'I guess it's well and truly popped now.'

'What do you mean? It's not like I'm going anywhere.'

'Aren't you? I'd understand if you did.'

'Don't be stupid. I love you. That doesn't change because you've got a problem with your heart. We'll face this together.'

His cheeks flushed and he looked down at the table. Reaching out, I brushed a tear from his cheek with my fingertips. 'What did you think? That I'd leave you?'

He shrugged. 'It affects everything, don't you see?'

I frowned at him. 'I'm never leaving you, Anthony. We've spent too long apart already and this has no effect on how I feel about you at all. The only thing I want is to be with you.' Covering his face with his hands, he started to cry more. 'Come here.' I slipped from my chair and knelt beside him, cradling his head in my arms. 'Please don't cry. There's no need. I'm here. I'll always be here.' I kissed his hair, his ears, his hands covering his face, desperate to convince him of my love. Eventually, he removed his hands from his face and wrapped his arms around me, hugging me back.

Chapter Eleven

The sky was grey when I awoke the next morning. I went to the window and watched five crows in the field opposite mob a buzzard, trying to get it away from their nests. I watched their black shapes wheel about in the sky as they cawed and croaked their alarm. Yawning, I looked back to where Anthony lay, still fast asleep among the soft mounds of the duvet. He wasn't in work today, and I hadn't wanted him to wake up alone after last night, so I'd phoned my mum and asked her to cover for me.

I went downstairs to make coffee. The cottage was so quiet that the roar of the boiling kettle was deafening. I found my phone in my bag and searched for hypertrophic cardiomyopathy. I soon wished I hadn't when it listed its complications as heart failure, irregular heartbeat and sudden cardiac death.

Sudden cardiac death?

Taking my coffee, I went into the lounge and curled up on the sofa to read more. I found a website that included lots of case studies of different patients. It seemed everyone had walked a different path and had a different story to tell, but I noticed many of them had lived for years with the condition. It reassured me that Anthony and I would have a future together so long as he was closely monitored and continued with his medication.

It was still shocking, though, to discover that someone who appeared so outwardly strong and healthy had something so serious going on inside them.

Anthony woke up about nine. He stopped on the stairs when he saw me. 'What are you doing here still? I thought you were at work today?'

'I was but I called my mum to ask her to open up for me.' I yawned and stretched. 'Is it all right if I stay with you today?'

'All right?' His face lit up. 'It's more than all right.' He came down the rest of the stairs and kissed me. 'What time did you wake up?'

'About six. Do you want me to make you a coffee?'

'I'll get it. You stay there.'

He disappeared into the kitchen and I could hear him clanking about and filling the kettle. I'd finished reading about his condition on the Internet and was now using his laptop to work on the new website for the shop. 'Thanks,' I said when he placed a drink down next to me on the coffee table. 'How are you feeling?'

'Fine. I've taken my morning tablet if that's what you're getting at.'

I smiled and leaned over to kiss him. 'It wasn't, but it's good to know. I've just been reading up about your condition, actually. I was reading something about an implantable cardiac defibrillator.'

'Oh, that.'

'What do you mean "oh, that"?' I asked suspiciously. 'Have you been offered one and turned it down?'

He sighed. 'Not really. It's something to consider in the future, though.'

'Well, I've been reading some people's journeys and some of them have had their lives saved by them.'

'Yeah. I know. But I've been fine, touch wood.'

I gasped. 'There's no touch wood about it! If the doctor's offered one to you, then he must think it will help you.'

'It's one course of treatment,' Anthony said calmly. 'My doctor's monitoring me and we'll see how we go.'

'Do you feel your heart racing?'

'Only when I'm with you.' He put his coffee down and moved closer.

'Don't change the subject.' I laughed and tried to move away but he caught me and held me tight.

'I feel fine! Honestly.' Anthony kissed my neck. 'I'm not dead yet.'

'Let's keep it that way, shall we?'

With a growl, he pushed me down on to the sofa, dropping kisses on my cheeks and mouth while I giggled breathlessly. I could feel him growing hard against me and his playful kisses grew more intense and serious. He tugged at my pyjama shorts, and I arched my back to help him ease them down over my thighs. Entering me slowly, he stared down into my eyes and I gasped as he started moving in and out. I'd never felt closer to him than I did at that moment. He continued to stare deep into my eyes and I felt something shift inside of me, overwhelming me with emotion. Tears slid sideways from my eyes and Anthony smoothed back my hair and kissed me. 'It's okay,' he whispered softly. 'I love you. It's okay.' His words were soothing, but they made me even more emotional and more tears fell from my eyes. Anthony looked uncertain. 'Do you want me to stop?' I shook my head, wrapping my legs around his hips to keep him inside me. He closed his eyes briefly, and when he opened them they burned with a fire and desire that touched me deep inside. I never wanted this moment to end.

***

We spent the rest of the day lounging around the cottage. I felt guilty I hadn't done as much work as I should have on the website. I knew I had to put the graft in if I wanted the business to succeed, but somehow spending time with Anthony seemed more important than ever. It wasn't because I thought he was about to die or anything, but because he'd opened up to me at last and I knew that, deep down, he was vulnerable and needed me.

The grey clouds lifted in the afternoon, revealing the bright sunshine. We went for a walk along the lake and I decided I wanted to take the rowing boat out. Anthony wanted to row, but I insisted and we floundered around on the still water for a while, until I finally got the hang of it and rowed us to the opposite shore.

'There you go!' I said, triumphant. I was knackered now and slightly dismayed that I was going to have to row back. Anthony had adopted a kind of Edwardian-gentleman stance and was now reclining in a leisurely manner with his eyes closed. I watched him fondly and he opened one eye.

'What are you looking at, Jones?'

I grinned. 'You, Bascombe.'

'Get rowing,' he laughed, trailing his fingers in the water and flicking it at me.

'Hey!'

'Hold on.' He sat up and stared up at the road. 'Is that your mum and Bobbi?'

I turned round to see Mum's car pulling up next to the Brew House.

'Oh, she's brought Bobbi!' I cheered, starting to row back to the opposite side of the lake.

'Do you want me to row now?' Anthony looked slightly anxious, as though he thought they might think less of him for making me do all the work.

'No, I'm doing fine, thanks.'

We jumped out and tied the boat back up at the jetty.

'Hello!' I called to them. 'How lovely to see you!'

'We were quiet so I thought I'd close up early and bring Bobbi to have a look.' She rubbed her hands on her beige trousers and looked at Bobbi. 'Isn't it lovely?'

'Yes.' Bobbi looked around her in amazement. 'I can't believe you live here, Anthony. What are you doing talking to the likes of us? I bet you think we're peasants. What are you? Some kind of duke?'

'Not at all. And I certainly don't think of you as peasants. My family aren't like that. None of us is.'

I smiled. 'It's true. His mother's lovely and bakes the most fabulous cakes. Here, let me show you inside.' Pulling the keys from my back pocket, I opened the door and gave Bobbi the guided tour, telling her where I planned for everything to go.

'I can't believe we'll be working somewhere so beautiful!' She walked slowly around, examining every corner. 'It feels like a dream.'

'Wait until you see the garden,' I told her.

As predicted, she completely loved all the varieties of roses.

'Wow, that's amazing!' she said. 'I can't believe there are so many.'

'I know. He's a marvel. I don't know how he does it all.'

'He spends his whole life in here, that's why,' Anthony said, looking round. 'I'm surprised he's not in here now, actually. He must be having his afternoon cup of tea. Shall we go in and see if my mother will make us one too? I bet she's got cake.'

'She's always got cake,' I laughed.

Cath and Arthur were drinking tea outside on the patio. They looked up as we approached, shielding their eyes from the sun.

'Hello, do you mind if we join you?' Anthony called.

'Of course not, welcome, welcome,' Cath said, rising to her feet. She kissed my mum in greeting and shook Bobbi's hand. 'Lovely to meet you,' she said warmly.

Bobbi smiled and tucked her pink hair behind her ears self-consciously. She sat quietly while we talked about Arthur's garden and Elena's wedding.

'I just don't know how I'm going to get here,' she said suddenly. 'I mean, I love it and everything, and I'd love to be part of it, but I really don't think I'm going to be able to.'

'I've already told you not to worry about that, Bobbi,' I said gently. 'We'll sort it out between us as we go along.'

'Perhaps you could stay here for a few days at a time, rather than travelling back and forth,' Arthur suggested. 'It's not like we don't have enough room.' He jerked his head back at the house. 'You'd be more than welcome. Everyone always is with Cath about.'

Bobbi smiled shyly and rubbed her nose. 'That's really kind and everything but…'

'But?' I prompted when she didn't say anything else.

I watched her take a deep breath, like she was gathering herself for some big announcement. I braced myself. 'I'm pregnant.'

There was a shocked silence in which we all stared at her as if waiting for the punchline. Arthur had gone beetroot red and Anthony just looked horrified. Bobbi scuffed her black Converse against the grass and sighed. 'Sorry.'

I was still too stunned to speak. Bobbi pregnant? But she couldn't be! She'd been ill, hadn't she? She'd had food poisoning!

It was Mum who spoke first. 'I told you! Didn't I say? See, I'm always right. It was morning sickness all along, you poor thing. How long have you known?'

'Only a couple of weeks. I'm sorry. I wanted to tell you but I didn't know how.'

'That's okay, Bobbi. Have you told Jayjay?'

She nodded. 'He's been really supportive, actually. He's not the problem, though, is he? My problem is that you're moving here and I'm losing my job.'

'You're not losing your job, Bobbi,' Mum protested. 'We want you to stay with us. Rachel needs you to help her with the business. We haven't worked it all out yet, but I'm sure we can find a solution to this. If you really don't want to, that's your choice.

But if you stay, then we'll look after you and you'll get maternity leave and maternity pay.'

Bobbi looked up, startled. 'Really?'

'Of course,' I agreed. 'And like Mum says, I'm not sure how it's going to work out here at the moment. The hours will be different to the shop and actually they might suit you better. And you'd be welcome to bring the baby to work with you.'

'Really?'

'Of course you could. I'd be completely flexible to suit you.'

Bobbi's brow furrowed. 'I still don't know how I'm going to get here, though.'

'Well, if I couldn't give you a lift, perhaps you could get the train and someone could collect you from the station. We're looking for solutions, not problems, Bobbi, and I really don't want to lose you.'

Some of the colour returned to Bobbi's face and she started to smile. 'Oh. Okay then.'

'Especially as you're always on about flower farming, and this could be our opportunity to try our hand at it. With Arthur's support, of course.'

Bobbi looked a little more hopeful than she had over the past few days. I asked her if she planned to move in with Jayjay or not and she said they'd talked about it but hadn't decided on anything yet.

'Hold on a minute!' I said, as it dawned on me that we were forgetting the most important thing of all. 'You're having a baby! A real, actual baby! And all we're talking about is boring practical details, like your job and where you're going to live. Let's take a moment to squeal excitedly about the fact you're making a brand-new human being in there!' Getting up from my seat, I gave her a massive hug. 'This is amazing news, Bobbi! Congratulations! I'm sorry, I was too stunned when you first said. Were you upset when you found out?'

'A little. It was a bit of a shock, but I'm happy now.'

'Good.' I stared at her, trying to see if she looked different in some subtle way I hadn't noticed before, but I couldn't really see anything. 'Wow! A baby!' I couldn't believe it.

Cath brought out more tea and we told her Bobbi's news.

'How lovely!' she said. 'Babies are always good news.'

***

In the weeks that followed, Bobbi became much more enthusiastic about the move to Willow Hall. Always the creative, she had loads of brilliant ideas on how to make our website look great. She also made suggestions about the kinds of workshops we could offer. I knew it would take time to build the new business up, but I was sure we could do it. Especially as the brides-to-be who had already booked with us had been fine when I explained about the move.

There was still lots to do, though. Packing up the shop was going to be a mammoth task, even with the removal firm we had booked. There was so much of our family history in there, I felt emotional every time I thought about leaving it.

It was weird to feel so sad and so excited at the same time. When I was in the Chester shop, I felt sad, and yet when I was at Willow Hall, I couldn't wait to move into our new space. And I was spending more and more time there. Despite saying I wanted to take things slowly with Anthony, I found myself there almost every night. I had clothes in his wardrobe and cosmetics in his bathroom. Though I denied it to everyone who asked, deep down I knew I'd practically moved in. I only returned to my house to do laundry and collect more clothes.

I wondered what would happen when the business actually did move into the Brew House. Would I just stay at Anthony's the whole time? Would that be weird for him, having me working and living in such close proximity?

If he was worried, he never showed it. He seemed relaxed and happy to have me around, often begging me to stay with him if I suggested going home to Chester. On the occasions I did stay at my own house, he'd insist on coming with me. I couldn't help but question where we were going. It felt serious. My love for him deepened every day. Had he really got over his fear of commitment? If he hadn't, I was in serious trouble.

He never gave any indication that he was less than one hundred per cent committed, though. He told me he loved me all the time, and he was so caring and sweet. He did thoughtful things for me all the time. One day I walked down to the Brew House and found a wrought-iron sign hanging outside. Shaped like a vintage birdcage, the words *The Birdcage* were written inside, with a swallow swooping above.

'Did you do that?' I asked, staring at it in amazement.

He wrapped his arms around me from behind and kissed my neck. 'Do you like it?'

'Like it?' I turned and wrapped my arms around his neck. 'I love it! Thank you so much!' I covered his face in kisses, hugging him tightly. 'It's the most perfect thing ever. Almost as perfect as you, in fact.'

'Oh, no, I'm sure it's not that perfect!' Anthony laughed.

'Well, no, nothing could ever be as perfect as you.' Laughing, I kissed him again then turned to gaze back up at the sign. 'Where did you get it made?'

'There's a metalworks not far from here. They do loads of signs like that.'

'It's beautiful. I couldn't have chosen anything better.'

A family of sparrows fluttered down from the hedgerow, pecking about in the damp grass. The air was full of the sound of birdsong and insects and smelt fresh from a recent shower of rain.

'I can't wait to move in.'

'What, with me?'

I laughed. 'I'm practically living with you now, anyway.'

'Yes, but you keep going home too. Are you still going to do that when you no longer work in Chester?'

'I'm going to have to pick up Bobbi.'

'You can do that without living in Chester. Besides, your mum will help and there's the train. It's silly to live between two places when you could rent out your house and get some kind of income. You could even rent it to Bobbi and Jayjay.'

I stared at the sparrows, thinking hard. In the end, there was no getting away from it. I had to say it. 'But what if you change your mind?'

'About what?'

'Me.'

'Oh, well, then you can stay with my mother. She's got plenty of room.' He laughed, and I felt his hot breath on my neck. 'Just kidding. Rachel, I'm not going to change my mind about you. I learned my lesson last year and I'm not going to do that again. I love you.' He turned me round so he could gaze into my eyes. 'I don't want to be alone any more. I want to be with you.'

I'd never felt so happy. It felt like everything was slotting into place. Could life really be this good?

***

Even the shop move went smoothly. We'd reduced the number of flowers we had in stock, and what we had left I transported in the shop's van. I loved driving the van about. It was a little white Renault Kangoo and had *The Birdcage Flowers* written in scroll writing on the side. Bobbi and I filled the back with all the flowers, careful not to damage them. Their scent was almost overpowering in the confines of the small van.

'It's a good job neither of us has hay fever,' I joked, taking my keys from my pocket and jingling them before locking the shop for the last time. I stared at the back door, memories crowding my mind. Now the time had come, I didn't want to leave. Bobbi

175

watched me press my hand to the door and then kiss it, her eyes full of tears.

She'd been crying on and off all day, blaming her hormones, but now I couldn't help but cry too. It was hard walking away from a place I loved so much. We climbed into the van and Bobbi passed me a tissue.

I blew my nose noisily and started the engine. Bobbi kept her face turned away, staring out of the passenger window, a hand over her mouth. It was a sad day, and I knew that was why Mum had kept away. She would come back and say her goodbyes to the shop tomorrow when I was safely out of the way. For now, she had gone ahead with the removals van, which was carrying the big floral refrigerator, shelving units, Welsh dresser, and the oak table and chairs from the back room.

It had been grey and dreary all day, but as we drew closer to Willow Hall the clouds parted and the sun came out. Everybody was there to welcome us and they all cheered as Bobbi and I climbed out of the van. I'd donned my sunglasses to hide my red, swollen eyes, but nobody was really fooled. Anthony smiled sympathetically as he passed me a glass of champagne.

'Everything's inside,' Mum said cheerfully. 'It looks good. Go and have a look.'

I stepped inside and looked around. It was amazing, but all the furniture from the shop looked like it had been here for ever. The refrigerator hummed in the corner, and the shelves stood against one wall. The big oak table where we'd be arranging the flowers stood in the centre of the second room, and the shelving systems leant against one wall. The vintage birdcages that had hung in the shop were stacked neatly in one corner. 'I think you'll need more chairs,' Mum said, her footsteps echoing on the stone floor behind me. 'And you could do with some sort of counter for the till. It was a shame we couldn't bring our old one with us, but we'll be able to find another. Don't worry.'

I nodded. Happiness was starting to filter back in and I

reminded myself I needed to be looking forward, not back. I sipped the ice-cold champagne and stared out of the window towards the lake, shimmering in the afternoon sunshine. This was the perfect place for a new start, especially when I was surrounded by such friendly, positive people as Anthony's family.

'What work have you got booked so far?' Julian asked, his blue eyes sparkling over his champagne flute. Anthony's hand snaked around my waist and he squeezed me against his side.

'She's got a workshop booked already!' he told his brother proudly.

'Have you? Well done!'

I nodded. 'It's next Wednesday afternoon. Five ladies who live not far from here.'

'Great. We should put the word out in Mother's WI group, too. You might get something from them.'

'Brilliant. I have a wedding at the weekend, too, and one the following week, but they were already booked, so…' I shrugged. 'It's going to be weird making up the bouquets in a different location.'

'I'm sure you'll be fine.' Anthony squeezed my arm. 'And if you need anything, just give us a shout and someone will help you.'

'Aww, thank you!' I kissed him. 'And thank you to everyone here, too,' I said, raising my glass. 'I couldn't have done any of this without you. I may be sad to be leaving the shop, but I'm really excited to be making a new start here.'

Chapter Twelve

Anthony was right about me being fine making up bouquets in a different location. It was just the same except that I had a wonderful view of the lake through the window and was surrounded by beautiful nature and the constant sound of birdsong. Bobbi loved it too. We had more bookings for workshops and they were great fun to do. I was really enjoying myself.

The weeks leading up to Elena and Daniel's wedding seemed to melt away. I had been really nervous about doing her wedding flowers as well as being her bridesmaid, and was sure I would mess up one or the other, or even both. But the beauty of making the bouquets and table centrepieces at the actual wedding venue was that we could place them in situ and relax, knowing they were ready for the wedding the following day. It was far more relaxed than I'd anticipated, and the flowers were all done by the time Elena arrived at Willow Hall with her family. I was really looking forward to having a lovely gossipy evening together.

Most of Elena's family were staying in the converted stable block so we all went for tea in the village pub together. Elena's brother had returned from Australia specially to see his little sister get married, so it was a real family reunion. Growing up, I'd spent so much time around Elena's house that her mum, Rosa, was like a second mum to me. It was lovely to spend time with her again. I could tell she was really nervous about being in such a big, grand house, not to mention the fact that her daughter was getting married the following day; but Cath was so lovely and welcoming that she soon relaxed. I couldn't believe Cath had been living at the hall with Arthur on their own for so long when she was so sociable and warm and welcoming. They should have started this wedding business years ago.

After our meal, we went back to the bridal suite, and Elena produced her Daniel Box. It was a shoebox she'd filled with souvenirs from the crush she'd had on Daniel when we were at school together. I shrieked with laughter at the sight of it.

'I can't believe you're marrying him after you spent all that time stalking him!' I said, taking it from her. 'And I really can't believe you've still got all this!' I rooted through the poems she'd written about him, the pencil sketches of his face and the leaf from his drive. A nail clipping got stuck to my finger and I shook it off with a shudder. 'Surely you can throw this rubbish away now you're actually getting married to him. I mean, you've got free access to his dirty boxer shorts. Why on earth do you need leaves off his drive and chewed-off nail clippings he left on his desk.'

Elena laughed and shrugged. 'I still can't bring myself to throw it away. I don't know why.'

'I think you should. What if he sees it?'

'He knows about it,' she laughed. 'I won't actually let him read the poems or anything, but I don't want to get rid of it. Looking through it reminds me of how lucky I am to have got him at last.'

'Oh, God, Elena, that's the soppiest thing I've ever heard.' I made retching noises over the side of the bed.

'Hey! You must know how I feel, now you have Anthony!' She rolled over on to her stomach and propped herself up on her elbows. 'You seem to really love each other. I saw those lingering looks you give each other all the time. I'm so glad you're back together again.'

I blushed and plucked at the bedspread with my fingertips. 'I know. Me too.'

We turned off the light and climbed into bed, whispering in the darkness like we'd done so many times when we were growing up. After a while, I heard her breathing slow and even out, and I knew she'd fallen asleep. I fell asleep soon after and awoke the following morning to the sound of Elena singing in the shower.

The hair and make-up artist arrived just after nine. I couldn't believe how calm and organised everything felt. All I had to do was sit while someone else did my hair and make-up, and then get dressed. I didn't even have to worry about what to eat because Cath prepared breakfast and lunch for us and brought it up to the room on a tray.

Elena's beautiful, long, dark hair was put into an elaborate up-do with loose strands that curled around her face. Her silver tiara sparkled as it was pinned into place. She already looked amazing and she hadn't even got her dress on yet.

'I suppose we ought to get you into your dress,' I said, trying to stop myself from getting all teary.

'Ooh, don't cry!' Elena pulled me into a hug. 'You'll ruin your make-up.'

'I know!' I fanned my face with my hand and tipped my head back, trying to blink away my tears. 'It's being in this bedroom with all our old teenage memories and that bloody Daniel Box. And here we are, getting you ready for your big day, and you're actually marrying Daniel Moore! It's amazing. Do you remember how many times you practised writing your signature as Elena Moore? At least you've got that down to perfection before you've even started your married life.'

Elena laughed. 'I know! Come on, then, help me into my dress. I'd better call my mum.' She went to the door and called Rosa, who bustled in, wearing a lovely pale-pink dress and jacket.

'Ooh, gosh! Is it that time already.' She fanned herself with a magazine and anxiously touched the mottled red patches that were growing on her neck.

'Calm down, Mum. It's going to be fine.' Elena hugged her tight and I laughed.

'I can't believe you're so calm, Elena. It's usually the bride that's freaking out, not the bride's mum and the bridesmaid.'

'Are you freaking out too, Rachel?' Rosa asked.

'No, I've just had a bit of a cry, that's all. I'm fine now. Right, let's get this dress on you, Elena.' I took down the big ivory gown that was hanging on the wardrobe door and removed the plastic cover while Rosa unzipped the back. Elena slipped off her dressing gown and stepped into the dress.

'Oh, my God!' I covered my mouth with my hands and stepped back to look at her. The sweetheart neckline with lace sleeves and bodice suited her perfectly, and the ivory silk swept down to the floor 'You look amazing!'

'Oh!' Rosa covered her mouth too, her eyes filling with tears as Elena stepped forward and looked at herself in the full-length mirror. 'My little girl. All grown-up.'

'Aww, Mum.' Elena hugged her. 'You'll set me off if you're not careful.'

'Daniel's a very lucky man.'

'He is indeed.' I smiled at Elena, my heart overflowing with love for my best friend.

The wedding photographer came to our room and took photographs of Elena. He was a happy, enthusiastic man and I liked him immediately. He took a number of natural poses of Rosa and I helping Elena get ready, adjusting her veil and doing up her dress. Then he took photos of her sitting on the window seat and gazing out over the parkland, and then some of her standing at the top of the stairs.

A white Rolls Royce adorned with white ribbons pulled up in front of the house and Elena's dad held her hand as she walked carefully down the steps. The wedding photographer continually snapped photos until the car carried them away down the drive to the church.

'I take it that's our car,' Rosa said, pointing to a burgundy Jaguar that was parked in front of the steps. 'Shall we go then?'

'Yes.'

I smoothed down the skirt of my dress. I really loved it. My hair had been done in a smooth, shiny chignon, and I felt very glamorous. I couldn't wait to see Anthony. I hadn't seen him since yesterday morning and, although I'd had lots of fun with Elena last night, it felt like ages.

The car drew up outside the church and we climbed out. The bells were peeling loudly and the guests were already inside waiting. The vicar was standing beneath the lychgate, his robes blowing in the breeze. My heart started up a slow, deliberate thump as I followed Elena and her father up the path to the church door. The warm breeze lifted her veil, and I straightened the train of her skirt as she paused in the doorway, waiting for the organ to strike up 'Here Comes the Bride'. Goose bumps rippled up my arms and I took a deep breath to suppress the emotion welling up inside me. I couldn't follow my best friend up the aisle sobbing my eyes out.

The polished pews were filled with friends and relatives all dressed in their wedding finery. Anthony was seated on one at the very back of the church. Spotting him immediately, the hairs on the back of my neck prickled. Glancing behind, his eyes locked on mine and he winked. I smiled, my tears receding as suddenly as they had started.

Daniel was waiting at the altar, looking handsome and nervous in his silver-grey suit and blue tie. As soon as he saw Elena, his face flooded with colour and he visibly filled with emotion. Elena took his hand when she reached him and looked up into his eyes. Their love for each other shone out of them as they exchanged their vows, and I had to fight to hold in the tears, so moved was

I by the whole ceremony. As the vicar proclaimed them man and wife and they kissed, a beam of sunlight shone through the stained-glass window and illuminated them.

'Well, that was lovely, wasn't it?' Mum said, sidling up to me afterwards and dabbing her eyes with a tissue. 'I do love a good wedding.'

'Don't! You'll start me off,' I said, my throat aching with the effort of not crying. Mum passed me a tissue and I blew my nose surreptitiously behind her back. Anthony appeared behind me and slipped a hand round my waist.

'Hello, hello,' he said, kissing my mum and then me. 'May I say how beautiful you're both looking today?'

'You may!' Mum said, laughing merrily. 'Although I fear you mean Rachel more than me.'

'Not at all. Like mother like daughter. Although you look more like sisters today.'

Mum laughed. 'Well, someone's feeling silver-tongued! And may I say how very handsome you're looking, too, Anthony? Although there's nothing unusual in that.'

'Mother! Don't flatter him so much. His head is big enough as it is!' I placed a hand on his chest and he drew me close. Mum melted away and he bent down to kiss me.

'Christ, you look gorgeous,' he murmured against my lips. 'It feels like ages since I saw you. I missed you.'

'I know. Me too.'

'Err, excuse me! Don't be smudging her make-up, please. We have photos to get through first.' Elena came and grabbed my hand, tugging me towards the group of people lining up by the church steps. 'Come on, group one first with everyone in front of the church.'

The photographs seemed to last for ever. After the group photos had been taken, most of the guests started to leave to drive up to the hall. Anthony disappeared too, saying he didn't want to leave everything to Julian and Liz. Elena and Daniel had more photos in the churchyard and beneath the lychgate before travelling up to the hall.

There were more photographs in the grounds of Willow Hall and, despite having had very little to do with how wonderful the house and grounds looked, I was immensely proud of it all. Elena and Daniel had one last photo in front of the car and then we were free to go.

I went to find Anthony, who was sitting with my parents at their table in the pavilion. It looked magical, with the tables all laid out and the fairy lights sparkling in the roof, and I looked around in awe.

'Hello! Are you having fun?' Mum turned to look at me as I stood by the table.

'Yes. Although my face aches from smiling so much.' I placed my bouquet on the table and sat down on Anthony's lap as his hand snaked around the back of my legs. Turning, I kissed him full on the lips and wrapped an arm around his neck. 'Are you okay?'

'Yes, I'm fine.' He smiled at me, showing his lovely white teeth. 'Feeling a bit guilty about not being much help to everyone in the kitchen, but they've already rejected my offers of assistance.'

'I'm sure everything's under control, and the caterers will be doing most of it now.' I looked around at the tables full of happy, smiling guests. 'I think it's gone really well so far.'

'We haven't even eaten yet. Nor had the speeches.'

'Don't be so negative.' I kissed his cheek. 'Willow Hall is bound to be a success as a wedding venue. It's perfect!'

A man wearing a pink shirt and tie had set up a tripod and camera at the side of the pavilion. 'Who's that?' I murmured. 'He's not the same photographer as before.'

'No.' Anthony peered round me to look. 'He's from *Country Weddings* magazine. He's doing a glossy double-page spread, apparently. Elena and Daniel have agreed to it, don't worry. There's also meant to be a bloke taking a video for our website. I hope he does a good job. Last time I saw him he was in the kitchen chatting up one of the waitresses.'

I laid my head on his shoulder. 'I'm sad I can't sit by you at the meal.'

'Well, that's just not good enough.' He squeezed my waist, his eyes sparkling with amusement. 'I'm going to move my chair so I'm sitting next to you at the top table.'

'Are you now?' I giggled, imagining Elena's face if her seating plan got changed. 'Well, you are the owner, I suppose.'

'Exactly. What the owner wants, the owner gets.'

'Ooh! Masterful! And what does the owner want?'

'You.' He pressed his lips against mine, making my head spin.

'Do you two mind!' Mum's voice cut through the air. 'There are other people in the room, you know. Not just you two.'

'Sorry!' I stood up and smiled, feeling slightly embarrassed when I realised it wasn't just my parents sitting with us, but Elena's brother and her aunt and uncle too. 'I suppose I'd better take my seat.'

'Okay.' Anthony squeezed my hand and winked. 'But remember, I'll be watching you like a hawk to make sure you're not flirting with the best man.'

'Who? Zach?' I glanced over at Daniel's best man. He was the lead singer in the band Daniel played guitar in. Zach was lovely, but a bit off-the-wall, and a surprising choice for a best man, I thought. Still, he was looking quite tidy today in his suit, with his hair all neatly cut. The last time I'd seen him, he'd been sporting a man-bun and was headbanging on stage. 'Zach's lovely, but not my type, I'm afraid.'

'Glad to hear it.'

'Besides, he's sitting at the opposite end of the table to me. I'm next to Daniel's father.'

I took my seat at the top table. Virtually everyone except Elena and Daniel were sitting down and the room was full of chatter and laughter. I noted with satisfaction that my table decorations of pink peonies and white roses still looked beautiful and fresh.

Julian stepped in and cleared his throat. He looked nervous to be acting as the toastmaster, and the microphone in his hand was shaking, but his voice was strong as he announced the arrival of Elena and Daniel.

'Ladies and gentlemen, would you please give a very warm welcome to our bride and groom, using their married name for the very first time: Mr and Mrs Daniel and Elena Moore.'

The room erupted in a storm of cheering, clapping and camera flashes as Elena and Daniel appeared through the doorway. Music boomed through the speaker system and, laughing, they made their way hand in hand to the top table. The crystals on the bodice of her dress sparkled and she looked so beautiful and happy that I felt tears sting my eyes once more. I couldn't believe my best friend was married, and to the boy she'd been in love with at school. It was like a fairy tale.

Anthony caught my eye across the room and smiled. Would we get our fairy-tale ending? I wondered.

'I guess it will be you next,' Rosa said, leaning past Daniel's father, after Elena and Daniel sat down.

'I wouldn't bank on it, Rosa,' I laughed. 'It's very early days yet.'

'But that is the chap you were with last year, isn't it?'

'Yes.'

'Well, then, there must be something special between you if you've got back together. It certainly looks like it anyway.'

I looked over at Anthony to find he was still watching me, smiling. My heart swelled with love as our eyes locked and held.

'I didn't think I was going to like this,' Daniel's father said to me as he spooned up his tomato and roasted sweet pepper soup.

'Don't you usually like soup?' I asked politely.

'No, I meant the venue. I was looking forward to having the wedding at our golf club, not this fancy-pants hall. But I have to admit, it is lovely.'

'You're staying over tonight, aren't you?'

'Yes, we've got a room in the hall. It's lovely. Got great views over the hills. One of my friends has a daughter who just got engaged. I'm going to recommend this place to him.'

'Excellent!'

A warm feeling settled in my stomach. I felt like everything was going to work out fine, after all. Willow Hall's wedding business would be a success, my flower business would thrive, and Anthony and I would live happily ever after. Just like Elena and Daniel.

Once the main course of slow-cooked confit of duck with honey-glazed parsnips and fondant potatoes had been consumed, and the dessert plates had been collected, the waitresses served tea and coffee before topping up everyone's glasses for the toasts. Elena's father looked nervous as he got to his feet to propose a toast to Elena and Daniel. He then went on to say what a lovely girl Elena was and what a lucky man Daniel was.

'Seriously, though,' he went on, when everybody laughed, 'they make a wonderful couple. Daniel's a great young man and I know he'll look after my little girl as they make their way through life together.'

Daniel stood up, looking slightly red in the face. He thanked his father-in-law and began, 'On behalf of my wife and I…' at which everyone clapped and cheered. Elena caught his hand and kissed it. He talked about how much he loved Elena and how he'd fancied her at school but never had the guts to ask her out, and everyone oohed and aahed. Rosa dabbed her eyes on a napkin.

Zach looked nervous as he got to his feet to do his best man speech. He kept one hand in his pocket as he regaled us with funny stories of Daniel's antics in the band and told us what a good man he was, and how many times he'd come to Zach's aid.

After the speeches, Elena and Daniel cut the cake. Cath had made a hexagonal three-tier cake like the one Elena had originally wanted, and the result looked amazing. I hoped the photographer for the magazine would take a nice close-up photo of it to promote Cath's work.

Daniel's band was playing at the evening reception. They had an extra guitarist so Daniel didn't have to play all night, and while they brought in their instruments, microphones and amps, the rest of the guests went outside to enjoy the early evening sunshine. To my horror, Elena announced she was going to throw her bouquet for all the unmarried girls in the room. Please, no! I knew she was going to target me, and I couldn't face the humiliation of catching the bouquet and having everybody looking at me and saying 'Ooh, you next!'

I didn't think it was fair on Anthony either.

'Come on, Rachel,' Elena called to me as the rest of her female friends and relatives started lining up excitedly on the green lawn, ready to catch the bouquet. Screwing up my face, I shook my head, but Elena was already on her way over to me, determined to make me join in. My heels sank into the grass as she grabbed my hand and pulled me over to the group of women. Thinking I really should have talked to her about this before the wedding, I found myself standing next to two of Daniel's teenage cousins, who were already pushing each other out of the way, determined to be the one to catch it.

'I'm going to catch it!'

'No, I'm going to catch it!'

'No, I'm going to catch it!'

Elena turned her back and, holding the bouquet in both hands, lobbed it backwards over her head and into the gaggle of girls. I took a step sideways to avoid the wild, two-headed beast that Daniel's cousins had suddenly become. It was quite amazing how high they managed to leap into the air but the bouquet sailed over both pairs of outstretched hands. Elena had never been the best at judging distances, and had chucked the bouquet with such force that it sailed in a high arc over all the girls and hit Anthony on the side of the head with a dull thwack.

He looked up at the sky, as if wondering what in the world had hit him, and then down at the ground, where the bouquet lay on the grass. Completely oblivious of what was going on, he had been innocently crossing the grass to get to the hall. All the girls and several onlookers roared with laughter, but I could only stand and look on in horror.

Poor Anthony!

Luckily, he saw the funny side. 'Has somebody lost something?' he called, stooping to pick up the bouquet. Some of the petals had been damaged and were now lying in the grass.

'Are you okay?' I asked, hurrying across to him. 'Did it hurt? I'm so sorry.'

'You didn't throw it, did you?' he laughed.

'No!'

'Well, then.' He took me in his arms and kissed me while all the onlookers clapped and cheered.

'Talk about stealing the limelight!' Elena laughed as she made her way towards us. 'Sorry, Anthony! I wasn't aiming for you, I swear.'

'No harm done.' He handed her back her bouquet and she gazed forlornly at the broken flowers as he walked away.

'Oh, look!' she said.

'Well, that's what happens if you chuck it about!'

She pulled a sad face. 'Sorry, Rachel.'

'It's okay.' I hugged her, feeling the stiff skirt of her beautiful gown pressing against my legs. 'It's been a beautiful day, hasn't it? Are you enjoying yourself?'

'Yes, it's amazing.' She hugged me again tightly. 'And we have you to thank for all this.'

'Me? I don't think so!'

'Yes, we do. If you hadn't wanted to have a nose around Willow Hall, we would never have attended that wedding fair. And if Anthony hadn't been in love with you, he would never have tried so hard to convince us to change the venue to here.'

'No, it wasn't like that at all!'

'It was.' Elena looked around at the hall and the pavilion and the surrounding countryside. 'This place is so beautiful. You're going to be so happy here.' She squeezed my hand and moved away as an elderly aunt came over to speak to her.

Mum and Dad were standing nearby watching the children chase each other noisily around on the grass. The girls were doing handstands, the skirts of their pretty dresses up around their ears.

'I remember you doing that,' Mum told me.

'Good job I'm not doing it now.'

She laughed. 'I had no idea Elena had so many young relatives.'

'I think they're mostly related to Daniel. He's got a big family.'

'It's nice to have children around,' Mum said wistfully. 'They make everything so much happier.'

Dad's lip curled, and I laughed at him.

'I wish we'd had more, but it never happened,' Mum went on sadly.

'Why, aren't I enough for you?' I quipped.

'Of course you are, but it would have been lovely to have had more, that's all. I hope you and Anthony have lots of babies.'

'Oh, listen!' I said, as Zach's voice made an announcement. 'Elena and Daniel are having their first dance. Come on.'

We went back into the pavilion and joined the other guests watching Elena and Daniel on the dance floor. They were swaying in each other's arms while the band played a gentle Bryan Adams track. I felt Anthony's arms sneak around my waist and he kissed my neck.

'I was wondering where you'd gone,' I murmured, leaning back against him.

'I just went to see how everything was going in the hall.'

'How is everyone? Frazzled or relaxed?'

'Surprisingly relaxed, actually. The caterers have been excellent, and everything ran like clockwork. They're just gearing up for the evening buffet now.' He kissed the side of my face again. 'Do we get to have a dance now too?'

'Perhaps.' I caught his eye and smiled.

We waited until some other couples joined the dancing before we took to the floor. Anthony held me close against him, looking deep into my eyes as we danced. I put my hand on the side of his face, stroking his cheek with my thumb, and he caught my hand and kissed my palm. The music changed to something faster, but Anthony still held me close as people jigged around us. I laid my head on his chest, thinking that life didn't get much better than this. What could be better than dancing with a wonderful man, in beautiful surroundings, at my best friend's wedding?

Chapter Thirteen

We danced for a bit longer, then went outside to get some air. The sun was setting over the rolling hills, turning them pink, then blue, then purple. We leaned against the fence to watch.

'It's so perfect here,' I said dreamily. 'This is the best wedding venue ever! Did I tell you that Daniel's father is going to recommend this place to his friend? His daughter's getting married.'

Anthony didn't respond and I glanced over at him to check he was listening. He was rubbing his chest, his face creased with pain. 'Anthony?'

'I'm fine,' he gasped. 'It's just indigestion.'

Fear shot through me. Was it really just indigestion, or was it his heart? I looked back towards the house. 'Can you walk?'

'Of course I can walk!' He tried to laugh to soften the sharpness of his words but ended up sucking in air as the pain overwhelmed him. 'I'll be all right in a minute.'

There was no way this was just indigestion. I looked around for help but everyone was inside the pavilion, dancing to the band. What should I do? Leave him and run back to the house? Make him walk with me? I didn't even have my phone with me. I put my arm around him. 'Let's go to the house.'

He shook his head. 'No. Everyone will fuss. It will pass in a minute.'

I felt like the sky, the fields, the pavilion, the house were all revolving around us, with just Anthony and me stuck in the middle. Just as I was starting to panic, Julian emerged from the kitchen door and I screamed his name across the garden. He took one look and started running, pulling his phone from his pocket before he reached us.

'You all right, old chap?' He gripped his brother's shoulder with one hand, holding his phone to his ear with the other.

'I'm fine. It's passing now. It's going.'

'Good. Hello?' Julian said, into the phone. 'Ambulance, please. Yes, he's conscious and he's breathing, but he has severe chest pains and hypertrophic cardiomyopathy.' He reeled off the address to the hall.

'I don't want an ambulance.' Anthony spoke through gritted teeth.

'I know you don't, but we do. Have you taken your tablets today?'

'Of course I've taken my tablets today!' He straightened up slightly. 'Look, it's passing now. It's just indigestion from that duck.'

'Let's hope so. Will you come and sit down inside?'

'No, I'll go around the front and wait for this bloody ambulance.' He shrugged his brother's hand off his shoulder and walked away.

'Okay. I'll bring you a glass of water.'

I walked with Anthony to the front of the house and sat down on the front steps to wait for the ambulance. He refused to hold my hand so I held on to his arm, probably more to reassure myself than to reassure him. The pained expression had gone from his face, and now he simply looked annoyed. He sat quietly, staring off down the drive to where it disappeared into the dark tunnel of trees. The front door opened and Julian

193

passed him a glass of water. Cath hovered worriedly behind, but nobody spoke. Instead we sat listening to the distant thump of music from the pavilion and the occasional bleat from a far-off sheep.

Julian scuffed his feet on the top step and sighed. 'Should have driven you there myself!'

But then we heard it: the thin wail of an ambulance siren in the distance, gradually getting louder as it drew closer.

'Oh, dear God!' Anthony groaned. 'Please let them turn the siren off before they get here. We don't want to alarm the guests.'

'Shh,' said Cath. 'Don't be ungrateful.'

As if they'd heard him, the siren switched off as soon as the ambulance turned into the drive. We watched as the blue flashing lights emerged from the tree tunnel and the yellow vehicle approached. With a sigh, Anthony stood up, as if to prove he was fine, and walked slowly down the steps as the ambulance crunched to a stop.

'Sorry to waste your time,' he told the paramedic as she jumped down from the cab. 'I'm all right. Just had some chest pain. Probably indigestion.'

Clearing my throat, I caught the paramedic's eye and shook my head.

'Okay, sir,' she said. 'I understand you have an existing heart problem, so we'll take you in just to be on the safe side. If you'd just like to climb into the back of the ambulance, I'll run some tests on the way.' She looked back at us. 'Are you guys okay to follow in your car?'

I would rather have gone in the ambulance, but the doors were already closing and Julian had said yes. Cath came slowly down the steps, twisting her necklace between her fingers. Behind her, Oscar the ancient Labrador appeared in the doorway and slumped down with a whine. I knew how he felt.

Cath went to explain to the caterers what had happened while Julian went to get his car. I was trembling all over and my teeth were chattering from fear. Liz came to the door and hugged me. 'He'll be okay,' she said. 'Try not to worry.'

I felt bad that she was being left with everything when she was pregnant, but Julian said he would just speak to the doctor and then come home. 'We know he's going to be all right,' he reassured me as we waited for Cath to get her handbag. 'He's had these pains before. They want him to have an implantable cardiac defibrillator but he's being stubborn about it.'

'Why?'

'I don't know. He insists he's fine. Maybe you can convince him.'

'Huh, that's if he even lets me see him.' I watched as Cath came carefully down the steps and climbed into the front passenger seat. Seeing her with her bag reminded me I didn't have anything with me, not even my phone.

'Of course he'll let you see him,' Julian said cheerfully. 'If he doesn't, I'll chin him.' His eyes met mine in the rear-view mirror and he smiled.

The hospital wasn't far away. Julian's car sped down the narrow country lanes as the sun slipped below the horizon. Everywhere seemed so dark until we got into the brightly lit corridors of the hospital. Julian asked at the reception desk and we were directed where to go.

Anthony was lying on a hospital bed hooked up to an ECG machine. He looked fed up.

'Hello,' Julian said cheerfully. 'Have you seen the doctor yet?'

'Well, obviously,' Anthony said, indicating the electrodes taped to his chest.

'Now, don't get upset. You know you're supposed to avoid spikes in adrenalin.'

'Thanks for that.' Anthony rolled his head to the side and looked at me. 'Hey,' he said. 'Sorry about this.'

'Don't be silly. You need to be checked over.' I bent and kissed him on the forehead. 'How are you feeling now?'

'Okay. The pains have stopped.'

'Good.'

'I told you it was indigestion.'

'That's not what the readings say,' the doctor said, appearing behind us in the room. He gave Anthony a severe look. 'We'll need to keep you in overnight for further testing.'

Julian nodded. 'I've got his stuff here,' he said, brandishing a small holdall he'd got from the boot of his car. 'Always keep a bag in the boot, just in case.'

Anthony rolled his eyes. 'Great.'

'You're welcome!' Julian said. 'I know how you hate those hospital gowns. There's a book in there too, in case you get bored.'

'Thank you,' Anthony said, grudgingly.

Julian checked his watch. 'I need to get back to support Liz with the wedding.'

'Of course. You should all have stayed. You know I'll be okay. I'm just going to lie here and they'll say the same things they always say and then they'll discharge me. It's fine. Go on, go. All of you.'

'Don't be silly. There's no way I'm leaving you!' I was horrified by the thought of it.

Anthony reached for my hand. 'It's your best friend's wedding and you're her bridesmaid.'

'Yes, and my bridesmaid duties have been fulfilled, thank you. Elena would be horrified if she knew I left you in hospital so I could go back and dance at her wedding.'

Anthony groaned. 'Oh, God, I feel so bad for ruining it all. I'm so sorry.'

'Don't be sorry!'

'Of course you shouldn't feel sorry!' Cath said angrily. 'The only thing that matters is that you're all right. The caterers have got everything under control anyway. They've been amazing. I'd certainly use them again.'

Julian nodded. 'They have, but I'd better check on Liz anyway.

I know how tired she gets and she'll probably be wanting to go to bed.'

'Okay, lovey. I'll call Arthur to pick me up later.' Cath kissed him goodbye.

The next couple of hours were spent waiting in Anthony's hospital room or the corridor outside. I felt a bit ridiculous sitting around in my bridesmaid dress, especially when I had to queue to use the coffee machine. Poor Cath looked worn out.

'So Julian has been tested, has he?' I asked her after a while of sitting in the corridor in silence. Anthony had been taken to another room for a scan. 'And he hasn't got it?'

She shook her head. 'Apparently not. He tested negative for the faulty gene that's caused Anthony's. We think that will mean Charlie and Grace won't inherit it either, but they're being monitored to be on the safe side.'

'But if Anthony has children, it's likely his children will have it too?'

'It's possible, but not definite. We don't know for sure if Anthony did inherit this faulty gene from his father, but if he did, then he inherited it and Julian didn't. It's all very complicated.' She shook her head. 'This past year has been such a nightmare for Anthony.' She took my hand and squeezed it. 'Thank goodness you're back in his life.'

'I'm just glad he was pleased to see me when I came in,' I said. 'I was worried he might send me away like last time.'

'I don't think he'd do that again. He's learned his lesson now.'

The doctor came to speak to us and told us that Anthony was being transferred to the coronary care unit and we should go home and rest. I didn't want to leave without saying goodbye, and they allowed us to take Anthony's bag up to him and wish him goodnight before he went in.

I cried when I left him. He smiled and said not to worry, but how could I not worry when his heart wasn't working properly?

Arthur collected us from the main entrance and drove us back to Willow Hall. I felt bone-weary but wide awake at the same time.

'Do you want to stay in the bridal suite where you stayed last night?' Cath asked as Arthur drew up outside the main entrance. 'You don't want to go back to the gatehouse at this hour. Not on your own, anyway.'

I was grateful for the offer. I'd been dreading the thought of going back to the dark and empty gatehouse without Anthony.

All was quiet at Willow Hall. The caterers had packed up and gone home and the guests were in their rooms. Only Julian was still awake, waiting for us in the kitchen, to see if we had any news. He didn't look surprised when we hadn't, and we all went off to bed to try and sleep. It felt strange to spend another night in the bridal suite, but at least all my stuff from the previous evening was still there. It was heaven to climb into my own pyjamas and remove my make-up. I thought about Anthony in the hospital; imagined being there with him and holding his hand. It made it easier to drift off to sleep.

Chapter Fourteen

It felt as though someone had flicked a switch on my life. One day everything was pretty much perfect, and the next it was all falling apart. Even the gloriously sunny weather had changed to grey cloud and drizzle. The last of the wedding guests had left and we'd waved Elena and Daniel off with a 'Just Married' sign in the back window of their car. They'd been distraught to find out about Anthony, but we assured them everything was fine and that he'd be okay.

I hoped so anyway. I couldn't lose him now.

'Anthony's very sensitive about his heart condition,' Cath said as Julian drove us to the hospital that afternoon. 'He won't talk to us about it at all. It was the main reason he moved out of the hall. He thought I was mithering him too much about his medication. Of course, his moving out only made me worry more, so it backfired on him really.'

'How many times has he had these chest pains?'

'Only once. They changed his medication that time.'

Julian turned into the hospital car park and I stared up at the windows, wondering which one Anthony was behind. It was horrible to think of him lying in his hospital bed with all those wires attached to his chest like last night. I knew he was in the best place, but I still wished it wasn't necessary.

Visiting him here reminded me of the awful night I'd rushed to the hospital after his accident. The rain had been lashing down and I'd been so frightened. Cath and I had sat for hours in hospital corridors while the emergency medical staff worked on his broken body. It had been the worst night of my life, not knowing if he was going to make it through. It had been worse even than receiving the letter, or being turned away by the nurses when I'd gone to visit him.

I hoped he didn't push me away this time. There was no way I'd let him.

'They want me to have an implantable cardiac defibrillator,' Anthony said as soon as we walked through the door. 'I'm not having one! I don't need it. This whole thing's ridiculous.'

'You're ridiculous!' Cath told him crossly. 'Why won't you have one? It could save your life.'

'The pills work fine. I've had enough time off work and I can't afford any more. My career's already suffered because of the accident last year.'

'It was because of your job that you had that accident,' Julian reminded him. 'And that accident is the only reason they found out about your heart. You were still running back then. You could have died if they hadn't picked it up on that scan.'

'Yes, and now I'm on the pills and I'm perfectly fine. I want to go home. It was just the stress of going to that stupid wedding that brought this on. You know how I hate them. In fact, it was probably the shock of being hit in the head by that wedding bouquet.' He glared accusingly at me.

'Why are you looking at me? I didn't throw it!'

'It was your friend that threw it. Why are you here anyway? I don't want you here. Get out.'

'*Anthony!*' Julian and Cath gaped at him in horror. 'Stop this now!'

I met his gaze levelly. 'I will not get out, as you so charmingly put it. Do you have some kind of allergy to hospitals that turns you into a monster? I'm not going anywhere.' I sat down on the chair next to his bed and crossed my legs. 'Just have the implant and get on with your life. If the doctors say you should have it, then you should have it. They're the ones that know about these things.'

Anthony scowled and Cath tutted. 'Honestly, Anthony, you're the worst patient. The look on your face could turn milk sour. Rachel's right; you need the implant.'

'Your job should be the last thing you're worrying about right now,' Julian said. 'You're already driving miles every day just to do what's essentially a desk job. I've told you to put in for a transfer to somewhere closer.'

Anthony scowled. 'I like working in Manchester.'

'No, you don't,' Julian said. 'You don't, not really.'

'I don't like you driving all that way either,' his mother said. 'What if you have pains when you're driving? What if you lose consciousness?'

'The ICD will control your heart rate more effectively so you'll be able to lead a more normal life,' I said. 'Surely that's what you want?'

He grunted and looked away across the room.

'Well, don't ignore her!' Cath snapped. 'She doesn't deserve that. You've worried us all half to death and now you're acting like a sulky child. In fact, you were never this bad as a child! You were good back then.'

Anthony sighed and shook his head slowly from side to side. I'd never seen him so stroppy and uncommunicative.

'Are you scared of the operation?' Julian asked. 'Because I hear it's not too bad.'

'Of course I'm not scared!' he scoffed. 'Don't be ridiculous.'

'Well, then, there's no reason not to have it, is there?' Julian said cheerfully. 'What have you got to lose? It'd only be a couple of days in hospital and then a short recovery period. You'll probably lose more time off work if you don't have it done. How many times have you ended up here in the past year? Twice? And each time you've had to be off work. And what if you have children?'

'I won't have children!'

'What if Rachel wants children? That's not fair, is it? You can't dismiss it out of hand without even discussing it.

'I don't want to pass this down to my kids.'

'But your children might not get it. I didn't, did I? We don't even know for sure that Dad had it. But you'd get genetic counselling and your children would be monitored. As long as you receive the proper care and treatment, my understanding is you can live a long and happy life. All right, you might never run a marathon or play contact sports, but there are worse things in life. You could still be happy with Rachel.'

'No, I can't. That's not the life I want. I don't want this.'

'Yesterday it was,' I pointed out. Outwardly, I was calm, but my heart was beating so hard I was sure it must be visible through my chest. 'Yesterday we were fine.'

'Well, today we're not,' he said harshly. 'Things change, Rachel, and not always for the better.'

'But I'm not sure what's changed,' I said. 'If you've been admitted here twice in the past year, and you're here again, then surely it's clear you were living on borrowed time anyway. The pills aren't enough and you need the implant. Has it been offered to you before?'

Julian nodded. 'Twice.'

'Well, that's just stupid,' I said. 'You can't gamble with your life; you mean too much to too many people. Think about how selfish you're being.'

'I'm selfish? Listen to yourselves. You're the ones trying to force me into doing something I don't want to do. I won't be able to drive for weeks after it. I won't be able to work. Who knows what further damage that would do to my career.'

'What if you drop dead trying to keep up with your precious career?'

'If my time's up, my time's up.'

'That is so stupid! What about your family? What about me?'

'What about you? I never promised you a future. We were just happy in the now, remember? And now it's all gone tits up, that's finished.'

'Finished? Oh, really? I don't think so.'

'Oh, you don't think so, do you? Well, I've had enough and I'm out of here. Pass me my bag, Julian.' Sitting up, he began ripping off the electrodes still attached to his chest before swinging his legs out of bed.

'Anthony! Stop!' Cath's hands went to her face as she watched her son in horror. Julian stood without moving, looking on in disbelief.

'Julian!' he barked. 'My bag.'

'Oh, just stop it!' I said, exasperated. 'You need to be here. What are you going to do? Just walk out?'

'That's exactly what I'm going to do,' he said, snatching the bag out of Julian's hands and pulling on his trousers.

'But you can't!'

'Oh, yes, I can. Watch me.' He was still pulling his T-shirt over his head as he walked out of the room, his trainers in his hand. A nurse came running up the corridor. 'Mr Bascombe, what are you doing out of bed? Mr Bascombe…'

'Discharging myself.'

Cath, Julian and I looked at each other in disbelief.

'Is he always like this?' I asked, bewildered. It was so preposterous that I wanted to laugh. What the hell was he doing? 'Where's he going to go?'

Julian went to look for him, but he'd already disappeared into the maze of hospital corridors. We waited in the main entrance until one of the receptionists told us they'd seen him leave through the front doors. I was really angry by the time we got back to Willow Hall. How could he do this? It was an outrageous way to behave.

Cath and Julian weren't impressed either. Cath had started to shake so I made her a cup of tea while she sat at the kitchen table. She didn't need all this worry. 'Shall I go and see if he's at the gatehouse?'

Julian shook his head. Even he looked shell-shocked. 'He'll be there. Leave him for a bit.'

'How do you think he'd have got home?'

'Taxi, I expect.'

We sat around the table, sipping our tea and not really speaking. There didn't seem to be a lot to say. It felt like we were all holding our breath. Rain beat against the kitchen window, adding to our general air of despondency. After about half an hour, Julian's phone pinged with a text message. He looked up from where he was slumped, chin in his hand, and stabbed a finger at the screen to open it. 'He's back,' he grunted.

'Does he say anything else?'

'Sorry.'

Cath sighed heavily. 'I should think so too.'

I got to my feet. 'Okay, I'll go and see him.'

The path to the gatehouse was wet and full of puddles, and my exposed toes in my summer sandals were cold and speckled with mud by the time I reached the cottage. Thunder rolled in the distance, low and ominous.

Anthony was in the kitchen when I walked in through the door. He looked over at me and smiled. 'Typical British summer,' he said, as though this was just an ordinary day and he hadn't just absconded from hospital.

I stared at him. Did he think we would just go back to normal after this? 'This isn't just going to go away,' I said. 'You have to face up to this.'

He shook his head slowly. 'This is my body. It's my heart.'

'Well, if you feel like that, then I'm leaving.'

It was strange, but I didn't know what I was going to do until I did it. I just knew I had no choice. He had to be made to see he couldn't hide from this. He had to have that implant. Without that, our future was uncertain, and I wasn't willing to live like that.

He blinked several times as though he couldn't believe what he was hearing. 'What? You can't leave. I'm sorry, okay? You know I love you. I don't want this to be over.'

'Well, I'm sorry, but like you said, things change and not always for the better.' I started up the stairs to get my stuff.

'So, what? You don't love me any more?' he said, following me up. 'You're going to leave me because I have a heart condition?'

'No. I'm going to leave you because you're behaving like an idiot.' My overnight bag was at the hall in the bridal suite, so I took his holdall from the bottom of the wardrobe and started stuffing in clothes and underwear. 'I'm leaving because I won't be pushed away and treated badly by you when something goes wrong.'

'All right, I'm sorry, okay. I'm sorry.'

'Sorry's not good enough.' I zipped up the bag and pushed past him to go downstairs. 'You're not calling the shots this time.'

'What do you mean? I just don't want you to go.'

'Exactly.' I paused at the front door and looked back at him. 'Have the implant or it's over between us. And go and see your mother. You've really upset her.'

I slammed the door behind me. The rain seemed to get heavier, as though it was trying to stop me leaving. It bounced off the roof of my car in a deafening roar as I drove away, and lightning split the sky, framing Anthony in his doorway, shouting for me to stay. But there was no way I was giving in now. He had to face up to this. I saw what an unwitting mistake I'd made when I'd told him we should only talk about the present. I thought I was taking the pressure off, but really I was giving him an excuse not to think about the future, when if he didn't, he could die.

Chapter Fifteen

Julian phoned me when I got home. 'Bit harsh, wasn't it?'

I rubbed a hand over my face and groaned. 'I know. I'm sorry if I've caused an upset there but I wanted to make him see that he can't get away with behaving like this.'

Julian sighed. 'What did he do to make you leave?'

'He just acted like nothing had happened, and then he started with the "it's my heart, my body" attitude, and made me furious. I don't understand how he can't see that we all belong to each other, and his crap choices affect other people, not just him. I mean, look at you, worrying over him like you're the older brother, not the other way round. You've got two kids and a pregnant wife to consider. Liz must be shattered after yesterday but she's still had to cope with Grace and Charlie on her own because Anthony decided to be a twat. I love him but I'm not standing for this.'

There was a pause and I thought I heard muttering in the background. I narrowed my eyes suspiciously. 'He says if you loved him, you wouldn't have left.'

'Wait a minute, are you there with him now? Julian! Leave him to his own miserable devices and go and spend time with Liz.'

'He's come up to the hall, actually. We're all together.'

'Oh. Well, good. I hope he's apologised?'

'He has.' Julian sounded surprised.

'Has he agreed to have the implant yet?'

'Err, no.'

'Well, you can tell him, if he wants me back, that's what he has to do.'

'But isn't that emotional blackmail?'

'Of course it is, Julian. But what do you think he's been doing to you and your mum this past year? He's behaved really badly, but because he's been in an accident and has this heart condition you let him get away with it. Well, I'm sorry, but he can't treat people like that and he needs to grow up.'

It was only after hanging up that I started to feel bad. What if I'd gone too far? Should I have stayed by his side, holding his hand and trying to talk him round? Maybe he just needed some gentle persuasion.

But he had been very unreasonable in the hospital. Walking out on me and his family like that was just awful. If he thought more of his career than having an operation that could prolong his life, that said a lot about the value he put on his relationships. He had his priorities all wrong.

Chapter Sixteen

If I'd thought Anthony would back down and agree to the implant straight away, then I was very much mistaken. I went to work on Monday morning feeling nervous about seeing him again and wondering what the day might bring, but I didn't see him at all. I assumed he was at work, which was madness considering he'd been in hospital on Saturday night.

The hall, too, was quieter than usual. I wandered down to say hello, but the kitchen door was locked. When I saw Arthur pushing his wheelbarrow, he said he didn't know where everybody was, and that maybe they'd just gone shopping.

Bobbi and I were busy anyway. We had a midweek wedding to arrange flowers for and we worked solidly all day so they'd be ready to deliver the following morning. Really, it was good timing for me not to be living with Anthony, because the wedding was in Chester anyway, so it made everything that much more convenient. It meant that getting Bobbi to work was simpler too. She had blossomed in the past few weeks and had taken to wearing denim dungarees with brightly coloured T-shirts underneath. With her hair plaited in two long, pink-tinged pigtails, she looked like some kind of children's television presenter.

'Do you miss him?' she asked later on that week, when I still hadn't seen him.

'Yes,' I admitted. It was starting to bug me that I hadn't seen him or his car all week now. I hadn't even seen Cath to speak to either. Only God knew where everyone had got to. It made me feel slightly paranoid. Was everyone avoiding me? Had I misjudged things so badly?

With no one around, it felt strange to be working there, and I began to wonder if I had made a mistake moving the business after all. All I needed now was for Julian to put up the rent and I'd be well and truly stuffed. I spoke to Mum about it, but she told me to wait it out, convinced all would come good in the end.

I wished I had her confidence.

We had another wedding flower order booked for the following Saturday, so I worked late on the Friday evening. Jayjay had driven down to pick Bobbi up and taken her out for dinner at a nice country pub in the village, so I was free to stay as long as I liked. The long summer evening meant it didn't even feel late when I finally packed up to leave.

A shadow fell across the doorway and I looked up to see Anthony standing there. The air seemed to disappear from my lungs. 'Oh! Hi.'

'Hello. You're working late.'

'Yes, we have a wedding tomorrow.'

'Great. Whereabouts?'

'Not that far from here, actually. I haven't seen you all week.'

'No, that's what happens when you leave someone.'

'I suppose so.' I put the last of the flowers in the refrigerator and shut the door. 'I didn't think you'd go back to work so quickly.'

He shrugged. 'I felt all right so I went in. I've been staying with a friend in Manchester, though, so I didn't have to travel.'

'Good.' I put my hands on my hips and looked at him, aware

I resembled some kind of fishwife. 'It's been very quiet around here. I haven't seen your mum at all.'

'She's been away, visiting an old friend.'

I sagged a little in relief. 'Oh, that's good. I was beginning to think everybody was avoiding me. I asked Arthur but he didn't say where she'd gone.'

Anthony laughed. 'That's because Arthur's on my side, not yours. My mother, on the other hand, has taken a leaf out of your book and isn't speaking to me.'

'Oh, really?' I winced. 'Sorry. And for the record, I am speaking to you. I'm just not living with you at the moment.'

'At the moment?' There was hope in his voice.

'You know what you have to do,' I said, not looking at him so I couldn't see the pleading look in his eyes. 'Anyway, I'm going home now.'

'Can I have a hug first?'

I hesitated before putting my arms around him. It felt so good to hold him again. I pressed my face to his chest, feeling the faint thud of his heartbeat against my cheek. I didn't want to let go, and neither did Anthony, so we just stood there, holding each other while the sun dipped and the birds sang around us.

'I'd better go,' I said at last, pulling away.

'No, don't go,' he groaned.

'I have to. It'll be dark soon.'

'Stay. Please.'

I shook my head as I locked the door and headed for my car. 'I'll see you soon, Anthony. Take care of yourself.'

He watched me leave, standing beneath a sycamore tree, his suit jacket flapping in the warm breeze. It would have been so easy to stay with him. He was all I wanted.

Chapter Seventeen

The following week, Anthony disappeared again. Cath was back from her friend's house, but she had caught a cold and was keeping herself to herself. I assumed Liz and Julian must have gone on holiday, because there was no sign of them, or Grace and Charlie.

The feeling of being cut off seemed to intensify, and I couldn't shake the feeling that I'd caused a giant rift in his family.

'But you don't know that for sure, do you?' Bobbi said when I confided in her later on that week. 'They're probably just getting back to normal after Elena's wedding, that's all.'

'You're right. I know you're right. And I suppose, if I'm not with Anthony, there's no reason I should know where everybody is.' I sighed. 'It just feels weird being here and not knowing what's going on.'

'You'll get used to it, I'm sure,' Bobbi said, gazing out of the window at the lake. I looked at her. I didn't want to get used to it; I just wanted Anthony to change his mind about the implant. I wondered what I'd do if he didn't. Would I give in and just get back with him? Or would I stay strong and find somewhere else to rent? Both options seemed inconceivable.

As if reading my mind, Bobbi said: 'It's so beautiful here. I saw a fox this morning down by the lake. It was still misty but the sun was shining and it was framed so beautifully against the water. I wished I had a camera, but even then I don't think I could have captured quite how special that moment was. I never want to leave here. It's magical.'

I sighed, knowing exactly what she meant. 'Yes, it is pretty special.'

When Friday arrived, I made sure I worked late again so that I could see Anthony when he arrived back from work, but there was no sign of him all evening. I waited until the shadows crept in and it was so completely dark that it began to feel eerie being there alone. He must have taken on an extra shift and be working later, or perhaps he was working the weekend too. It wasn't unusual for him to work weekends, after all, but the fact he'd been away all week meant he was surely due a day off.

I drove down to the gatehouse and stopped outside. The whole cottage was in darkness, save the hopeful security light that lit up as soon as it sensed my car passing. I couldn't help thinking that perhaps he was back in hospital again. Hot beads of perspiration broke out on my forehead just imagining it. He might not be so lucky next time. I wouldn't even know because we weren't together any more.

But then, he could equally be out with friends.

Perhaps he had met someone new who could give him a good time without nagging him to get a heart operation.

Perhaps.

Perhaps did no one any good, I reasoned. There was nothing I could do here. I just needed a shower and a good night's sleep.

The same feeling of disquiet followed me around all the next morning too. I delivered flowers to another wedding before driving to Willow Hall and sitting in the Brew House, just waiting to see if he would turn up. There was no sign of his car. No movement from the cottage. And then, around lunchtime, I heard the crunch of his footsteps from outside. I froze, resisting the urge to bound out and throw myself at him like some kind of overexcited Labrador. It could still be someone else, I told myself, preparing to be disappointed.

It was Anthony. I couldn't help the smile that spread across my face at the sight of him again.

'Hello! I was hoping you'd be here,' he said. He came straight up to me, standing so close that I put my hand up to his chest because I thought he was going to walk into me. He flinched slightly before starting to undo the buttons of his shirt.

'Steady on!' I laughed. 'What are you doing?'

'What you wanted me to do.' He pulled open his shirt to reveal a small red scar above his left pec and a slight bump beneath his skin. My hands flew to my face and I gasped. 'There you go. One ICD, all fitted and ready to shock me back to life should my heart decide to stop.'

'What? But why didn't you tell me you were having it done? I would have come with you and supported you.' Tears spilled down my cheeks.

'You're not going to have a go at me about that now, are you?' He rolled his eyes theatrically. 'I didn't tell anyone until afterwards. I just decided to go and have it done.'

'But why?'

He smiled. 'So I could get you back, Miss Jones. And so that I have the best chance of living a long and happy life with you. If that's what you want, that is?'

'Of course it's what I want.' I hugged him gently, careful not to press against the implant. I had so many emotions flowing through me. Relief, elation, and just a tiny, tiny smidgeon of guilt that he'd felt he had to do it alone. 'I just wish you'd told me.'

He shrugged his right shoulder. 'Oh, well, it's done now and it wasn't so bad. I just have to not lift my left arm for a while. And, the other piece of news I have is that they're going to transfer me to the local branch. They've found a nice, boring desk job for me.'

'That's fantastic news!'

'Is it?' He pulled a face. 'I can feel the cobwebs growing on me already.'

'Don't be silly. It's much better for you. I'm sorry your career hasn't gone the way you wanted recently, but I'm sure it will pick up again.'

'Well, I doubt I'll ever get promoted now, but as long as I have you, that's all that matters. So, are you going to come home?'

I smiled up at him. 'Of course I'm coming home. I've missed you so much.'

'Even though I behaved like a twat, as you so eloquently told Julian?'

'Even though you acted like a twat,' I confirmed. 'I love you.'

He stroked my hair back from my face and I saw so much love in his eyes that it made my heart soar. 'I love you, too,' he said. 'And I promise never to act like a twat again.'

Chapter Eighteen

'What are you doing on Sunday?' Anthony asked a few weeks later.

'I don't know. What are *you* doing on Sunday?'

'This.' He held up a flyer for a hot air balloon ride. 'My friend runs this company and he said there's availability if we want to go.'

'Really?' I put my plate on the table and took the leaflet from him. It showed a big colourful balloon floating above beautiful green fields and trees. It looked idyllic. 'But I'm scared of heights.'

'Are you?' He looked alarmed. 'Really? You never said.'

'No, well, it never really came up.' I passed the leaflet back to him. 'Nice thought, though.'

He came and sat down next to me, looking crestfallen. 'Are you sure? You'd be in a massive basket, you know. And it's really sturdy.'

I gave him a look. 'Massive? Really?'

'And it's very safe. You've flown in an aeroplane, haven't you?'

'Well yes, but that's a massive steel construction, not a picnic basket dangling from a balloon.'

'It's not a picnic basket! Honestly, they're very sturdy. And they don't go as high as an aeroplane.'

I gave him another look. 'Oh, good.'

'It's a once-in-a-lifetime opportunity.'

'If he's your mate, I doubt that! I bet you've been up before, haven't you?'

'Well, yes, but he's invited me this week and I'd really love it if I could share it with you.'

I groaned. 'That's emotional blackmail, you know. Are you even allowed to go up in that thing? You've not long since had an operation.'

'Of course I'm allowed,' he said, looking shifty. 'I've been up before and it's not like I'm going to get really excited.'

'Are you sure?'

'Of course I'm sure. It's really relaxing, floating along. Come on, we haven't done anything fun for ages.'

'You don't have fun with me?' My heart stuttered in alarm.

'Of course I have fun with you!' he said quickly. 'You know I do. But you've been working so hard recently, and what with my operation and all, I thought it might be nice to get away from everything for a couple of hours. We can just go and watch if you'd rather. I promise I won't make you go up if you don't want to, but I said I'd go and see Mark.'

'Mark? I've never heard you mention him.' I narrowed my eyes suspiciously.

'That's because I haven't seen him for ages!' He laughed, incredulously. 'I went to school with him. Don't you believe me?'

'Of course I believe you,' I said, backing down. 'I was just surprised, that's all. I've just never heard you mention anyone called Mark or hot air balloons.'

He looked disappointed and a little bit sad.

'I'm sorry,' I told him, squeezing his leg and shifting closer. I was still careful not to put any pressure on his chest or left arm. 'I'll come. I'm sure it will be lovely.'

He smiled. 'Good. And it will be lovely, I promise.'

Sunday was a lovely sunny day. We were in September now

but it was still warm. Part of me had been hoping for high winds so I wouldn't have to go up in the balloon, but the conditions were perfect. The airfield wasn't far away. We parked in the small car park and walked through the gate into the field. One hot air balloon was already rising up into the sky, and another was still on the ground, its basket lying sideways on the grass, with the red fabric of the balloon spread out beside it. A tall man with dark hair and a blue-checked shirt was standing next to it. He waved when he saw us and came over to shake Anthony by the hand.

'You must be Rachel,' he said, turning to me with a smile. 'The lion tamer.' He glanced at Anthony and winked.

'Oh, I don't know about that. Hello, Mark. Lovely to meet you.'

'Anthony tells me you're a bit nervous about going up. Please don't be.'

'Well, Anthony's had me watching videos online so I feel a bit braver now.' I grimaced slightly and looked up at the balloon that was already floating high in the air.

'Great! Let's inflate the balloon then. Come on.' We followed him over to where the balloon was lying on the grass, and another man came over to help.

'Is it just us going up today?'

'Yes, just you two and me,' Mark said cheerfully. The blowers started up with a deafening roar and the balloon started to billow and rise as it filled with hot air. I stood nervously by, listening to Anthony and Mark chat about old times and how their friends and families were. When the balloon was sufficiently inflated, Mark climbed on to the basket and used his weight to tip it upwards as the balloon rose up into the sky. I stared up at the rainbow-coloured silk, thinking how beautiful it looked.

'Come on, jump in,' Mark called. 'I promise you, we'll bring her back down if you don't like it. No worries.'

Anthony took my hand and helped me climb into the basket.

The heat from the burners warmed my skin and I looked up into the vast chamber of the inside of the balloon, fascinated by the way the air shimmered and rippled in the heat. The man on the ground released the ropes, and before I knew it we were rising into the air, slowly and gracefully. My knees felt a little wobbly and I gripped the basket for support, but the feeling of floating up, up, up above the treetops was also exhilarating. The basket felt so sturdy beneath my feet that I began to forget there was nothing but air beneath us. I didn't dare look over the side of the basket. It felt safer to keep my eyes on the horizon and admire the patchwork quilt of fields all around us.

Anthony put his arms around my waist and kissed my head. 'Are you okay?'

'Yes. Yes, I think so.'

'You're shaking.'

'I know, but I'm getting used to it.'

'We can go back down at any time. Just say the word.'

'No. I'm enjoying the view. Isn't it beautiful?'

'It is. We should be able to see Willow Hall soon, too.'

'Really? Will we fly over it?'

'I don't know. Mark? Will we fly over Willow Hall?'

Mark turned and grinned over his shoulder.

'Just so happens the wind is blowing us that way. Who knows, maybe we can land in your field.'

Anthony laughed. 'Well, that would be nice. My mother would love to see you again. We could drop in on her, literally.'

'Do we not land where we took off?'

'No, the steering's not that good on these things.' Mark grinned. 'We go where the wind takes us. Well, within reason, anyway. Don't worry, we have a team that comes out and picks us all up to take us back to the launch spot.'

'Oh, good.'

He laughed. 'It's a beautiful evening for it. Great conditions.' He stared around him contentedly. 'Shall we keep going higher?'

'Okay.'

'Are you starting to relax now?'

'Maybe.'

Mark laughed and Anthony rubbed my shoulders. The burners blasted more hot air into the balloon and Mark and Anthony chatted about what they had been up to recently. I watched the fields stretch out around us as the view got bigger and bigger. It really was breathtaking. I marvelled at the tiny cars moving along a winding road, and the miniature village that looked like something out of a toyshop. Feeling braver, I peeked over the edge of the basket, then wished I hadn't when my stomach flipped.

'Hey, don't look down!' Mark laughed at the expression on my face and cut the burners. The sudden silence after the steady roar was almost a shock and we drifted peacefully through the air, with the English countryside stretched out below us. I felt humbled by the vastness of the landscape, moved by its beauty. I stared around me, as wide-eyed and awestruck as a child.

Anthony was leaning on the side of the basket, watching me with a smile on his face. I looked over at him and smiled.

'This is amazing. Thank you so much.'

His smile widened and he moved closer and took my hands, staring down into my eyes. I felt my heart shift as it always did when he looked at me like that.

'Rachel.' He said my name softly and chills ran down my spine. Smiling, I moved closer and he smoothed a strand of hair behind my ear. 'I want to spend the rest of my life with you,' he continued. 'I want to wake up with you every morning and fall asleep in your arms every night. I want to grow old with you, and be there for you through the good times and the bad.' I blinked up at him, smiling. I felt the same way, but why was he telling me this now? 'Rachel…' He sank down on one knee and my heart began to beat wildly as he opened a small black box to reveal a sparkling diamond ring. 'I love you. Please, will you marry me?'

I gasped, completely and utterly shocked. This couldn't be true. It was too good to be true. This must be a dream.

But in dreams, you can't feel the wind in your hair. Or the heat of the blowers on your arms.

'Yes!' I shook myself and squealed before throwing myself at him and covering his face with kisses. 'Yes! Yes! Yesyesyesyesyesy esyesyesyesyesyesyesyes!' I was so overwhelmed by emotion that I started to cry. 'Of course I will! *Of course* I will! Oh, my God, I'm so happy!'

Tears studded Anthony's eyes and he laughed with relief. I let go of him and fanned my face, trying to stop the tears. Taking my left hand, he slid the ring on to my third finger. It was beautiful. A rose gold band with a large round diamond, surrounded by smaller diamonds to form a flower.

'It's perfect!' I stared at it on my finger. I was in love with it already. 'Thank you so much.'

Anthony rose from his knees and kissed me. The pop of a champagne cork reminded us we weren't alone, and we looked round to see a beaming Mark pouring out three glasses of champagne. 'Congratulations!' he said, passing them out to us. 'That's wonderful. I'm so pleased someone's going to make an honest man of you at last!' He winked at Anthony and laughed.

The sun was sinking lower in the sky and streaks of pink and orange were seeping across the horizon. This was such a perfect moment. I had never been so happy or surprised. I kept looking at the ring, twinkling on my finger.

'You couldn't have picked a more beautiful ring,' I said.

'And I couldn't have picked a more beautiful girl.' He smiled down at me.

'Hey, look, there's Willow Hall. Just coming into view down there.'

We turned to see where Mark was pointing. Willow Hall lay surrounded by fields and trees, its tall chimneys reaching up to the sky. To the side, we could just make out the walled garden and Julian and Liz's house. And if I squinted, I could see the white walls of the gatehouse peaking above the trees.

'Shall I bring her down?'

'Yes, please.' Anthony took my hand and smiled down at me. 'Let's go home.'

I'd expected the landing to be the scary part, but it was actually quite smooth. With the burners blasting intermittently to control our landing, we settled gently on the grass at the back of Willow Hall.

Cath was sitting on the patio, enjoying the last of the evening sunshine. She got to her feet as we landed and came towards us, shielding her eyes, her white hair glowing pink in the reflected rays of the setting sun.

'Hello! Did you have a nice time?'

'Yes! It was fabulous!' I climbed out of the basket and ran to her. 'Look! Look!' I said, showing her my ring.

She gasped and covered her mouth with her hands, before throwing her arms around us both. 'That's wonderful! I'm so happy for you both. Congratulations.'

'Did you know he was going to ask me?'

'He said he might, but he wasn't sure if you were going to like the balloon ride.'

'Yes, there'd have been no point asking if you were cowering in fear at the bottom of the basket.'

'Oh, so this ring is a test of my bravery skills, is it?'

'Not at all. I'd have had to think of another way of asking you, that's all.' He put his arm around my shoulders and kissed me.

'Will you get married here?'

'Ooh, well, I don't know about that!' I put my finger to my lips, pretending to think hard. Everyone laughed. 'Of course we'll get married here. There's no place better!'

Cath beamed with pleasure. 'Wonderful! I can't tell you how happy this makes me. You're perfect for each other.' Cath kissed

221

me on both cheeks and squeezed my hands. 'Thank you, Rachel. You have brought sunshine back into our lives.'

'Oh!' I laughed in surprise and glanced up at Anthony. He grinned.

'Here, here,' he said.

'I'd better go and say hello to Mark,' she said. 'Goodness, he's changed since I last saw him.'

'That was about ten years ago, Mother.'

'What's going on here then?' Julian and Liz appeared with Charlie and Grace trotting behind them. Charlie was staring up at the balloon with an awestruck expression on his little face. In answer, I held out my left hand and Liz squealed and reached out to hug me. Her pregnant tummy was huge now, like a big, hard cushion between us.

'Aaargh! I'm so happy for you both! That's amazing news!' She grabbed my hand and examined the ring closely. 'Wow! That's a beautiful ring. Did you choose that yourself, Anthony?'

'Of course I did.'

'Well, I'm very impressed.' She stretched up to kiss him on the cheek. 'Congratulations. You're a lucky, lucky man!'

He laughed. 'I know I am.'

Julian had just about managed to shake Anthony's hand before being dragged away by Charlie to get closer to the hot air balloon. He looked back over his shoulder at me. 'Congratulations, Rachel!'

'Thanks, Julian.'

Grace patted me on my leg. 'Congratulations, Auntie Rachel.'

'Aww, thank you, sweetie. Shall we go and look at the balloon?'

She nodded and I took her hand and led her over to it. Mark had got back into the basket and Julian was climbing in with Charlie in his arms.

'We can just go up a few feet,' Mark was saying.

'Are you sure you don't mind?'

'Not at all.'

'Can I come, Daddy?' Grace piped up.

'Okay, come on then.'

I helped Grace into the basket and she gripped the top with her little hands, peering out over the sides.

'Are you coming in, Mummy?'

Liz shook her head and grimaced. 'No, thank you.'

'Go on, it's amazing.'

Liz laughed and shook her head.

'Some other time, maybe?' Mark laughed and fired up the burner. Grace jumped, her eyes opening wide as she stared at her mother.

'Hold on tight, sweetie.' The colour drained from Liz's face as she watched the basket containing her husband and children rise up into the air. Mark only went up a few feet, before slowly coming back down again and settling on the grass.

'Again! Again!' Charlie cried.

'That's all for today, little man,' Mark said, while everyone else laughed. 'The van will be here in a minute to pick me and the balloon up so I can go home for my tea.'

'Say thank you to Mr Mark, Charlie.'

'Thank you, Mr Mark,' Charlie said solemnly as his father passed him to Liz. My heart squeezed with love. He was such an adorable little boy. The whole family was lovely, and I felt so blessed I was going to be a part of it.

The back door opened and Arthur appeared, closely followed by my mum and dad.

'Hello! What are you doing here?' I said in amazement, going over to kiss them both. They both looked flushed and excited.

'Oh, well, that's charming, that is!' Mum rolled her eyes in mock indignation. 'I heard a rumour that there might be something to celebrate, so we thought we'd call in.'

'Did you now?' I said, turning to look at Anthony. 'Did everyone know he was going to propose except me?'

'Yes,' everybody chorused amid much laughter.

'Well, it's a good job I said yes then, isn't it?'

Mum laughed. 'We never doubted you for a second, my darling. Now, have you got some glasses? I've brought champagne.' She produced a bottle from her handbag and placed it on the table.

'Ooh, lovely! Thanks, Birdie. I'll just get some now.' Cath went into the kitchen and came out with a tray of champagne flutes. Anthony slipped his arm around my waist, drawing me against his side.

'You don't mind all this, do you?' he murmured into my hair. 'I hope you don't think I've been too presumptuous or pushy.'

'Of course not!' I tipped my head back to look at him. 'You've made me so happy, Anthony. Thank you.'

He smiled, staring deep into my eyes. 'And I hope I make you happy every day, for the rest of our lives together.'

We kissed, with the clink of champagne glasses and the cheers and laughter of our family ringing in our ears.

'Hey, you two. You've got the rest of your lives to do that. Come on, let's have a toast. To Rachel and Anthony. May you find many years of happiness in each other's arms.'

'Aww!' Anthony squeezed me and I nestled into his side as everyone raised their glasses to us.

'To us,' Anthony murmured, clinking his glass against mine. 'I can't wait to spend the rest of our lives together.'

The sun had dipped below the trees and Cath switched on her patio lights so that we could see better. Music was playing from the kitchen and Anthony took my glass out of my hand and placed it on the table before pulling me into a dance hold. He danced me round and round on the grass, and we laughed and kissed as the world spun around us. There had never been a more perfect moment in my life. Like Anthony had said before, I couldn't wait to spend the rest of our lives together. I felt like the luckiest woman alive.

Acknowledgements

To my brilliant editor Charlotte Mursell and the HQ Digital team for all of their hard work in the making of this book.

Massive thanks to the wonderful book blogging community who give their time to read and review so enthusiastically, especially Kaisha (The Writing Garnet) and Rachel (Rachel's Random Reads), although there are many more that have made me smile with their supportive words.

Thank you to all my lovely author friends on Facebook and Twitter who are always on hand with advice and support.

Love and thanks to my husband, Ian, and children, Isobel, Tom and Cassie for keeping me anchored to the real world, as well as to my wider family for cheering me on. Special thanks to my dog, Barney, for making me venture out into the fresh air once in a while.

To the builders Chris, Louis and Jayjay who worked on our conservatory. Thanks for the use of your name (only), Jayjay!

And huge thanks to you, the reader, without whom there would be no point writing these words. May you all live happily ever after.

One of the characters in this book suffers from cardiomyopathy, which affects around 1 in 500 people in the UK. For more information about this condition, please visit www.cardiomyopathy.org

Dear Reader,

Thank you so much for taking the time to read this book – we hope you enjoyed it! If you did, we'd be so appreciative if you left a review.

Here at HQ Digital we are dedicated to publishing fiction that will keep you turning the pages into the early hours. We publish a variety of genres, from heartwarming romance, to thrilling crime and sweeping historical fiction.

To find out more about our books, enter competitions and discover exclusive content, please join our community of readers by following us at:

🐦 *@HQDigitalUK*

📘 *facebook.com/HQDigitalUK*

Are you a budding writer? We're also looking for authors to join the HQ Digital family! Please submit your manuscript to:

HQDigital@harpercollins.co.uk.

Hope to hear from you soon!

ONE PLACE. MANY STORIES

Turn the page for an exclusive extract from *Meet Me Under the Mistletoe*, another heartwarming romance from Carla Burgess…

Chapter One

Anthony Bascombe walked into my life one Thursday afternoon in the middle of November. The bell above the door tinkled violently and a gust of wind accompanied him into the shop, making the flowers quiver in their buckets and the fairy lights shiver on the shelves. The shifting air carried the scent of his aftershave as it lifted my hair from my shoulders, and I had to place a hand on the sheets of wrapping paper on the counter to stop them flying away.

'Sorry!' he said, shutting the door behind him quickly. 'It's a bit blustery out there.'

'It's okay.' I laughed and tried to ignore the fizz of attraction that surged through my veins as he smiled across at me. All kinds of customers came into my flower shop, including plenty of attractive men buying gifts for their loved ones, but it wasn't often that they were dressed so well or had such lovely, twinkly blue eyes. He wore a beautifully cut navy suit and his short, dark-blond hair was styled into a neat little quiff at the front. Self-consciously, I smoothed down my flowery tea dress and tried to remember if I'd applied my winged eyeliner straight this morning. 'How can I help you? Are you looking for anything in particular?'

'I'm looking for you, actually,' he said, still smiling as he walked towards me. 'If you're Rachel Jones, that is?'

'Oh! Yes, that's me. What can I do for you?' I cleared my throat, mortified that my voice had gone all squeaky when his was so pleasantly deep.

'I just came in to introduce myself. My name's Anthony Bascombe.' He extended a hand to shake. 'I'm the new tenant in the apartment upstairs. I believe your parents are my new land-lords.'

'Oh!' I gazed at him wide-eyed, delighted that I was going to be seeing him around a lot. He had such a lovely warm smile; it lit up his whole face. I couldn't take my eyes off him. 'Of course! You moved in on Sunday, didn't you? I was wondering when we'd get to meet. Have you settled in okay? Is everything to your liking?'

'Yes, everything's perfectly fine, thank you. The apartment's lovely.'

'It is, isn't it?' I said, eager to keep him talking. 'We had it renovated recently so it's all fresh and new. I'm quite jealous you're living there, actually. I felt like moving in myself.'

Raising his eyebrows slightly, he looked at me with interest. 'Why didn't you then?'

'I have my own house already. It's only a ten-minute walk down the road and over the river. Close enough.' Realising I was on the verge of giving him my home address and inviting him round for tea, I shut up and then noticed my fingers were still wrapped around his big, warm hand. Trying to pretend it was normal to hold a handshake for this long, I let go and tucked my hands into the pockets of my cardigan instead. To his credit, Anthony pretended not to notice and turned his attention to the shop.

'It's lovely in here. I love the whole vintage vibe.' He turned around slowly, taking in the shelves of flowers, the display of scented candles on the shabby-chic Welsh dresser in the corner and the floral birdcages hung at different levels from the ceiling.

'I like the fact you haven't got any Christmas decorations up yet.'

'Oh, they'll be going up this weekend, don't worry.'

He glanced back over his shoulder and raised an eyebrow. 'Still too early.'

I laughed. 'That's the way it is in retail, I'm afraid. Some shops put them up as soon as Halloween's out of the way.'

'I know,' he said, grudgingly. 'So, why's this shop called The Birdcage, then? You're not trapped here, I take it?'

'No, it was my mum's shop. Her name's Birdie. I take it you haven't met her yet. She's on holiday with her sister at the moment. Dad won't fly.'

'Yes, I've only met your dad. Nice man.' He turned back to face me and smiled. 'Well, if you're not trapped here, perhaps you'd like to take pity on the new boy in town and come out to dinner with me?'

'I'm sorry?' I blinked in surprise, thinking I'd misheard him.

He smiled. 'No pressure or anything. I just can't stand the thought of spending another night sitting in the flat sorting out boxes and I'd quite like to see a bit of Chester. That's unless you already have plans, and only if your boyfriend wouldn't object, of course?'

'Oh! No, not at all. What time is it now?'

He looked at his watch. 'Half past five. What time do you close?'

'Half past five.' I smiled, suddenly excited. This was a vast improvement on my original plans for the evening, which involved a microwave meal for one in front of *Emmerdale* and a bubble bath. 'Let me bring the flowers in from outside and then I can lock up.'

'Oh here, I'll help you,' he said, following me out of the shop to where more buckets of flowers stood just outside the door.

'You don't have to. It'll only take a minute,' I said, bending to lift a container of roses.

'No, here, pass it to me.' He held the door open with his back and took the container out of my hands. 'Do I just put them in front of this shelf?'

'Yes, please. That's perfect,' I said, passing him another container. There were only half a dozen or so containers of flowers out today. It had been too windy and cold to risk more. Leaves scuttled along the pavement and my skirt flapped around my legs, lifting and billowing ominously as I passed Anthony the last container. I clamped it down with my hand, pink with embarrassment, but Anthony either didn't or pretended not to see to spare my blushes. 'Thank you,' I said, as he stood back to let me through the door. I caught another waft of his aftershave and resisted the urge to sniff him all over like my parents' spaniel. 'I'll just lock the back door and get my coat,' I said, breathlessly, walking through the archway into the back of the shop where we created the flower arrangements. I'd intended to clear the stalks and leaves from the large wooden table before I left tonight, but it could wait until the morning. Locking the door, I set the alarm and grabbed my blue pea coat from the peg. Anthony turned the sign to closed as I dashed round switching off fairy lights and blowing out candles, and then held the door open for me when we were ready to go. I was seriously impressed by his manners. I wasn't used to such gentlemanly behaviour.

'So, where have you come from, Anthony?' I said, as we walked up the street towards the city centre. I raised my voice over the sound of cars and buses rumbling past, and he bent his head closer so he could hear.

'I'm originally from Shropshire, but I've just moved here from Manchester.'

'So, not too far away then.'

'No.'

'Why Chester? Do you have a new job here?'

'No. I just like to move around. See new places.'

'Really? Blimey, I don't think I could be bothered with all the hassle of moving my stuff from place to place.'

He shrugged. 'I choose furnished rental properties and keep my belongings to a minimum.'

'Oh, okay.' I raised my eyebrows, a little surprised by his answer. I couldn't imagine a life where I moved around from town to town. The only time I'd left Chester was to go to university in Liverpool for three years, then I'd moved straight back home. Presumably, that would seem boring to a man like Anthony. I remembered my dad saying he'd only signed a three-month contract. Dad would have preferred six but Anthony had seemed like the ideal tenant so he'd gone along with it. It was a shame he wouldn't be sticking around for longer. 'So, what do you fancy to eat? Anything in particular?'

'Mmm, something with potatoes and gravy. Preferably a pie.'

I looked up at him in surprise. He was so posh, I'd half expected him to say venison or something, although to be fair he hadn't specified what type of pie. It could well be a game pie he was craving. He looked at me and laughed. 'What?' he said. 'I've been starving all day! Don't tell me you're one of these women that nibbles on lettuce leaves and calls it a meal.'

'Not at all. I just… I don't know.' I laughed and peeled a strand of hair away from my face. I didn't know him well enough to start joking about how upper class he was. 'There's a pub up here that serves nice food. We'll go there.'

It was only a few minutes' walk, which was a relief because the cold wind was making my eyes water and I didn't want mascara all down my face. I couldn't believe I felt so nervous and excited about going to dinner with this man I'd met less than half an hour ago. This wasn't me; I didn't go all fan-girl crazy over men I'd just met. I was sensible and practical. The fact that I'd got engaged to my last boyfriend rather too quickly was beside the point. That had been a big mistake and one I would not be repeating any time soon.

Anyway, this wasn't a date. I was just being neighbourly, that's all, and taking care of my parents' new tenant. It wasn't nice to be all alone in a new city, especially with Christmas approaching. No matter how much he liked to move around and be in new places, he was bound to get lonely sometimes. And he might even have a girlfriend already. Just because he lived alone didn't necessarily mean he was single.

I breathed the cool night air deep into my lungs as we approached the pub to try and calm my nerves. Anthony opened the door and stood back to let me enter first. The pub was quiet so finding a table was no problem. We sat at a table for two next to the window. He smiled as he passed me a menu and my stomach fluttered.

'See, they have pie,' I said, pointing at the menu.

'Mmm, so they do.' He smiled.

A waitress came over and took our drinks order. I noted that he spoke just as courteously to her as he had to me and it made me like him even more. I found myself watching the way his eyes crinkled at the corners when he smiled up at her. At a guess, I'd have said he was about ten years older than me. Probably thirty-five, or thirty-six. The waitress jotted down our order and walked away.

'So, I take it your boyfriend won't mind you being out with me tonight?' he said, turning back to me.

'I haven't got a boyfriend.'

'You haven't?' He raised his eyebrows in surprise. 'I find that hard to believe.'

I narrowed my eyes at him to hide the fact I was flattered. 'What about you? Will your girlfriend mind that you're out with another girl?'

'I haven't got a girlfriend.' He rested his chin on his hand and smiled.

I raised my eyebrows. 'Wife?'

'Absolutely not.'

'Boyfriend or husband?'

'Nope.' He shook his head, slowly.

I sat back and looked at him. 'I find it hard to believe no one's snapped you up yet. A handsome, eligible man like you? You must have hordes of women after you.'

'Not so far as I'm aware, but thank you. I'll take that as a compliment.' His cheeks flushed slightly and he laughed as he fiddled with his menu with his long, elegant fingers. Realising I'd embarrassed him, I blushed and glanced down. Maybe that had been a bit much. I'd have to watch myself; I hadn't even had a drink and I was showering him with compliments. 'I've been single for quite a while, actually,' he went on. 'I'm not very good at relationships.'

'Really? Why not?'

He shrugged. 'I work too much. So, what about you? How long have you been single?'

'Four months or so. We broke up in July.'

'What went wrong?'

I smiled ruefully. 'He worked too much.'

Anthony laughed lightly. 'What did he do?'

'For a job, you mean?' I winced slightly. 'I was never completely sure, to be honest. He ran an IT company or something. Whatever it was required him being out of the country a lot.'

'Where did he go?'

I shrugged. 'Places with no phone signal, usually.'

Anthony raised a sceptical eyebrow. 'Surely if he worked in IT he'd be going to towns and cities that had good network coverage?'

'Exactly. I'm quite ashamed at how long it took me to realise he was stringing me along, but at least I got there in the end.'

'How long were you seeing him?'

'Just over seven months, but if you condensed that into the time we actually spent together, it would probably be more like one or two. He lived in London, so even when he was in the country it was difficult.'

He wrinkled his nose. 'London's not exactly the end of the

earth, is it. There are fairly regular trains, for a start. Did you go and visit him or did he come here?'

'He came here.'

'Always?'

'Yes, apart from when we went to Paris one weekend.'

The waitress appeared with our drinks and took our food orders. He thanked her before turning back to me. 'You never got to see where he lived? Did that never strike you as odd?'

I shrugged. 'I was more concerned with when I was going to see him again. If we'd spent more time together, then maybe I would have. I suppose it doesn't matter now anyway.'

'You're over him, are you?'

'Yes.' I reached for my drink and took a sip.

'You don't miss him at all?'

'Not really. We didn't spend enough time together for me to really miss him. I suppose I missed the idea of him at first. The possibility that he would come and visit me. But it didn't take too long for me to realise that my life was pretty much the same as it had always been. If anything, it was easier because I didn't have the agony of waiting for the phone to ring or the disappointment when he couldn't see me, yet again.' I sighed heavily and shook my head, more at myself than anything else. 'It's strange because, at the time, I was mad about him, but he feels like some kind of dream now.'

'Dream? Or nightmare?'

I laughed. 'Oh, he was a dream. When he was around he was lovely. It's just that he had no substance. He just came and went like some kind of stray cat. Anyway, let's not talk about Patrick. What about you?'

Anthony's eyes flickered and he shook his head. 'Nothing much to say really. I live a very boring, simple life. I run, work, eat and sleep, and that's the way I like it.'

I cocked my head to one side. 'What job do you do?'

'I'm a detective.'

238

'You are?' My eyebrows shot up in surprise. 'Wow! I didn't expect that.'

'What did you expect?' He laughed as he took a sip of his beer.

'I don't know.' I shrugged. 'Just not that.'

'Does it bother you?'

'Of course it doesn't. Why would it bother me? I just didn't expect you to work in the police at all, really. I thought you'd be something like... I don't know... a barrister, or something?'

'Why?' He looked amused.

'Because of your suit and your manners and how well-spoken you are.'

'And detectives can't wear good suits and have nice manners? What about Inspector Morse and Inspector Linley?'

'I was thinking more of Rebus, but okay then.'

He laughed. 'We come in all shapes and sizes.'

'Do you like your job?'

'Yes, I love it.'

'Does it get you down? Dealing with murderers and paedophiles?'

'Of course. I wouldn't be human if it didn't. I'm primarily fraud at the moment, though.'

'Oh, okay. Presumably that's less emotionally traumatic to investigate than some other crimes?'

'Yes, I suppose it is.' He drummed his fingers on the table. 'There's no such thing as a victimless crime, though.'

I nodded, and waited for him to continue, but he just looked at me. I didn't know what to say next. I didn't know much about fraud really. 'Are you investigating anything at the moment?' I said at last, slightly bewildered by his silence.

'Of course. Fraud's a massive problem.'

'I expect you have to work long hours?'

'Yes.'

'Hence why you're really bad at relationships?'

'Absolutely.' He smiled and took another sip from his glass of beer.

'Not all detectives are single, though, are they?' I sat back and moved my cutlery to one side as the waitress appeared with our plates of food. 'Surely some of them are married and have families?' I smiled my thanks to the waitress.

'Thank you. Yes, of course they are. My friend John is very happily married.'

'So, I suspect the problem is more you than your job.'

He laughed. 'That's true. So, why has your mum gone on holiday without your dad? Are they splitting up?'

'Oh no. At least I hope not. She's gone with her sister to celebrate her birthday. They don't go every year or anything. Mum and Dad still go on holiday together, but only in this country. Dad won't go abroad. He's terrified of flying.'

Anthony laughed. 'Your poor dad.'

'Mmm, I know. I think he's enjoying having the TV to himself.' I cut into my salmon and carefully pushed it onto my fork. 'I've been round to keep him company a couple of evenings but I think he's coping okay. Have you been on holiday this year?'

He shook his head as he chewed his mouthful of food. 'I had a week off in the summer but I didn't go away anywhere. I just visited family really. What about you? You mentioned Paris before?'

'Yes, I went to Paris with Patrick for a weekend but other than that I haven't been anywhere. I usually go somewhere with my friend Elena, but she's bought a house with her fiancé so she couldn't afford it. Besides, I doubt he'd have let her go anyway. They can't be apart for more than a few hours before they start pining for each other.'

Anthony wrinkled his nose slightly. 'That sounds a bit nauseating.'

'They're very sweet, actually. She was obsessed with him at school. It's lovely that she finally got together with him.'

'So, was Paris nice?'

'It was lovely, yes. Have you been?'

'A couple of times. Where did you stay?'

'In a hotel near the Champs-Élysées. It was lovely. I'd never been to Paris before so it was lovely to see all the sights I'd read about and seen on TV.'

'Did Patrick know Paris well?'

'He seemed to, yes.' I smiled a little sadly. 'It was very romantic. He proposed to me, actually. He pulled out all the stops: violins, champagne, roses.'

'He proposed?' Anthony's fork paused on its way to his mouth. 'But I thought you'd only been together a short time?'

'Yes.'

Anthony put his fork down and looked at me. 'You said no, of course.'

I stared at him, wishing I could agree and say 'of course I said no!', but I'd said yes, so I couldn't. I felt a quiver of shame and regret run through me and decided that, in future, I should just lie, or preferably not discuss Patrick at all. Especially with extremely handsome men who were practically strangers.

Anthony raised an eyebrow. 'You said yes? So, let me get this straight. You hardly saw or spoke to him, but you still thought it would be a good idea to marry him?'

'I know, it sounds awful.' I passed a hand across my face, feeling embarrassed.

'Hey, it's not my place to judge.' Anthony held up his hands and laughed. 'I'm just wondering how he got away with behaving like that when I've never been able to.'

I smiled and rubbed my head, still embarrassed. 'Well, he was behaving better at the time. When I first met him, which was just before Christmas last year, he was really full-on. He phoned me all the time and showered me with gifts. He made me feel special. And then it seemed like as soon as I started falling for him, it all stopped and he started not being able to see me. We had a big row about it around March time, and he said I wasn't being fair because he had to make time for his daughter too, which made me feel like a monster. Anyway, we sorted that out and he allowed me to meet his little girl, and I felt like he was letting me into his life at last. It was just after that he took me to Paris and proposed. I must have been mad to say yes, but I thought he'd changed and that he must be serious about me to go to all the effort of organising a proposal that grand. I was swept away by it all. But when I got home, he was worse than ever. I hardly heard from him again at all.'

'When did you finish it?'

'He was supposed to come to my mum's sixtieth birthday party but he let me down at the last minute. Said he was stuck at work. It was a big deal because he hadn't met any of my friends or family.'

'Really?' Anthony looked astounded. 'I need to talk to this man, get some tips from him.'

'What do you mean?'

'He kept you hanging on for months while avoiding spending any quality time with you, and managed to avoid meeting your friends and family. That's quite a genius manoeuvre. How did he do that? Can I have his number?'

I knew Anthony was joking, or at least I hoped he was, but his words stung and I felt a frisson of anger pulse through me. 'He has a big personality and he's hugely generous. But I can't give you his number because I don't have it any more. I made a point of deleting it when we split up.' I put my knife and fork down and reached for my wine. 'It also requires your girlfriend to be gullible and slightly mad. I mean, I must have been mad, mustn't I? I even agreed to get married abroad, knowing my dad won't fly. What was that all about? I have no clue.' I took another gulp of wine and blinked away the sudden tears from my eyes. 'It's funny because I'd never been taken in by men's bullshit before. Patrick was the first man I ever really cared about and he played me for a fool. People warned me our relationship didn't make sense but I wouldn't listen. I suppose I wanted to believe him.'

Anthony reached for my hand with a sympathetic smile. 'I'm sorry. I didn't mean to upset you.'

'It's okay.' I looked at his kind eyes and was unable to imagine him taking advantage of anyone's trust. 'Anyway, I can't believe I'm telling you all this. I feel so ashamed of myself for being taken in by him like that.' I picked up my knife and fork again as Anthony removed his hand from mine. 'Suffice to say, it is not a genius manoeuvre to string people along like that and leave them feeling duped.'

'Is that how you feel? Duped?'

'Pretty much. And used and stupid. When I finished with him he said he didn't want to leave it like that and that he'd phone me and we'd talk everything through. And guess what? He didn't phone. So, even though I said the words "It's over", I still feel like he had the last laugh by making me wait for a phone call that never came. It's like he's play-acting all the time. Everything that comes out of his mouth is a lie.' I shook my head. 'I'm sorry, I shouldn't be talking about him. This must be very boring for you.'

'Not at all. It's my fault, after all. I did ask you about him.'

'That's true.' I smiled at him. 'What about you then? How did your last relationship end?'

He looked startled for a moment. 'Oh, err, with me leaving, I expect. That's usually how they end.'

'Were you living together?'

'Oh God, no. Nothing like that. Like I said, I just like to move around.'

'Does that have to mean leaving everything behind, though? Like you said before about me and Patrick, London isn't the end of the earth, so if you're staying in the UK, surely it's easy enough to carry on seeing someone?'

'Not if you work all the time, it isn't.'

'But didn't we already discuss that your colleague John is happily married?'

He laughed. 'I suppose I've never met anyone I wanted to keep in touch with like that.'

'Does that mean you've never been in love?'

He cleared his throat and shrugged. 'Define love.'

I gaped at him. 'You've never been in love? How old are you? Thirty-five?'

He shrugged a shoulder. 'Thereabouts.'

'How have you managed to get to thirty-five and not fall in love? Are you a robot or something?'

Laughing, he put his knife and fork together on his plate before pushing it away. 'I don't want to fall in love. I generally leave before it gets to that stage. Love is time-consuming and painful.'

'It's also wonderful and exhilarating and joyful.'

'Says the woman who's had her heart broken.'

'But I will love again.'

'Wow! You said that like it's a slogan or something. Have you had that printed on a T-shirt?'

I laughed. 'Just think about all the women whose hearts you've broken in your time.'

'Funny, I'm pretty certain I haven't broken any hearts.'

'I bet you have, Anthony.'

'No, I haven't.'

'Even if you don't think you have, I bet you have. Just look at you. On top of being handsome and intelligent, you have beautiful manners and seem really kind too. Not that I know you, of course. But you seem lovely.'

'Maybe that's the problem. Women don't want a lovely man with beautiful manners. Women want a bad boy in motorcycle leathers.'

'Erm, not really.' I looked up as the waitress came over to take our plates.

'Do you want another drink?' he asked.

'Oh, I shouldn't.'

'Go on. I'll walk you home.'

'You don't have to do that. It's only up the road.' I felt slightly flustered as I looked up at the waitress. 'I'll have another wine, please.'

Anthony ordered his drink and then turned back to me. 'You kind of proved my point with Patrick.'

'What point?'

'About women preferring bad boys. You said you'd never met anyone you cared about before Patrick. He didn't exactly treat you well, did he?'

'He did when he was with me. And the boys I'd seen before weren't super nice or particularly horrible, they were just immature. Patrick was older, so maybe I just prefer older men.'

'He didn't treat you well, Rachel. You never knew where you were with him. And he didn't meet any of your friends and family. I'm pretty sure I've met at least some of the friends and family of every girl I've ever been in a relationship with. And I'm always upfront about the fact I'm not looking for anything long-term or serious.'

'Really?'

'Really. I'm not out to mislead anyone or make false promises.' He scratched his face and looked at me. 'I wouldn't like to think I'd broken anybody's heart. That's just sad.'

I smiled at him. 'You're very sweet. And that's exactly why I find it so hard to believe that nobody has fallen in love with you.'

He rolled his eyes, looking embarrassed. 'Anyway, this is getting a bit deep. Let's change the subject now.'

'Okay. What do you want to talk about?'

'I don't know.' He laughed. 'Tell me about yourself.'

'Me? We've talked enough about me. Why don't you tell me about you? You're the new boy in town.'

'I'm really not that interesting.'

'I disagree. I think you're quite fascinating, actually. You have a very bizarre attitude to relationships and I'd like to know why.'

'Ah, but we're not talking about that any more.'

I leaned my elbows on the table and smiled at him. 'Let's start with your family. Are you an only child?'

He hesitated for a moment, a smile playing on his lips as he looked at me through narrowed eyes. 'No. I have a younger brother.'

'How much younger?'

'Three years.'

'Is he married?'

'Yes. And he has two children.'

'Aww, so you're Uncle Anthony. Are they cute?'

'Very.'

'You like kids?'

'I love kids.'

'But you don't want any yourself?'

'No. Look, what is this? The Spanish Inquisition?'

'I'm just making conversation.'

He laughed and took a sip from his drink. 'Yes, I love my niece and nephew but I don't get to see them very much.'

'You mentioned your mother before?'

'Yes. I have a mother.'

'Are your parents divorced?'

'Look, I know what you're doing, you know. You're trying to find out about my relationship issues by asking about my family. You can save your pseudo-psychological analysis of me for another time, thank you. My family are great. Now, are you an only child?'

'Yes.'

'I thought so.'

'Why?'

'Because you're bossy and like to get your own way.'

I laughed in disbelief. 'Oh, really? How would you even know that about me when we've only just met? Besides, is that what only children are meant to be like?'

'I have no idea, I'm just winding you up.' He sat back and laughed. 'What do you like to do in your spare time?'

Shrugging, I ran my finger around the top of my wine glass. 'I don't really have that much free time with running the shop, and when I get home I'm tired.'

'But you're only twenty-six. You can't just work and sleep.'

'I don't. I watch TV in between.'

'Don't you go out dancing?'

'No. All my friends are settling down with their boyfriends and can't afford it. Besides, how did you know I was twenty-six? I didn't tell you, did I?'

'I think your dad mentioned it.'

'Oh.' I frowned. That was odd. Why would my dad be telling the new tenant how old I was? But then I suppose he might have been talking about me running the shop. 'Anyway, what's this about dancing? Who says dancing these days? Clubbing is the word.'

'Dancing sounds nicer. I like dancing.'

'Can you dance?'

'Of course I can dance!' He looked offended at the very notion that he might not be able to.

I raised an eyebrow. 'Do you fancy yourself as a bit of a Fred Astaire? We should call you the dancing detective.'

'Ha ha, I like that.' He looked like he was going to say something else but changed his mind and took a sip of his beer instead.

I smiled at him. 'What's the time?'

'Nearly eight.'

'Already? I should go.'

'Why? Is your Horlicks calling to you?'

'No, but my bed is. I've got to be up at five to go to the flower market.'

'Five? That's crazy! I can't believe you have to go that early. What time does your shop open? Nine?'

'Half past eight.'

'So, why do you have to be up at five?'

'Have a shower, get dressed, put my make-up on, then I drive

247

there, choose the flowers, have a chat, drive back, make up any orders.'

'Can't you get them delivered?'

'Yes.'

'So, get them delivered.'

'I like to go and see what's there. They always have new things in. It's exciting.'

Anthony frowned at me. 'But, do you really need to go tomorrow? Couldn't you get them delivered? Just this once?'

'For a policeman, you're a really bad influence, you know!'

He grinned. 'Is that a yes?'

I looked at his smiling face and decided I'd much rather have an evening out with a handsome man than get up at five and start work early. 'Well, I suppose it's not essential that I go tomorrow. But I'm not sure about going dancing. How about we just go to another bar?'

'Okay.' He turned and called the waitress over for the bill. I got my purse out of my bag but he waved me away. 'I'll get this as a thank you for coming out with me tonight.'

'You don't have to do that. It's my pleasure, honestly.'

'No, let me. Please.'

ONE PLACE. MANY STORIES

If you enjoyed *Meet Me at Willow Hall*, then why not try
another sweeping historical from HQ Digital?

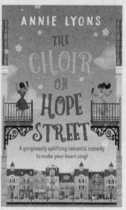